"I said, thanks for your time." JJ left it at that, but her smile suggested what she left unsaid. *Though it wasn't your choice.*

"Not a problem." Another of those annoying phrases. When had people stopped saying "you're welcome"? He couldn't recall.

She dug out her car keys and used the remote to unlock the Challenger before she opened the door. He watched her slide into the seat, a fluid movement of heavy brown coat and snug-fitting denim. When she moved to close the door, he hastily spoke.

"If you have any trouble with the neighbors..."

Now, why had Quint gone and said that? He was done. He'd followed Sam's orders—had gone beyond them by going shopping and having lunch with her. Why give her even the faintest idea that he might be willing to do it again?

But he couldn't take back the words, and when that naughty-little-girl grin lit up her face, he wasn't sure he wanted to.

* * *

If you're on Twitter, tell us what you think of Harlequin Romantic Suspense! #harlequinromsuspense

Dear Reader,

There's an old saying to write what you know, which is one of the reasons I write so many small-town books, but not the only one, mind you. I know small towns, and I love them. Though our few big-city years created great memories—hello, San Diego—I can't see myself living anywhere now but the little Oklahoma town where I grew up. Granted, there's a shortage of restaurants, and shopping's limited pretty much to Walmart and the farm-supply store, but I can cook, and shopping's overrated, anyway. Besides, where in a big city can you buy fried frog legs to munch on while you fill your gas tank?

This particular little town, Cedar Creek, is my hometown in disguise. Well, maybe not fully disguised. *Slightly camouflaged* might be more accurate. There are a few fictional places mixed in with enough real ones that the locals recognize it in spite of made-up names. It makes writing the books feel like...well, coming home.

In this book, I combined a second love—heroine JJ is from South Carolina. We lived there three times while my husband was in the navy, and it's a special place. Of course, by the end of the story, JJ is willing to leave home and settle in Cedar Creek with Quint, just like I once moved from Oklahoma and settled a lot of places with my husband.

Because, after all, home is where the heart is, isn't it?

Happy reading,

Marilyn

DETECTIVE ON THE HUNT

———

Marilyn Pappano

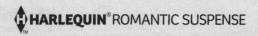

HARLEQUIN® ROMANTIC SUSPENSE

Recycling programs
for this product may
not exist in your area.

ISBN-13: 978-1-335-66227-9

Detective on the Hunt

Copyright © 2019 by Marilyn Pappano

Printed in U.S.A.

Oklahoma, dogs, beaches, books, family and friends: these are a few of **Marilyn Pappano**'s favorite things. She lives in imaginary worlds where she reigns supreme (at least, she does when the characters cooperate) and no matter how wrong things go, she can always set them right. It's her husband's job to keep her grounded in the real world, which makes him her very favorite thing.

Books by Marilyn Pappano

Harlequin Romantic Suspense

Copper Lake Secrets
In the Enemy's Arms
Christmas Confidential
"Holiday Protector"
Copper Lake Confidential
Copper Lake Encounter
Undercover in Copper Lake
Bayou Hero
Nights with a Thief
Detective Defender
Killer Secrets
Killer Smile
Detective on the Hunt

Visit the Author Profile page at Harlequin.com for more titles.

To my childhood partner in crime, my cohort and conspirator, and one of the very few people I know who really would be sitting beside me if I ever wound up in a jail cell, saying, "Dang, that was fun!" You're the best cousin ever.

Yes, Hope Cooper, I'm looking at you. Love you!

Prologue

"Give me one reason why I shouldn't fire you."

Quint Foster kept his gaze steady on the upturned Stetson on Sam Douglas's desk, kept his jaw shut tight and every muscle in his body wound like a spring. If he tried to answer the chief's question, if he relaxed his control just that little bit, he would fall apart in a way he never had before. Never could.

Because he didn't have the courage to put himself back together again.

"Damn it, Quint, you showed up drunk at a crime scene. You assaulted a prisoner in custody. What the hell—"

Sam broke off. Quint knew the question: *What the hell is wrong with you?* Just as Sam knew the answer: Belinda. The day she'd died, so had Quint. His body just hadn't been smart enough to catch on. His brain functioned enough to keep his heart beating, but not enough to make him care about a damn thing. He'd lost everything that mattered except his job, and that was coming.

The thought echoed through the hollowness inside him. Losing his job... All he'd ever been, all he'd ever wanted to be, was a cop. For nearly twenty years, he'd been a good one. He'd advanced through the ranks to assistant chief. If things had continued as they'd been, he likely would have succeeded Sam as chief, if he didn't retire before the boss.

Now, in another ten minutes, maybe fifteen if Sam was pissed enough, he would be turning in his badge and commission. He would walk out the front door for the last time, and he would truly have no reason to get out of bed again.

Sam remained silent, his steely glare unwavering. Quint didn't have what it took to look at him, but he could feel the disapproval and disappointment and disgust radiating around him. He'd never imagined the day he would lose his boss's respect, but here it was. It was only by the grace of God that Sam hadn't thrown his ass in jail.

By the grace of *something*. Quint didn't believe in God anymore. Maybe he was real, maybe he wasn't. Maybe he existed for other people but not for Quint. Every prayer, every plea, every moment he'd spent begging on his knees had been for nothing. Linny had died. He hadn't.

"Damn it, Quint." This time the words sounded more sorrowful than angry. Sam raked his fingers through his hair. "What am I supposed to do?"

For the first time in seventy-two hours, Quint made eye contact with his boss. His gut was knotted with dread at losing that last part of himself. He wanted to go to the men's room and puke up everything in his stomach, then he wanted to go to the nearest bar and refill it with the cheapest crap they had. He wanted to die.

What he did was stand up very carefully. He pulled his badge from his belt, took his credentials from his back pocket and unholstered the gun on his hip. He had to clear his throat twice to make his voice work. "I'll make it easy for you, Sam. I quit."

Sam wasn't surprised. "I don't want you to quit. You're a good cop, and I need good cops. I just need you to…"

If he said, "Get over it," Quint would punch him in the face, and if he hit him once, he wouldn't stop until he was pulled off.

"I need you to deal with it, Quint," Sam said quietly. "I can't even begin to guess how hard this is for you. Belinda was your world, and it's unfair as hell that she's gone, but you're not. You can't just crawl into your grief and wait to die. It's not what she'd want. It's not even what you want, or you would have already done something."

Quint didn't know if he should argue that last statement. He felt every year of his forty years twice over. He was tired. Worn-out. Hopeless. Faithless. Alone. Every morning since her death, he'd woken up and thought, damn, he'd survived another night. For a while, it had been a good *damn*. Everyone had told him—his family, his friends, Linny's pastor—that recovery was a one-day-at-a-time deal. He was supposed to be grateful for each day he made it through, and in return, God was supposed to make each successive day a little easier.

It hadn't happened.

"I don't want you to quit," Sam said again, "but I

can't keep you as assistant chief. I have to put you on probation. Back in uniform. Back on the street. Are you willing to do that?"

A sound halfway between a snort and a laugh escaped Quint. He sank into the chair again, rubbing hard at his eyes. He hadn't been in uniform since he'd met Linny twelve years ago. He didn't even own the current uniform; suits or tactical pants and polo shirts had been his work clothes. Everyone in the department— hell, in the whole damn town—would know he'd been demoted. They would scorn him or pity him. No one would ask his opinion, respect his judgment or even acknowledge all his years of good work. He'd be a patrol officer again, writing tickets, filling out reports on inconsequential incidents, turning the important cases—the cases he'd handled himself the past twelve years—over to detectives to investigate.

But he would still be a cop. He would still have a reason to get out of bed in the morning. And given what he'd done, that was a hell of a lot more than he deserved.

His jaw didn't want to unclench. His mouth didn't want to form words, but he forced them out. "Yes, Chief. I'm willing."

Chapter 1

The sixth sense that JJ Logan considered as much a tool in her line of work as any of the physical, tangible ones made the back of her neck tingle. She lowered the binoculars from her eyes and shifted her gaze to the rearview mirror. A police vehicle, its lights on, was pulling to the side of the road behind her. She'd half expected this— a stranger with out-of-state tags on her car surveilling a local's house just screamed for police intervention—but it gave her an odd feeling, being on the wrong side of the flashing red-and-blue lights.

A tall, lean man dressed in khakis got out. He seated his hat before he began walking toward her, tipping it so it shadowed most of his face, then stopped far enough away from her car that she couldn't open the door and knock him off balance.

She liked caution in a cop. That was why she kept her hands resting loosely on the steering wheel. She waited, prepared to tell him right up front that she was a cop herself, to show him her ID, driver's license and proof of insurance and tell him that she had a pistol in the console and a Taser on her hip.

Before she had a chance to even say hello, though, he surprised her.

"Are you Jennifer Jo Logan?"

She blinked, her mouth quirking the way it always did when she was called by her full name. Growing up, it had meant trouble, with consequences she deserved. Today, though, she couldn't possibly have done anything to earn consequences. She didn't know a soul in Cedar Creek, Oklahoma, and no one knew she was here besides her parents, her sisters and a few people back home. While watching someone's house might provoke curiosity, it wasn't actually illegal.

Except...one of those people who knew she was here and why was the person she trusted least in the world. Police Chief Bryan Chadwick. Her boss.

The officer was waiting, his expression immobile, and she forced a smile. "Yes, I'm JJ Logan. Can I help you?"

His carved-stone features didn't shift. "Chief Douglas would like to have a word with you. If you'll follow me, I'll show you to the station." His voice was deep, reminding her of the long-ago times of midnight radio broadcasts, sultry music and a honey-sweet, soothing voice. This morning, the voice was a little short on the honey. Instead it was raspy, heavy, what she would expect from someone who didn't talk a whole lot.

"I know where it is, Officer..." Her gaze flickered to the brass nameplate on his shirt. "Foster." She'd studied online maps of Cedar Creek, familiarizing herself with the places that would be important while she was here:

the hotel, the police station and sheriff's departments, the house she'd been watching just ahead and, of course, restaurants. Creek Café had a zillion five-star reviews, and there were Chinese, barbecue and steak places that were similarly popular. She was a real fan of food that someone else had prepped, cooked, served and cleaned up after, so she intended to visit every one of them.

Her smile, her cooperation and her friendly use of his name didn't soften him one bit. "Then I'll follow you."

Ah. The chief's request to see her wasn't a request at all. Like a lot of small-town police chiefs, he probably didn't play well with others, especially when those others wandered into his jurisdiction and didn't show the courtesy of dropping by to introduce themselves. She'd told Chief Dipstick—er, Chadwick—that she wanted to check in with the locals, but he'd instructed her not to. This was family business, private—no need to involve anyone else.

That hadn't been a request, either. Chief Dipstick considered himself so far superior to women that asking them for something would never cross his mind.

Suppressing a sigh, she looked up at Officer Foster again. Barely visible under his hat, his hair was blond, streaked with lighter strands that would be a definite gray in a few more years. Dark glasses hid his eyes, but with the blond hair and golden skin, she would put her money on blue. She would also bet they were as steely as…well, steel. To match the hard line of his jaw. He looked like a guy who was having a bad day. A guy who made other people have bad days.

Don't get confrontational with a cop who is armed. One of her personal rules. With a thin but notoriously compliant smile, she said, "I appreciate the escort, Officer. Okay if I make a U-turn?"

His response was a slight tilt of his head.

As she started the engine, he stepped back, then returned to his vehicle, a huge black pickup truck emblazoned with the usual police stickers. A drug forfeiture? Or was Cedar Creek more generous with its police budget than Evanston, where her official car was a beater practically as old as she was?

The thud of Foster's door sounded through her window as she shifted into Drive. The house holding her interest was the last one on this lonely street. Its nearest neighbor was half a block behind her, and the street ahead ended a hundred feet past its driveway, the pavement abruptly chopped and blocked to traffic with steel barriers. She'd intended to drive up there when she left, to use the driveway to turn around. To see whether there was a gate, any obvious security system, possibly a security guard.

She would have to come back to find out. This job required a face-to-face visit with Maura Evans, and JJ never left a job undone.

There were no curbs on the sides of the street, the newly greening grass growing right up to the concrete. Her Challenger didn't require a lot of room to turn around. Frustrated, though, that the locals knew she was here—and pretty sure it was Chadwick who'd told them—she vented by expanding what should have been an easy three-point turn into five or six points.

"Yeah, no passive-aggressiveness in you, Detective Logan," she murmured as she drove past the scowling Officer Foster with a half-hearted wave and back down the block.

She'd seen nothing worth seeing in her hour at the house Maura was renting, unless she counted the cat sunning on the patio table. Funny. She remembered Maura as a fierce dog lover with no interest in felines whatsoever. Granted, that was over fifteen years ago, and Maura had been a little kid. She'd changed, like all little kids did when they grew up, and JJ knew next to nothing about the woman she'd become.

Except that, according to the Evans family lawyer, she'd gotten lost in her grief after her parents' deaths. She'd closed up the family mansion and hit the road in the überexpensive Mercedes that had been their last gift to her, and six months ago she'd settled in Cedar Creek. Three months ago she'd cut off all contact with her past life.

And now JJ was here to make sure everything was okay with her. According to Chadwick, she'd been his first choice to look into the matter. If she didn't detest the man so much—and if he didn't detest her even more— she might have taken that as a compliment. But she knew better. From his first day on the job, he'd made it clear that women had no place in his department and certainly not in his detective squad. The only problem: he couldn't fire her without cause, and she was damn well determined not to give it to him.

Which left him one option: making things bad enough that she would quit. He'd alternated between assigning her cases so simple a brain-dead squirrel could close them and ones so lacking in evidence they would stump Sherlock Holmes, Columbo and Steve McGarrett combined. He nitpicked everything she did and everything she didn't do. He disrespected her within the department and encouraged the *real* officers—read: male—to do the same. Publicly he was gracious, but privately he made her work life hell.

He hadn't realized he was butting heads with the most stubborn person in town. JJ intended to outlast him, and the odds were in her favor. He'd come to Evanston after retiring from a small North Carolina police department. He was seventy-two, believed fervently in the Southern food adage *If it ain't fried, it ain't done*, drank like a fish and had high cholesterol, heart disease and high blood pressure. Sooner or later, he would retire again or die, and she would be there to wave him off—or throw the first shovel of dirt into his grave.

With a surprised look around, she realized she'd driven the few miles to the police station without noticing. When she'd worked traffic, she'd made a small fortune for the city of Evanston writing tickets to inattentive drivers, and now she didn't remember how she'd gotten here.

Officer Foster in his big truck followed her to a parking space, left a couple of empty spots between them, then got out and met her at the rear of the vehicles. Though the morning had started off nippy, it had turned into a glorious March day. Things were greening, coming back to life. The sun was warm, and she would swear she could smell the fresh, sweet, woodsy fragrance of the flowers thirty yards ahead of them.

Unless… She weaved a bit closer to Officer Foster and surreptitiously took a deep breath. Yep, it was him, not the flowers. The scent made her mouth water and her stomach do a little butterfly twirl. Lovely, lovely.

There might be an upside to this gig, after all.

Probably in defense of her gleaming little car, Jennifer Jo Logan—JJ, Quint reminded himself—had parked at the farthest end of the lot from the station, six or eight spaces from the next nearest vehicle. Though she was half a foot shorter than him, she matched his strides without complaint. He was long out of the habit of slowing down to accommodate anyone with shorter legs—*Don't think of Linny*—but now he made a conscious effort to shorten his steps.

Which gave him an opportunity to study JJ.

From a purely professional viewpoint.

She would have to stand on tiptoe to pass five foot six, and she was slender, curvy, soft, but she had an assured don't-mess-with-me air about her. Her hair fell to her shoulders, nothing special, brown with a few reddish streaks, and her eyes were hazel, again nothing special.

And somehow, in spite of all that nothing special, she was pretty. Not beautiful, not the sort who would stop guys in their tracks, not like—

His jaw tightened, and he forced the thought to its conclusion: not like Linny. Linny had been gorgeous, with silky black hair that fell straight and sleek to her waist, skin so pale it might have never seen the sun, delicate and fragile and breathtaking.

JJ Logan wasn't any of that. But neither was any other woman in the world.

Quint was comfortable with silence—had made himself become comfortable—but not so much her. It wasn't more than a minute before she spoke. "How long have you been a cop?"

"A while."

"You a local boy?"

"Yeah."

"You like patrol?"

He lifted one shoulder in a shrug, realized she wasn't looking and grunted instead.

An annoyed tone came into her voice. "Is your chief good, bad or indifferent?"

As if any cop who cared about his job would honestly answer that question from a stranger. Sam was damned good—Quint wouldn't have a job if he wasn't—but if the truth was one of the other two answers, no way he'd admit it. "Good."

He thought he heard a sigh from her in response, but when she didn't respond, he turned his attention to the police station ahead of them. The building was three stories, constructed of huge blocks of sandstone, with broad concrete steps leading to the double doors. More than a hundred years old, its purpose wasn't just function; it provided beauty and solidity, elegance and grace—a quote from the city's tourism brochure. It had been built to last, and it gave him a sense of...

He wasn't sure how to identify the feeling. He'd spent sixteen months learning to ignore feelings, and it was hard, once a habit formed, to give it up again. Satisfaction wasn't quite the right label. Neither was comfort. Security, maybe. It had stood there strong and whole his entire life, and it would still be there, strong and whole, long after he died. Unchanging. Constant.

They stepped onto the curb, walking between flower

beds planted with hardy petunias, when JJ broke her silence. "Just for the record, I'm armed."

He stopped. So did she. He wasn't surprised. Most cops he knew didn't go anywhere without some form of weapon. His surprise was that he hadn't thought to ask her. Now he faced her, his gaze focused tightly as it moved down, then back up her body. Almost immediately, he spotted the slight bulge beneath her jacket on the left side indicating something holstered there, but he didn't assume it was the only weapon.

Her white shirt was fitted, hugging her breasts and stomach, and couldn't have concealed a thing. Her jeans, faded soft blue and showing signs of long-term wear, were snug over her hips and clung to her muscular thighs and calves, all the way down to the brown leather boots peeking out from beneath the hems.

Nothing special, he reminded himself.

"What is it?" he asked with a nod toward her caramel-colored suede jacket.

She pulled back the left side to reveal the black-and-yellow Taser holstered grip forward on her waistband. An easy position to draw from for a right-handed person. No doubt she normally wore her pistol on the right. No chance for a mix-up unless a person was an idiot.

"Is that all?"

A smile crinkled her eyes. "Where could I hide anything else?" Then a nod toward the Challenger. "My weapon's locked in the car."

Confirming what he suspected: JJ Logan was in Cedar Creek on a job—the reason Sam had sent him out to retrieve her in the first place. Sam liked to know what was going on in his town. Quint…he didn't care that much anymore.

"Should I leave the Taser in the car?"

Quint shook his head. "Everyone inside is armed, too. You're not a threat."

She gave him a look halfway between hurt and insulted. "Don't be so sure of that. You don't even know me yet." Smiling, she began moving again, reaching the bottom step before he gave himself a mental shake and followed.

He knew one thing: he didn't want to know her. His life was steady. Predictable. Not happy, but the normal that had been forced on him. He didn't need any upsets to his routine. He was going to deliver JJ Logan to Sam's office, go back to his vehicle, forget he'd met her and get back to work. Back to the solitude he preferred.

Maybe not actually preferred, but had chosen. Or had it chosen him?

You can't change the world, someone had told him, *but you can change the way you react to it*. And he had changed the only way he knew how. No reactions whatsoever. If he didn't lose control, then he didn't have to struggle to regain it.

JJ reached the double doors before he did, opened one and stepped back so he could enter first. It didn't bother him. In Cedar Creek, courtesies like that weren't assigned by gender. Whoever was there first did the honors, and sooner or later the honoree would do it for someone else.

She stopped a few feet inside the door to look. He was in and out of here five or six times a day. He rarely noticed the furnishings anymore, but JJ certainly did.

The lobby was marbled, high-ceilinged, chandeliered and grandly staired. Behind the gleaming wooden counter, though, the ceiling had been dropped to a regular height with ugly acoustic tiles, and so much furniture had been crammed in that there was little breathing room.

Quint used to have his own office. Now, in the event he needed a desk, he used one of the two unclaimed ones against the back wall. One had two uneven legs, and the other was so scarred on top that it was impossible to write legibly without borrowing a solid surface from elsewhere.

The chief's secretary, Cheryl, looked up and over the top of her glasses. "Sam's in his office."

Quint acknowledged her with a nod, seeing that everyone else was looking at them, too: Daniel Harper and Ben Little Bear, two of the detectives who'd once answered to him; Morwenna Armstrong, dispatcher and coqueen of local gossip along with Lois Gideon, their first female and first turquoise-haired officer; and three other patrol officers checking in for something or other. Quint knew they were interested in the visiting detective, not him, but bitterness stirred in his gut anyway. That sourness—regret or, more likely, shame—made its presence known damn near every time he came into the station.

He gestured to the hallway this side of the staircase. Too narrow to be called a corridor, it had been chopped out of other spaces and just barely allowed two people to pass without bumping shoulders, and that was only if one of them wasn't Ben Little Bear. It was lighted by cheap ceiling fixtures circa the '70s, and two of the

four had burned out. Waiting for someone else to do
something about them hadn't worked, so maybe Quint
would drag out the ladder before he went home today
and change the bulbs. It was something to do.

Something to put off that moment of pulling into
the driveway of his and Linny's house. Of climbing
the steps knowing the house was empty. Of opening
the front door and walking into a space where her fragrance didn't sweeten the air, where her laughter didn't
ring, where her presence was insubstantial.

The first door down the hall opened into Sam's office.
Quint rapped a little sharper than necessary, feeling
the sting in his knuckles, then opened the door. He'd radioed in when he parked outside, so Sam was expecting
them. This time, Quint stepped back and let JJ enter
first. "Chief Douglas, Detective Jennifer—"

She cleared her throat.

"Detective JJ Logan," he finished. "I'm headed back
out—"

"Come on in, Quint. You should probably hear this."
Sam rose from his desk and shook hands with JJ, then
directed her to one of two chairs in front of his desk.

Quint stiffened. No, he shouldn't probably hear this.
Whatever JJ was doing in Cedar Creek couldn't have
anything to do with him. Sam—he needed to know.
Little Bear, Harper, the other detectives—they might
need to know. But Quint was just a patrol officer. He
wrote tickets, broke up brawls, handled domestic dis-
putes. He didn't need to be in the loop on the important
stuff any more than the newest rookie out there did.

But he wasn't about to argue with Sam, especially in
front of a stranger. Reluctantly, he pivoted back into the

room, closed the door and, ignoring the empty chair, leaned against the edge of the table butted up to one wall. It gave him a good head-on look at his boss, with only a peripheral view of JJ.

"I bet you got a call this morning from South Carolina," she said pleasantly.

"I did," Sam agreed.

"From Chief Chadwick?"

"It was."

Though JJ's tone hadn't changed when she spoke her boss's name, something about it, or about her, reminded Quint of the question she'd asked out front. *Is your chief good, bad or indifferent?* Not idle conversation, then. His intuition was willing to bet that she put Chadwick as squarely in the second category as Quint put Sam in the first. Personality conflict? Professional differences? Was Chadwick a bad chief, was JJ a bad cop or did the truth fall somewhere in the middle?

That feeling rousing in his gut felt vaguely like curiosity, maybe even plain old interest. How long had it been since he'd been interested in anything?

Maybe he'd been wrong outside. Maybe he did want to know more about JJ Logan.

JJ tried to not let her nose wrinkle with distaste at Chief Douglas's last answer. She'd known Chadwick couldn't be trusted. If she told Douglas—and the handsome Officer Foster—that Chadwick had specifically told her to not touch base with them, she would seem petty or defensive. Besides, no cop bad-mouthed her chief to cops she'd just met. That would be a big step toward giving Dipstick the reason he needed to fire her.

So she put on her best trust-me face—a smile that was neither over- nor underwhelming, her gaze clear and steady—and added a bit of sheepishness to it. "I really did intend to come by later today. I was just eager to get to work."

"Work," Chief Douglas repeated. "What's your interest in Maura Evans?"

Had Chadwick told him the truth about that or tried to screw her there, too? Was she going to tell her story only to find his had been totally different and thereby look like an idiot—worse, an untrustworthy idiot—in front of these fellow officers?

Nothing she could do but be honest herself. If the boss had muddied things between her and the local department, she would just have to make the best of it.

"Maura's a local girl. She left town a few years ago after her parents' deaths. She's twenty-five, single, still grieving…and very wealthy. She settled here in Cedar Creek about six months ago and, three months later, cut off contact with everyone back home—friends, relatives, the family attorney who also happens to be her godfather. He wants to know what's going on with her."

She saw a flicker of expression—negative—cross Officer Foster's face, making it easy to guess what he was thinking. Spoiled rich girl, selfish, entitled, the center of her own universe—her influential lawyer godfather taking advantage of the system, the chief giving in to political pressure to treat Maura as if she were *special*.

It was harder to tell with his chief, though. Douglas's expression gave away nothing, and neither did his tone. "Your department must be blessed with detectives—and funds—if they can send one halfway across the country to do a welfare check on one of our residents." Then came a faint whiff of disapproval. "A check that we would have happily handled for you if you'd just called."

Her smile thinned. Hey, she wasn't onboard with this, either. She had much more important cases she could be working on, cases where there was actually a police interest. "Did I mention that the town Maura Evans left is named Evanston? The Evans family have been rich and powerful since they founded the town in 1804. They donated land, set up charities, ran businesses, built schools and libraries and churches and hospitals. The men were war heroes, and the women were social workers ahead of their time. They are one ridiculously wealthy family that everyone in town respects and cares about."

She hesitated, then corrected herself. "They *were*. Maura has distant relatives, but she's the last one in the direct line." People would have treated her like their greatest, most fragile treasure if she hadn't fled town after the funerals. But no one blamed her for that. How could she have stayed in that town with its all memories, in that house knowing...?

With a suppressed shudder, JJ shifted her gaze to Officer Foster. Quint, the chief had called him. She liked the name. It was neither overly common nor trendy nor so unusual as to be unspellable, unpronounceable or unmemorable. "I really was just having a look around out there this morning."

His only response was the smallest of shrugs. The chief, on the other hand, raised one brow. "That's what you call surveillance back in South Carolina? Having a look around?"

"All right, yes, I parked down the street from her house this morning for fifteen minutes…maybe thirty… maybe an hour." She couldn't resist a rueful grin, the one her sisters called her mischief grin. Standard when she'd been caught with the cookie jar in her hands and chocolate chips smeared across her face, saying, *Yes, I'm guilty, but I'm just so darn adorable, you have to forgive me for it.* Dad always had. Mom usually had. She achieved varied success with others, and it looked like none whatsoever with Quint Foster.

Aw, she'd really like for him to find her adorable. If not him… She remembered the other officers she'd seen when they'd come in. Good-looking, every last one of them. Hopefully, between work, she'd manage some play on this trip, too.

"Along with a pair of binoculars, a map of the city, a camera, a large cup of coffee and an empty bag from Ted's Doughnuts."

JJ was impressed that Quint had been so observant. With those dark glasses he'd had on, of course, she couldn't see where his gaze was directed, but it had felt as if it was on her the whole time. Obviously not.

"Didn't take her long to figure out where the best doughnuts in town are, did it?" Douglas murmured.

Though the comment wasn't directed at her, she responded with a little shrug. "Cops and doughnuts. What can I say?"

He smiled briefly at the stereotype, then opened the laptop and began clicking away. She'd never had a chief who was anywhere near her age, but she would bet Sam Douglas was even a few years younger. He didn't wear a uniform—Chadwick always wore a uniform with four shiny gold stars on his collar to ensure everyone recognized him as the head honcho—but instead was dressed in jeans and a button-down shirt. A soft-looking gray cowboy hat was on the file cabinet to the left of his desk, leading her to expect cowboy boots on his feet if she could get a peek.

You're definitely not in Carolina anymore, JJ.

"Okay, Detective Logan—we don't stand on ceremony much around here. All right if I call you JJ?"

She nodded.

"I'm Sam, and he's Quint."

Wow. She'd never had a chief who was that casual, either. Even the last one, her mentor, had never invited her to use his first name. He'd believed in good work relations, but there was a line that should never be crossed.

"You didn't ask what we know, but we'll tell you anyway. You have the address of the house Maura's renting. You know she drives a little red car that cost more than a lot of people's houses around here. I've never met her myself, but my officers have handled four disturbance calls at that address for loud parties and given her three—no, four citations for speeding."

Disturbance calls at that big house at the end of that lonely street. Those must have been some parties.

"Quint gave her three of those tickets."

She shifted her gaze to Quint. He hadn't changed position—he still leaned against the table—but his posture seemed fractionally more rigid, his expression harder. She was half surprised he could open that taut jaw to add, "I also answered one of the disturbance calls with Ben."

Sam frowned. "Why was Ben answering a disturbance call?"

"He was in the office when it came in. Loud party, forty or so people, lot of booze."

JJ called to mind the area across the hall that served as reception, dispatch and detective squad, including a very tall, very broad-shouldered muscular man. "I'm going to guess Ben is the big guy out there at one of the desks."

Sam nodded. "Six foot four, solid muscle, can make you confess to anything just so he'll go away and stop looking at you. No matter how drunk people are, they never want to take on Ben Little Bear."

She envied that. When she was in uniform, all the drunks had wanted to take her on. She'd been forced to perfect her combat skills and had developed quite an affection for her nonlethal resources: baton, pepper spray and Taser.

"When was the last time you saw Maura?" Sam asked Quint.

"The day I gave her that last ticket." Quint's scowl was slightly more fierce than his normal expression. "About two months ago. She was doing forty-eight in a twenty."

JJ smiled faintly. "That sounds like Maura. The day her parents gave her that car, she got stopped for speeding in town and again in the county. Notice I said stopped, not ticketed. The officer and the deputy let her go when they realized who she was. I wrote her father a ticket once. Got called back to the station and royally chewed out."

"Must be nice to have so much influence." Cynicism made Quint's voice dry as parched sand.

"I can live without it." She crossed her legs and let her foot tap air a few times. "At home, we have a dispatcher named Carla and a patrol officer named Patrick who know everything there is to know about everyone in town."

Quint and Sam exchanged looks before the chief answered. "That would be Morwenna and Lois. Quint, why don't you show her the conference room and I'll get them."

Quint straightened to his full height easily and fluidly. She, on the other hand, felt the stiffness of two days' driving and another few hours' sitting. While she was here, she needed to make time for regular runs, long walks or—her gaze slid from his golden hair over his chest, his narrow waist and narrower hips, down long legs to the black tactical boots he wore—ah, yes, physical activity of some sort.

Without realizing it, she'd registered at some point that, unlike Sam, he wore no wedding ring. She had only two hard-and-fast rules in her romantic life, and one was that she didn't dally with married men. She'd pulled enough enraged wives off their husbands' girlfriends, hands filled with hair and fingernails leaving deep gouges, to know the best sex in the world wasn't worth that.

The other rule was that her butterflies had to twirl and her heart had to pitter-patter.

Check on the butterflies. And—she caught the slight increase of her heart rate—check on the pitter-patter.

But what were the odds she'd be here long enough to thaw him out?

Showing JJ to the conference room took about five seconds: out the door, turn right, go to the next door. Quint flipped on the overhead, then went to open the blinds on the tall windows. The light flooding the room illuminated the intricate crown molding, original to the building, along with the battered table, cast-off chairs and unwanted desks bunched against one wall.

"Interesting room," she remarked as she made her way to a chair. "The marble floor is gorgeous, and the moldings are incredible."

"But everything in between sucks."

"Except for the windows, pretty much." She sat at the far end, where sunlight filtered through the blinds. The position would give her a good look at everyone else while she would be shadowy when they looked back. He bet she had all kinds of similar tricks up her detective's sleeve.

He should ask Sam if he could go now, but Sam hadn't included that in his instructions. For whatever reason—probably because Maura lived in Quint's patrol district—he wanted Quint to know all this, and because Quint was damn grateful to have his job, he was going to obey. But he'd still rather be outside, alone in his vehicle, with nothing for company but the radio broadcasts.

JJ's chair was pushed back from the table, leaving

her room to cross her legs again. Her spine was straight, barely touching the back of the chair, and except for the heavy jacket, her clothing clung, shirt hugging her breasts just short of straining the buttons, denim stretching over her thighs. Most women he knew with that kind of posture had suffered through years of ballet or gymnastics. He tried to imagine her in leotards or tights, tumbling or pirouetting on her toes, but the image wouldn't form. Swinging a baseball bat or breaking a board with her bare foot seemed far more likely.

She brushed her hair back, and sunlight flashed on a stone on her left hand. It was on her ring finger, fiery orange set in gold. A nontraditional engagement or wedding ring, or just a piece of jewelry she liked? He wouldn't find it hard to believe she was unconventional. Wouldn't find it hard to believe she was married, either.

Didn't matter to him either way.

"What is your impression of Maura?"

Embarrassment heated Quint's neck but luckily burned inward instead of out. From the moment the dispatcher had passed on the call to check the stranger on Maura's street, he'd known in the back of his mind that this had to do with Maura. Who else on that street was interesting enough for surveillance? The young couple with four kids in the house fifty feet behind where she'd parked? The elderly sisters? The two college girls down the street or Jamey Moran, the deputy fire marshal who was so clean he squeaked?

But the front part of his brain hadn't wanted to give it any thought. Now he had no choice, so he gave the most superficial answer that came to mind. "She's a bad driver with too much time and money on her hands."

JJ tilted her head to one side. "That's it?"

Acknowledging that he seemed to be getting further away from returning to his vehicle instead of closer, he swallowed a sigh and took a chair near her end of the table, leaving an empty space between them. "I don't know her. My interaction with her has been less than thirty minutes, all calls combined."

That was true. But he was leaving out the fact that the last time he'd stopped her, Maura had offered to remedy the not-knowing-each-other thing if he wouldn't write the ticket. He'd stood there in her driveway—she'd refused to stop until she reached the house—and smelled the sweet scent of her perfume, watched the breeze mold her already-tight dress even closer to her body, and sweet hell, he'd been tempted. He'd been alone so long. So damn alone. Sometimes he'd missed human contact so much that he'd physically hurt with it, and he'd thought...

It had shamed him then, and it did now. He'd thought Maura was no one special. She would never mean anything to him. He could use her to ease his pain and never have to bother with her again. He'd never treated women as disposable, but it had held a strong appeal that day.

Then she'd touched him, and it had had the effect of a gut punch, slamming home one important truth: he didn't want human contact. He wanted Linny. No one could ever replace her, not for a night, for an hour or a minute, and certainly not some rich girl who thought avoiding a hundred-dollar ticket was worth trading sex for.

Disgusted with himself, he'd removed her hand, a bit of a struggle when she'd already insinuated her fingers inside his belt and didn't want to let go. She'd pouted, called him a few names, torn up the ticket and let the wind scatter the pieces. And after that, he'd turned a blind eye to her driving infractions, just like those South Carolina cops did. Don't poke the bear, his father used to say. The next time he might not walk away with his dignity intact.

"She was self-centered. Used to getting her way. She fluttered her lashes and smiled real pretty and expected problems to go away. I have no idea why she settled here. There aren't a lot of restaurants, no clubs that would appeal to someone like that, no shopping besides Walmart, a couple of small clothing stores and the antique stores downtown, and name-dropping wouldn't get her anywhere this far from home. Cedar Creek doesn't have anything to offer her."

That was the most he'd said at one time in months. His chest was tight, his lungs empty from putting together so many words. It was an odd feeling, hearing so much of his own voice when he generally got through the day with minimal talking.

He drew a breath and turned the question around. "What is your impression of her?"

Her smile was easy. "She was self-centered and used to getting her way. But I don't think she could really help it, given who she was and where and how she was raised. I don't think she was strong enough to develop any independence or real sense of character when every soul in her life expected her to be a princess.

"I babysat her one summer. I had graduated from college, and her mother was busy, and I had some time on my hands before the academy started. She was spoiled, of course, but not rotten. She just expected things to go her way because they always had. It never really occurred to her that they wouldn't until her parents…"

Quint watched as JJ's mouth thinned, her affect darkened. "How did they die?"

She bit her lower lip, full and soft peach in color, then blew out her breath. "They were murdered five years ago. Home invasion. I had stopped by my parents' house a few blocks away, so I was the first officer on the scene. Their bodies were found by the housekeeper, but Maura came in a few minutes after I got there and saw…everything."

The twinge of sympathy Quint felt surprised him. He'd always been empathetic—most cops were—but the only person he'd felt sorry for in the last year and a half had been himself. Maura had been twenty at the time. How deeply had that sight scarred her? If she hadn't been strong before, that experience certainly wouldn't make her any stronger. So she'd coped by running away, by living fast and partying hard and trying her damnedest to forget the memories. By drinking and using drugs and having meaningless sex.

But sympathy didn't mean he wanted any contact with her again. It didn't mean he particularly cared what state her life was in. He just didn't have it in him to care right now.

He shoved back the discomfort that admission caused and refocused his attention on JJ. "So, you're going to go talk to her, make sure she's okay and go home." He said it as a statement because that was what he wanted to happen. Like he'd thought earlier, he didn't want upset in his life. It was routine that got him through the days—and quiet desperation that carried him through the nights—and like a cranky old dog, he needed to stick to that routine as much as possible.

"Actually, I'm going to look around first. Talk to your dispatcher and your officer, maybe visit her neighbors, her landlord." Her lips thinned again, but thoughtfully this time. "As I said, she's very wealthy. Her godfather is executor of her parents' estate. About ten million went to their favorite charities, but Maura got the rest. I don't know how many zeroes are tacked onto her net worth, but she gets an allowance of $100,000 a month, which she never completely spent until she came here. She's young, rich, grieving, vulnerable."

Quint ignored the statement that she was going to stay around longer than necessary—he wouldn't have to deal with her—and laced his fingers together. "So her godfather is concerned because this spoiled rich kid is spending more money than usual?"

"No, not just that. For all her flaws, Maura was very close to her parents. She left town after they died and traveled constantly until she came here, but no matter where she was, she remembered every holiday—their birthdays, anniversaries, Mother's Day, Father's Day— with deliveries of extravagant flowers. Even when she was trekking in Nepal and on a tourist expedition to the South Pole, she sent the flowers. But she missed both their birthdays last month."

"Maybe she's coping better now. Maybe she realizes flowers don't change anything." They made the grave site prettier, let people know that the person who occupied that grave had someone who loved them in death as much as they had in life. But they didn't ease the pain.

They didn't make life any easier. They didn't help you survive another day or another week. They were a gesture, but a pretty meaningless one from his experience.

"It was important to her," JJ disagreed. "Also, in the last three months, she's only gotten in touch with Mr. Winchester, her godfather, twice by text. The first time, she demanded more cash, and the second, she threatened to sue him for control of the money. Mr. Winchester and his wife are also important to her. They're her second parents. It's out of character for her."

Quint wasn't convinced anything was out of character for someone like Maura. Pretty, entitled, spent her money freely, shared herself freely… Unpredictable seemed the best word to describe her. Hell, she'd gone from South Carolina to the South Pole to Small Town, Oklahoma, where her name meant nothing. *Out of character* seemed to be the only constant in her character.

But it wasn't his problem.

That was the best part of the situation. Once he left the station, he was out of it.

Chapter 2

JJ rose from her chair when Sam escorted two women into the conference room. She'd noticed both women when she and Quint had arrived and had presumed Sam got busy on the way back or Lois had gone back on patrol and he'd had to wait until she returned. The women greeted her with friendly smiles and very curious gazes. Oh yeah, they were just like Carla and Patrick at home. In seconds, they'd summed her up, cataloging her from head to toe as efficiently as any machine.

After shaking hands, she sat down again and told them why she was in town, watching their faces when she named Maura. Recognition lit both pairs of eyes.

"Wild child," Lois said immediately. She was the officer, the older of the two, compact and competent, her short hair colored a blast of fresh blue that suited her perfectly. "Lot of money, lot of parties, lot of spending. Drives a flashy little red convertible that I would look so good in—" she preened accordingly "—and thinks speed limits and red lights are more suggestions than actual laws."

Morwenna, the dispatcher, was young enough to be Lois's daughter, pretty, soft, her clothing bright and mismatched enough to present a danger to everyone's vision. A faint hint of an accent came and went from her voice as she agreed. "I don't think she's a bad person. She's just spoiled. But she's very generous, too. We've run into her and her friend a couple times in Tulsa, and she paid for everyone's drinks all night long, then took us to a late dinner—er, early breakfast when we were done. And her parties are always popular. I went once—too loud and too much booze and—" she glanced at Sam "—and, uh, weed for me. And the police show up at least every other time, and I didn't want a lecture from you, Sam, for being at a party where the cops were called."

Nothing new there, JJ thought. The cops at home had often gotten called to Maura's parties. She'd held them at other kids' houses because the Evans family home would have shaken on its foundations at such goings-on. She'd invited a few friends, who invited a few friends and so on, until two or three hundred people from all over that part of the state showed up. The liquor had flowed freely, the pot had perfumed the air and who knew what else the kids had been doing?

"You mentioned a friend," JJ said to Morwenna. "Man or woman? Do you remember a name?"

The dispatcher propped her foot on the seat of her chair, wrapping her arms around one leg covered in Easter-patterned tights. The yellow chickies, white bunnies and pastel eggs were cute, but the lime-green shirt over a fiery-red tank… It would give Chadwick apoplexy if one of his dispatchers showed up dressed that way.

JJ liked the outfit for that reason alone.

"It was a girl, but her name was a guy's name." Morwenna pressed her lips together and quirked her mouth to one side while tugging on her ponytail. "Mick, Mike…no, Mel. The last name was common. Smith, Jones, something like that."

Lovely. There was nothing so tedious as searching for someone with a common surname. It was one of Chief Dipstick's favorite jobs for JJ. "Is Mel a local girl?"

"Not Cedar Creek. We thought she was a cousin or something. Blond hair, blue eyes, cute little nose—" Morwenna tapped her own less-than-little nose "—little Cupid's bow mouth. Same attitude, same entitlement."

"There was definitely a resemblance," Lois said.

"They were really tight for a while. Mel was at her house all the time. She practically lived there. Maybe she did live there, at least for a while."

That made sense. Maura had never been a quiet, rely-on-herself sort of person. She needed companionship and entertainment. All that traveling… JJ had thought she was getting acquainted with herself, plumbing depths that no one knew she had, but maybe not.

"What happened to Mel?" Sam asked.

"Maura said she went home. She was getting bored with Cedar Creek. She never mentioned where home was for either of them."

"When was that?"

Morwenna shrugged, her vibrant image blurring in

JJ's gaze. "Three or four months ago. I'm not sure. We aren't really friends. We just hung out a few times."

JJ made a mental note to ask Mr. Winchester if there was an Evans relative named Mel—Melody, Melinda, Melanie. As far as she knew, the Evanses had no close relatives. Neither of Maura's parents had had any siblings, and she'd been an only child herself. But in a lot of Southern families, the Logans included, a cousin was a cousin, no matter how many times removed.

Sam handed out notepads and pens from the battered desk and asked everyone to make a list of Maura's associates. While the women started writing, Quint declined. "She was alone when I stopped her, and I didn't know anyone at the party." He shrugged. "I'm more likely to recognize those kids' parents than them."

JJ's gaze settled on the stone in her ring. It was a Mexican fire opal, orange-red, her birthstone. It was a lucky stone, her mother had told her, symbolic of hope and innocence, a god's tears turned to stone and colored with the fire of lightning. JJ wasn't sure about any of that, but touching it did help her think better.

One of Mr. Winchester's concerns that she hadn't brought up earlier was the possibility that Maura was being influenced by someone. Con artists were always on the lookout for easy targets, and between her sorrow, her dependence and her immaturity, she would be one of the easiest. The payoff for the crook could be in the tens of millions of dollars. Was that Mel's role in her life? Manipulating all that lovely money into her own greedy hands?

Or maybe she really was a relative. Or a friend. Maybe more than a friend. Mel had left Cedar Creek about the time of the change in Maura's behavior. A broken heart could certainly explain a lot, especially with a twenty-five-year-old who'd already lost so much.

But shouldn't that have strengthened the tie to her godfather? Would she actually threaten the only person left in her life because her girlfriend had left her?

Maybe. If she was distraught enough. If she'd thought he was too conventional to understand.

The women finished their lists at the same time and passed them to her. Morwenna's, written with loops and swirls, was longer, while Lois's, in graceful old-school cursive, was more detailed. JJ thanked them as they stood and, after a moment's chitchat, left the room.

Sam slid a piece of paper down the table toward her. "She owns the house Maura's renting. Quint will go with you."

Annoyance flickered across Quint's face, and for an instant, JJ was half insulted on two fronts. She had conducted hundreds of interviews all by herself and didn't need help with this one. And Quint should have realized by now that she was fun. Smart. Could carry a conversation all by herself. She was an easy companion. And adorable.

And he was cranky. Not a people person. Not thrilled with the idea of giving up a good part of his day to babysit the out-of-town cop when he had better things to do. She totally got that. She had lots of better things to do than make sure Maura was coping. With all that money, Maura could buy everything she needed: someone to pamper her, take care of her, entertain her, have sex with her, clean up after her. She could even buy someone to love her.

She and Mr. Winchester had managed to temporarily buy JJ herself, though against her will.

"I don't really need an escort," she said, standing to her full height, unimpressive as it was with men who both topped six feet.

Sam's smile was part genuine, part sly. "I promised your chief we'd do all we could to help out."

She was considering baring her teeth at him when he went on.

"Besides, Mrs. Madison doesn't take kindly to many cops. Quint happens to be one of the exceptions. She'll be more likely to talk to you if he's with you."

So instead, she bared her teeth at Quint, disguising it as a smile. "Then I appreciate the offer. And I thank you for your time, Sam."

Folding the notepaper into a neat rectangle, she tucked it into her hip pocket, slid the chair under the table and followed the two men out of the room. Sam turned immediately into his office. Quint moved toward the front door with long, natural strides, making for a pleasant view as she followed him.

Momentum carried her to the edge of the first step, where she stopped cold. "Holy cats, what happened with the weather?"

Quint drew up as he realized she'd gone stationary. "Cold front moved in."

"Damn." The sky had darkened, and the breeze had morphed into a merciless wind with a bite that made her so-cute-and-comfortable jacket totally inadequate. Too bad she hadn't brought anything warmer. Too bad she didn't *own* anything warmer.

She hugged herself tightly as she hustled down the

steps and started across the lot. Her exposed skin was seriously cold, and the kind of bone-deep shivers that were actually painful were starting. She had no clue how many degrees the temperature had dropped while they were inside—thirty or more?—but it was way outside her comfort zone. She needed protection from the wind, and she needed it now.

Quint easily matched her stride. She knew a lot of men who used their longer, faster steps as a passive-aggressive outlet when they dealt with her five-foot-five-inch self. She'd long since stopped trying to keep up, especially when they were traveling in the same vehicle. Let them dawdle at the car, she'd decided, because generally they couldn't leave without her.

At the black pickup, he beeped the doors, slid inside and moved his black duty jacket from the passenger seat while she climbed up. Adjusting the mounted laptop to give herself an extra couple of inches of space took a second longer than it should have because the chills had worked their way from the inside out, and ditto with the seat belt. "Heat, please," she requested before her teeth started chattering.

He gave her a sidelong look as he started the engine. "Are you that cold?"

"South Carolina has a humid subtropical climate. In Evanston, fifty degrees is a frigid winter day. I break out my jackets at sixty."

He grunted before turning the heat on high. "Wind-chill's supposed to drop to around ten. You might want to put on those jackets before we go see Mrs. Madison."

"I didn't bring them. It's *March*. It's springtime." She tucked her fingers underneath each arm to stop them from turning blue. He didn't even seem affected, and he was wearing short sleeves.

"Here, winter's not over until summer."

She luxuriated in the rapidly warming air blowing from the vents, finally loosening her self-hug so she could hold her hands out. When her heart had recovered from the shock and started pumping warm blood again, she settled back. "Why does Mrs. Madison not like police officers?"

"Family tradition. None of them were very good at walking the straight and narrow."

They had plenty of those families in and around Evanston. Some of them were belligerent about it, but others, at least, disliked the police from the right side of the law. "And why does she like you?"

"She doesn't exactly like me. She tolerates me. She and my mother's family were neighbors."

JJ doubted the first part of his statement. Once people got past his stiff, stern exterior, she figured, they liked what they found. Sam, Lois and Morwenna certainly seemed to have a bond with him.

She gazed out the window at the sometimes pretty, sometimes shabby, sometimes overcommercialized town that Maura had chosen to live in. It really wasn't so different from Evanston. Smaller, not quite so prosperous, but she was certain it had its charm when the sun was shining and the air was sweet and warm.

She'd studied the Cedar Creek map, but it was always good to see exactly where to find the ice cream store and the grubby little hamburger joint that surely made the best burgers in town. In this particular case, they were south of downtown on Main Street. Another mile down, they passed a Whataburger, and her mouth started watering.

When she was a kid, every time they visited their grandparents in Florida, Grandpa had taken her and her sisters to Whataburger for a burger, fries and shake. Given that her mom and Grandma both had an unnatural aversion to fast food, it was always an absolute delight.

She intended to delight all over one later today.

When the street ended a moment later, Quint turned right. Three blocks later, he pulled into the parking lot of an assisted-living facility. *Who's going to take care of you when you get old if you don't have kids?* Mom routinely asked. *You'll wind up in one of those old folks places.*

This one didn't look so bad. The outside was well maintained, and inside, the lobby smelled of flowers and wood polish and, faintly, Italian spices, tomatoes and onions. Large windows let in a lot of light, and plants brightened even the darkest corners.

Quint signed them in, and they took the elevator to the third floor. Their strides weren't so evenly matched this time. In fact, if she were a suspicious person, she would think he was practically skulking along the far wall, head down, shoulders hunched, face turned to the left. When he actually raised his right hand and pulled his hat even lower as they passed an open door, she made a quick note of the room number—318—then watched him revert to normal. Or, at least, his variant of normal.

Interesting.

* * *

With a silent sigh of relief at passing room 318 unnoticed, Quint stopped at 327 and rapped on the door. The voice that called a response was soft, frail, sounding like a fragile old lady summoning up her dying breath to invite them in.

He knew better.

Georgia Madison's apartment consisted of a tiny kitchen that went mostly unused, a small living room and, visible through an open door, a bedroom. It was brightly lit to offset the gloominess outside, with table lamps and hanging globes of vivid colored glass. They were every shape and size: royal blue beside an orange the shade of JJ's ring, sunny yellow and green and a red that set the standard for all reds.

Georgia was sitting in a recliner near the floor-to-ceiling windows. Her hair was a mix of faded black, steel gray and white, her face lined with wrinkles, her eyes displaying her perpetual distrust of the unexpected. When she recognized him, some of the distrust faded, only to return in intensity at the sight of JJ.

"First time you come to see me in months, and you bring a copper with you?" She shook her head with mild disgust. Then she broke into a smile for him. "How are you, Quint?"

"I'm good, Georgie." It was a blatant lie, and going by her second head shake, this one with mild sorrow, she recognized it.

He gestured to JJ, who'd stopped beside him. "Mrs. Georgia Madison, this is JJ Logan. You're right, she is a cop. But she's not out to get you."

"All cops are out to get everyone." The old lady gave

JJ an appraising look, then nodded. "Sit. Ask your questions."

JJ chose the couch, settling naturally into that perfect posture he'd noted earlier. Quint sat with a creak in the rocker a few feet to her left. The chair was old, the finish faded, but it was comfortable in ways a brand-new one could never be. He'd always sat in this chair when he'd visited the Madison home as a kid. It had squeaked badly even back then, and rocking in it had been one of his pleasures, until the inevitable warning from whichever adult was closest to *please stop that*.

He hadn't thought about the chair, or those visits, or that time of his life in a very long while.

"How did you know I'm a cop?" JJ asked.

"Really? That's the question you want to lead with?" Georgie gave an eye roll and a sigh, both heavily exaggerated. "It's the look. Quint has it. That good-looking Little Bear kid he works with has it, that little guy, Harper—hell, everyone down there at thug headquarters. All good cops have the look."

JJ considered, then accepted her answer as a compliment if her satisfied look was anything to judge by. "Do you prefer that I call you Mrs. Madison, Miss Georgia or Georgie?"

"Quint's the only one in this room who can call me Georgie. For all other coppers, it's Mrs. Madison."

"All right, Mrs. Madison, can I ask you a few questions about the woman renting your house on Willow Street?"

"You can ask whatever you want, and I'll answer whatever *I* want. And of course it's my house on Willow Street. It's the only house I own." She humphed.

"So? What do you want to know? I'm ninety-six years old, honey. Time's a-wasting."

JJ muttered, "And they say the good die young." Her voice was barely a whisper, and her mouth hardly moved, but that wasn't going to save her, Quint knew. Georgie heard everything.

Georgie's brows drew together in a frown. He thought for half a second about intervening but decided against it. The old woman was more than happy to spread her ire around, and he was more than willing to let her. Instead, he sat back, rested his ankle on the other knee and rubbed at a scuff on his boot.

"Let me tell you something, little girl. Disrespecting a fragile elderly woman that you want information from isn't the smartest way to go. My hair may be gray, my bones may be weak and my body may be giving up while I'm still using it, but my hearing is as good as ever, so a little politeness is in order here."

Quint waited for JJ's flush, for her eyes to widen with dismay and words of apology to tumble out of her mouth. That was how people always reacted to Georgie, especially coppers. But not this one. JJ arched one brow and fixed her steady, challenging gaze on her adversary. "That politeness extends both ways. Besides, I bet you never aspired to be good or die young, so that's probably more of a compliment than an insult."

Okay, she'd surprised him. He wouldn't be surprised by Georgie's response, because he had zero idea what it would be. He'd never known anyone who, when dressed down by Georgie for her attitude, displayed even more attitude.

He should have left JJ downstairs in the lobby. Better

yet, he should have just called Georgie and asked about Maura. But hell, who ever would have thought *he* would be the more tactful of any two people in the world?

Georgie's stare simmered for a long moment, then she pointed one long, thin finger JJ's way. "You should be scared of me."

"Ha. You never met my grandmother Raynelle. She was a lot like you, only she was *really* scary."

Georgie considered the name a moment. "I don't know any Raynelles. Where are you from?"

"South Carolina."

"And they say Southern women are genteel. Apparently, they never met you." Georgie snorted before relenting. "You're right. I never did aspire to be good, just like you never cared about being genteel. And you can call me Miss Georgie. I like the la-di-da sound of that. So what do you want to know about Maura Evans?"

Quint blinked. He'd seen Georgie chew up grown people and spit 'em out. If she'd been a cat, she would have been the sort who tormented the mouse mercilessly before killing it. JJ should have been lucky to walk out of here with her skin intact.

Instead, they both looked smugly satisfied. Like they'd come to some kind of agreement and would now make nice of their own accord. He'd never seen Georgie make nice with anyone outside her family or his.

JJ set her clasped hands on her lap. "Have you met Maura?"

"Of course. I'm not going to let someone move into my own house without getting a good look at her. My granddaughter showed her the house." Georgie's faded gaze darted to Quint. "Twenty-three and hasn't been to jail once."

"Yet," he tacked on, making her grin. Truth was, none of her family had been to jail in his lifetime. They'd gotten tamed before he was even born. But they'd still nursed that family animosity toward the law.

"She's going to be a schoolteacher. Graduates from OSU next December." Georgie rummaged in the drawer beside her chair and drew out an electronic cigarette. Her smoking had been the nastiest habit under the sun, his mother used to declare, even though Georgie had never smoked in anyone's house, not even her own. At her age, he figured, she was entitled to a few vices. Smoking, a glass of whiskey before bed and terrorizing the other old folks in the home were all she could manage.

"When Maura decided she wanted the house, I had her come over here to sign the papers. We had lunch, just me and her and that obnoxious little friend of hers. Mel. I hope her real name was something like Mellissandriennalou. That twit walked through the door—" she gestured with her e-cig toward her own door "—took a sniff and said old people smell like death. Like she even knows what death smells like. Rude kid. I should have pinched her ear."

JJ grinned. "You are like Grandmother Raynelle. I was convinced my right ear was going to be bigger than the left because of all the times she tweaked it."

"Sounds like you needed it."

Quint couldn't quite see JJ as a disrespectful kid. Disobedient, sure. She struck him as someone who acted first and apologized later—sweetly, innocently and even faintly sincerely—if it was necessary. Even in her earlier exchange with Georgie, he suspected she'd already known how the old woman was going to react, so there'd been no real disrespect intended.

"Do you remember Mel's last name?"

"Wasn't even polite enough to offer it."

"What did you think of their relationship?"

With the push of a button, Georgie reclined the chair, stretched out her legs and crossed her ankles, propping hot-pink running shoes on the footrest. "I thought they were family at first. Mel's hair and eyes were brown, and Maura was a blue-eyed blonde, but other than that, they could have been sisters.

"But you could tell Maura had always had money and Mel never had. Maura was all elegant and confident, and Mel... There was a sort of hunger about her. Not physical, you know, but more as if life had been tough and she'd never known anything better. She didn't *look* like money, you know? And telling me I smell. Twit."

The image that formed in Quint's mind didn't create a warm-and-fuzzy feeling. Rude, disrespectful, didn't know how to behave and eager to trade her tough life for something better. And that was apparently the only friend Maura had had. And then Mel had left her.

As unsympathetic as he intended to be, that thought told him he wasn't succeeding.

Because that was just damn sad.

JJ tipped her head back and gazed at the ceiling. The mysterious Mel sounded like Maura's friends back home, except that the Carolina friends mostly came from money, like her. JJ was familiar with some of them because of their run-ins with police that never resulted in consequences, some because of their parents' friendships with her parents. Most of them she could recognize, maybe even identify by name, but that was all. She couldn't recall a brown-haired, brown-eyed hard-luck kid who'd infiltrated the Evanston crowd and stuck with it.

The two women could have met in college or on the road. It didn't seem possible Mel had toured a winter's full of ice palace hotels in Norway or cruised the Mediterranean, but Maura had spent plenty of time in American cities, as well. They could have run into each other in any number of ways, hit it off and decided to roam together with Maura picking up the tab. She was very generous, Morwenna had said.

Because her companions had let her thoughts wander undisturbed—Quint probably preferred her silence, but as Miss Georgie had said, time was a-wasting—she filled the silence with an absentminded comment. "Your glass is beautiful."

"It is. That swirly red-and-green one there—that was a Christmas gift from Maura. She brought it when she delivered the December rent. We had lunch together every month when she paid the rent, but after that, I never saw her again. The rent started coming in the mail."

JJ studied the lamp with new interest. Maura had noticed the collection and taken the time to find a beautiful icicle-shaped addition. For a woman she didn't really know and expected nothing from in return. That was the kind of thoughtfulness one expected of an Evans a few generations ago, not from the current one. If she made the right friends, fell in love with the right person, would Maura discover something of substance inside herself?

Possibly. But it didn't seem likely that maybe-Melanie, maybe-Mellissandriennalou was the kind of friend who could anchor Maura in the real world. Instead, she appeared to have been along for the ride, enjoying the luxury until she'd gotten bored and moved on.

Leaving Maura one more loss to cope with.

Her muscles protesting too much sitting, JJ got to her feet. The rocker squeaked as Quint followed suit. "One last question, Miss Georgie. Did Maura say why she'd decided to stay in Cedar Creek?"

A rather sad look claimed Miss Georgie's features. "She said it reminded her of home. You know, I never saw a person more lost than her."

JJ felt a little sad, too, as she approached Miss Georgie and offered her hand. The old woman's skin was dry and cool, marked with what Grandmother Raynelle had called wisdom spots, and her fingernails were painted a sparkly midnight blue.

"It was a pleasure to meet you, Miss Georgie."

"For a copper, you're not too bad." The effect of Miss Georgie's scowl was dampened by her sly wink.

"You're not half as bad as you think you are."

Miss Georgie chuckled. "You can come back sometime. We'll see if I can change your mind about that."

"I'd love to see you try." JJ gave the thin hand a gentle squeeze, then turned toward the door.

She was halfway there when Miss Georgie spoke again. "Come over here, Quint."

There was no doubt it was a command, and no doubt that he would obey it, JJ thought, hiding a grin, because that was the kind of person he was. She waited at the door while he did, indeed, obey and Miss Georgie took both of his hands in hers.

"How are you? Really?" Her voice was a murmur, but JJ shared one thing with the old woman: excellent hearing.

He looked as if he wanted to pull away, rush out the door and let the cold air drive away the flush to his cheeks. He didn't, though. Instead, he muttered, "I'm okay. Really."

Okay about what? It clearly wasn't the throwaway question everybody used a dozen times a day. Something had happened in his recent past that worried the crusty old woman—something he didn't want to discuss.

JJ turned her back, deliberately tuning out their conversation. She didn't feel guilty for being curious. She wouldn't be a police officer if she wasn't curious about things, and she wouldn't be a woman if she wasn't curious about *him*. But she didn't stoop to eavesdropping, not unless it involved a case.

After a moment, his footsteps sounded behind her. She opened the door and stepped out into the corridor. He closed the door and stopped beside her, looking to the right, the way they'd come, then to the left, where a red exit sign marked the stairwell. He looked like a man who very much wanted to take the stairs.

"Who's in 318?"

His scowl wasn't as fierce as Miss Georgie's, but it was more sincere. "You noticed that."

"I'm a copper." The word made her grin. She might never call herself a cop again. "I get paid to notice things." Turning 180 degrees, she started toward the stairway exit.

She was pretty sure that was relief radiating off him as he fell into step beside her. No answer was forthcoming, though, so she prompted him. "Family?"

The closing of the stairwell door was muffled by the sound of their boots, hers sharper, his more solid, descending the steps. He didn't answer until they reached the second-floor landing. "Practically."

It wasn't much of an answer, but that was okay. She didn't have the standing to insist on more. Though they'd spent half the morning together, they were still strangers. His life was his, and he got to choose what he wanted to share.

Besides, it wasn't his life she wanted him to share.

She had a healthy regard for sex. She was thirty-seven and unencumbered by relationships. She'd come close to marrying once, a decade ago. Ryan had been a fellow officer who moved to Evanston after two years with the Columbia Police Department. He'd been sweet and smart and funny and everything she wanted in a guy...until she made detective before him.

When he'd broken the engagement and moved back to Columbia, it had stung her pride and made her doubt her judgment, but it hadn't broken her heart. Which meant he really hadn't been even close to everything she wanted in a guy.

Since then, she hadn't gotten within squinting distance of marriage. She'd dated her share of men, had sex with some of them and not with others. She didn't indulge in one-night stands or stranger sex because of the inherent risks. She still had a yearning, not necessarily for marriage but for commitment. For that one special man who would brighten her day just by being in it, who would love everything about her the same way she would love everything about him and would make her heart flutter when she was eighty.

But if she waited to meet Mr. Forever before she had sex again, she would be a very grumpy and cranky JJ, and that wasn't a pretty sight.

The air broke over her, offensively cold, when she walked out the front door. This time, though, she didn't stop in shock. Her steps lengthened as she practically jogged across the lot to Quint's vehicle. The exercise, brief as it was, felt really good to muscles cramping from the same position for so very long. On another day, she might even have told Quint she would walk back to her car, enjoying the exercise, the fresh air and the budding of the trees. Today, spending one instant more than necessary outside was out of the question.

"What now?" Quint asked as they fastened their seat belts.

"Where can I buy a coat?"

"Walmart. Atwoods. It's a farm and ranch supply store. Or there's a little store about a mile north. We can stop there on the way back to the station."

Ooh, she liked a man who didn't whine about shopping. Her father and both her brothers-in-law acted as if their fingernails were being torn out with pliers every time they had to hang out in a women's clothing department. Though, truthfully, JJ felt the same way when she accompanied her middle sister. Kylie could spend an hour choosing between two pairs of nearly identical jeans.

"Little store sounds fine. When it comes to warmth, I have no vanity."

He reached into the back, snagging his duty jacket, and offered it to her. "Until the truck warms up."

She hesitated half a second before accepting it, huddling beneath it like a blanket. It was big and heavy and smelled enticingly of scents undiluted by cologne. Shaving cream, detergent, fabric softener, soap. No floral or woodsy intruders, but plain, simple Quint. She drew a deep breath, then sighed happily, her chin tucked into the faux-fur collar.

It was a quick drive to the shopping center where the clothing shop nestled between a coffee shop and a grocery store. The air blowing from the truck's heating vents wasn't much warmer than outside when they parked, but she handed the jacket back, anyway. He didn't insist she keep it, didn't pretend he wasn't finally feeling the cold himself, but shrugged into it as he got out.

She appreciated that fact. She'd never understood why men always offered their jackets to women who'd failed to dress warmly enough. Like the chill didn't cut through their clothes just as easily? She had never been a Boy Scout, but she knew all about the consequences of not being prepared. You don't take an umbrella on a soggy day, you get wet. You wear a sweater on a hot day, you get sweaty. You don't take a heavy coat to a place known for its iffy weather, you get frozen lungs and blue skin.

Sadly, blue wasn't really her color.

They hustled from the parking lot to the store. On the other side of the glass doors, warm air, an explosion of colors and rock music greeted them, along with a pretty girl sitting at the checkout counter and texting. Her hello was perfunctory until she glanced up. Then a smile split her face, she clutched her cell phone, jumped to her feet and rounded the corner to approach them. "What are you doing here? Did that six-pack of T-shirts you bought five years ago finally wear out? Can I take your picture and send it to everyone as proof of life?"

Curious, JJ looked from Quint to the girl. She was way too young for anything romantic between them. Sure, some older guys had to go young for an emotional-needs match, but he seemed far too stolid to date someone he could have fathered. Besides, with the blond hair, blue eyes and the square angle of both their jaws, she'd put money on a relative. Much younger sister, niece, cousin.

"If you take my picture and send it to everyone, there won't be any life left in your phone by the time I finish grinding it into the ground," he said, gaze narrowed, voice gravelly enough to give some weight to the threat.

But the girl wasn't the least bit threatened. "Uncle Quint, you haven't scared me since the time you caught me and my friends drinking beer at the park. That was ages ago."

"Four years."

"Like I said. Ages." Her gaze shifted to JJ, raking up and down. "I love that jacket, but it's way too cold for it today."

"That's why I'm here." JJ saw racks of coats near the back of the store and headed that way. A murmured conversation drifted behind her—Quint's voice low and raspy, the girl's higher and lighter—then came the click of high heels on the tile floor. JJ lifted a black wool coat from the rack to examine it, and when she lowered it, the blonde was on the other side.

"Hi, I'm Lia, and though my job is to sell the merchandise, that coat is something my grandma would buy. We have a great plum one, and a persimmon one, and a gorgeous fuchsia. Even something like this brown does so much more for you than black. Plus, it's more fitted, like your jacket, so you still have a shape when you're wearing it, instead of being padded and curveless like the black one." Lia held up the brown coat, flashed a smile at Quint, waiting by the register, and lowered her voice. "So you're a friend of Uncle Quint's."

JJ couldn't help but smile at both her fashion advice and her conspiratorial tone. "We just met this morning. I'm in town on business." She patted her Taser after removing her own jacket and before pulling on the brown coat. The shade was rich and dark and reminded her of hot cocoa with just a sprinkle of cinnamon. Its luxe lining embraced her with warmth.

Lia smoothed the collar, then turned JJ to face a mirror. "See, the color plays up the reddish tints in your hair and those freckles you do a decent job of hiding. You really shouldn't be hiding them. They're there, they're cute, and Uncle Quint likes freckles. And you can be warm without adding so much bulk." Without a breath, she shifted gears again. "How long will you be here?"

"No idea. A few days, maybe a week." She shrugged.

"Oh. Too bad…or maybe not. I mean, not everything's got to be forever, right? You're pretty, and you have good taste, and a week of innocent—"

Quint cleared his throat, and Lia literally jumped.

Her face went pale, then a few shades darker than his own flush. "I'm telling Grandma you eavesdropped."

"Grandma was the one who taught me that when your voice got quiet, you were up to something."

Lia sniffed. "She should have been the cop in the family." Her pout turned immediately to a smile when she turned back to JJ. "Do you like this coat, or would you like to see the persimmon one? And do you need a scarf or gloves to go with that? They're right this way—"

The glimpse JJ got of Quint's aggravated face as Lia pulled her away was sweet. He wasn't terminally cranky, after all; he was kind to old ladies and fond of his niece. Chief Dipstick had clearly sent her here as punishment, but the universe had smiled on her by putting Quint in her path.

Wouldn't that make the old man spit nails?

Quint stayed nearby while Lia rang up JJ's coat, scarf and gloves, then cut the tags from them. The only way to stop a Foster woman from talking about anything and everything was to stand watch, ready to put the fear into them. He'd forgotten that when he'd let his niece wander off to wait on JJ. He hadn't heard everything when he joined them, but he'd heard enough to get the impression that Lia was trying to set up JJ with someone, and since he was pretty much the only single guy in Lia's life right now—definitely the only single one in JJ's age range—he figured he'd been Lia's target. All the Foster women—and, sadly, most of the men— thought another relationship was the best way to get him over the one he'd lost.

He rubbed idly at the center of his chest where it ached. There had been a few times in the beginning when he'd thought he was having a heart attack. Had hoped he was. He hadn't wanted to live without Linny. Had never even imagined it. She'd been the best part of his life for so long, and the idea that he would have to live without her had been incomprehensible.

Forty was too young to die. Sure, it happened all the time—accidents, suicides, homicides—but natural causes fell pretty low on the list. Linny had never had surgery before. How could anyone have known she would have an adverse reaction?

Adverse reaction. A nicer, neater way of saying *stroke.* How in the hell had a healthy forty-year-old woman having a minor surgical procedure had a stroke and died on the table? How could anyone have prepared for that?

Slim fingers caught his hand and pulled it away from his chest. His vision was fuzzy when he focused, slowly clearing to show concern on Lia's face as she gazed up at him.

"Uncle Quint?"

How many times had she spoken to him? Her expression suggested several. He squeezed her hand reassuringly. "What were you saying, Bean?"

As he'd expected, she rolled her eyes at her childhood nickname. "Mom is gonna call and see if we can have Easter at your house."

Easter. Was it already time for that? Then came Mother's Day, Father's Day, the Fourth of July and enough birthdays to tire out a partier like Maura Evans.

"She knows I prefer family get-togethers where I can go home when I'm done."

She laughed. "That's why she wants to do it at your place. So you can't make an early escape."

Quint tugged at his ear. He didn't want a celebratory dinner at his house. Cleaning it to meet his mother's standards wasn't a problem; he kept it neat. An overgrown yard wasn't an issue, either. He would surely mow it between now and then. But instead of saying no flat out and wiping that sweet grin from Lia's face, he said, "I'll think about it."

"All right! We're partying at Uncle Quint's! I'll tell Mom." She folded JJ's suede jacket and handed it to her. "Thank you for the business, it's nice to meet you and have fun while you're here." She'd whipped her phone out before finishing the words and was already texting when they turned away. No doubt telling her mom that Easter was a go.

He walked behind JJ through narrow aisles to reach the door. Before she opened it, she pulled the new orange wool cap over her head and slid orange gloves onto her hands. This time, when they stepped outside, she didn't act as if she were the loser in a game of freeze tag. "Your niece is cute."

"Huh. How did 'I'll think about it' turn into 'Sure, bring the whole gang'?" He zipped his jacket, then shoved his hands into the pockets.

"When my mom said, 'I'll think about it,' that was exactly what she meant. With our dad, my sisters and I heard what we wanted. And because we were so adorable, it usually worked for us."

Adorable. That was his niece. She'd had him wrapped

around her little finger when said finger was only an inch or two long. He could see some adorability in JJ, too. Some prettiness, too. He'd always thought of brown as kind of a noncolor, like white or black, but the brown coat looked good on her. It made him aware, even in the dreary lack of sunshine, that her hair wasn't entirely brown but threaded through with strands that would gleam like copper in bright light. The color warmed her face and the fabric hugged her body, showing only a faint bump where her Taser was holstered.

She wasn't so nothing special as he'd thought just a few hours ago.

Scowling, he climbed into the truck. Sam, JJ, Georgie and Lia he'd talked to more people today than he usually did in three or four days combined. He was ready to take JJ back to her car and regain his usual solitude, but when he opened his mouth, that wasn't even close to what he suggested.

"Want to get some lunch?"

Chapter 3

JJ beamed, well aware that growls would start echoing from her empty stomach if she didn't eat soon. "I'm glad you asked. Can we go to Whataburger? The nearest one to Evanston is a couple of hours away, so I haven't had one in years, and that's way too long."

He took the back way out of the strip mall, passing a Chinese restaurant and a hot dog place, then turned back onto Main Street southbound. In a couple of minutes, he was parking in the restaurant's lot. The dining room was warm and smelled of beef and onions and French fries and the best ketchup in the world, and she breathed in deeply, appreciating every happy, sweet, treat-with-Granddad bit of it.

When they placed their orders at the counter, she swiped with her card before Quint got his out of his wallet. "Expense account," she explained.

His gaze narrowed. "Your department must have a bigger budget than ours."

"The lawyer's expense account." She wouldn't abuse

it—she was meticulously documenting every penny she spent—but buying lunch for an officer who'd been pulled away from his regular duties to help her was definitely a legitimate expense.

They got their pop, then chose a table by the plate glass window on the side where they'd parked. Sitting across from each other, they were able to keep an eye on each other, the other customers, the employees and the pickup outside. Cops like expanded horizons.

When she sat on the hard bench, the papers in her hip pocket crackled. Shifting her weight, she pulled them out. "These are the notes Morwenna and Lois did for me." She smoothed them on the tabletop and scanned over them.

Morwenna had listed a few dozen names, half of them only first or last, with additional data when she had it. *Tanya West—works at Starbucks on Taft. Landon Jonas—mechanic at the garage on First. Lily Ransom— day shift at the local ER.*

"Anything interesting there?" she asked, sliding the page to Quint.

He scanned it as quickly as she had. "I know some of these kids' parents or grandparents. Tanya is a friend of Lia's. Giggly, goofy, doesn't have any ambition. Jonas does the routine service on department vehicles. My own truck, too. He's okay, except that he's got a motorcycle that goes really fast and a need to prove it occasionally. He's got a string of tickets for that, but nothing else."

Another long conversational piece from him. She was reminded of a conversation with her aunt, the mystery author. Jada had hefted a dictionary and said, "My entire book is in here. I just have to pull it out one word at a time." Was more than twenty words at once a sign that Quint was warming up to her?

"I was first in my academy class in pursuit driving," she said, "but motorcycles make me scream like a girl. Way too exposed. All the protective gear in the world can't really protect you. Give me a four-thousand-pound cage wrapped around me any day."

She took his grunt as agreement before turning her attention to Lois's list. It was shorter but had more commentary. Like Quint, she knew most of the kids' parents and had filled in ages, vehicles and job information. She dedicated an entire paragraph to one Alexander Benson: oldest of three kids, twenty-six, arrests for bar fights, possession, reckless driving, driving under the influence of drugs and alcohol, harboring a fugitive—his sister—and three counts of assaulting a police officer. All three times, he'd gotten between a relative and the cops trying to arrest said relative. *Where Maura and Mel went, he followed.*

He went by the nickname of Zander, and he was definitely, according to Lois, *the boy our mothers warned us about.* Bad boys. Every town had them, and every good girl managed to meet them.

"Do you know Zander Benson?" Then, remembering his comment, she teased, "Or should I ask if you know his parents?"

His gaze narrowed again, almost as if from habit. "Yeah, I went to school with his dad. Hank had better things to do than spend every day in school, so he went to class when it suited him. He was a senior when I started my sophomore year, and he was still a senior when I started my senior year. He did manage to graduate that time. Marisa was sitting in the audience, holding Zander and pregnant with number two."

That image could have been inspiring. She loved underdog stories, people who never gave up until they achieved their goal. After three senior years, Hank had graduated, but had it really been an accomplishment, or had the school given him the diploma so they could be done with him? If his son was anything to judge by, probably the latter.

"I'm guessing marriage and fatherhood didn't turn Hank into father of the year material." Though her cynical cop side snorted at the idea, she believed it was possible. Hank could have learned his lesson about the value of education and staying out of trouble. He almost surely would have wanted better for his kids. It happened. Sometimes. On occasion. And Zander and his sister might have simply rebelled.

"Nah, Hank's still the overgrown idiot he was back then, and Zander's just like him. Too lazy to work, likes his drugs and his booze, rude and surly and looking for someone to take it out on."

JJ rolled one corner of the paper tightly, smoothed it, then rolled it again. "So Maura's best friend is rude, obnoxious and disrespectful, and her other friend is rude, surly and finds trouble everywhere he goes. Not that Maura didn't have obnoxious and surly friends at home, but they came from money. They were just like her."

"You mean they were her own kind."

That sounded ugly and made her nose scrunch and her mouth wrinkle. "I don't mean they were better because they were rich. God knows, that's not a plus for most of them. Just they all had money, so none of them took advantage. One day it was Maura blowing five grand on a party, but the next time someone else stepped up. They took their turns."

"But none of these people—" he gestured toward the lists "—have money, which would explain why $100,000 a month is no longer adequate for her expenses. Friendship doesn't come cheap."

A pang twinged around her heart. Was that what Maura had sunk to? Buying friends? She was a pretty girl. She'd been taught perfect manners, all the social graces. She would be as comfortable at a White House state dinner as a regular person was at McDonald's. She was smarter than average, had an enviable prep school education and all the potential in the world. And yet grief and sorrow had led her to a spot where she had to pay big bucks for the barest of friendships.

"My dad used to joke that he and Mom had me so my sisters would have someone else to torment, but now they're my best friends. They drove me crazy—still do on occasion—but they also stood by me, no matter what. If Maura had had a brother or sister to lean on, to grieve with and recover with, maybe…" Maybe that brother or sister would have been her rock. Or maybe he or she would be floundering with her, dragging her even farther down.

The woman who'd taken their order delivered their meals on two orange trays, and despite her momentary sadness, JJ's mouth instantly started watering. She smiled her thanks, picked up her burger and took the first groan-inducing bite. Oh, ten years between Whataburgers was entirely too long. She couldn't let that happen again.

"How many sisters do you have?"

The sweet-spicy scent of ketchup tickled her nose as Quint tore open a half dozen packets, sliding them to the space between their trays to share. Before her time, there'd been a fuss in the public schools about whether ketchup constituted a vegetable. Though she was well aware of the nutritional value of kale, brussels sprouts and such things, she would have given ketchup two enthusiastic thumbs up.

"Two." She swallowed, then grabbed a couple of hot, salty fries, coated them in ketchup and ate them. "Kylie and Elle. Kylie's a firefighter, Elle's a roofing contractor and they each have two little girls."

For a second, she thought he might smile. The lines around his eyes and mouth eased, and everything about him seemed just a tad easier. But the second passed, and the smile didn't form. "I take it your mom taught you that you can be anything you want if you put your mind to it."

"She did. It sort of backfired with me, though. I missed the part about being a cop *and* a mother. I just wanted the cop part. Even though she's got four grandkids already, she acts like life won't be complete if she doesn't also have a little JJ to spoil."

This time the corner of his mouth quirked. "My mom's got eight, and she still thinks I need to contribute my share."

"You're not married?" Sheesh, it felt good to talk about something less depressing and irritating than Maura Evans and her current issues, and what could be more normal than discussing parents and kids?

He shook his head, then broke eye contact, taking extra care dipping fries into ketchup. He didn't look down quickly enough, though, to hide the hurt that shadowed his eyes. He'd had his heart broken and still wasn't over it. Was that what Miss Georgie had wanted to talk to him about? Why Lia had been surprised to see him and quick to suggest a hookup to JJ?

Her first thought was what kind of woman walked away from a man who looked like Quint. Her second was less shallow. Looks meant nothing when it came to a person's character. The sexiest, most gorgeous man she'd even seen was one she'd arrested her first year on the job—a fugitive from California on a murder warrant. It had been a really grisly murder, too.

And Kylie's firefighter husband was really buff but could easily pass for a Kewpie doll. He was almost bald, what little hair he had was thin, wispy and colorless, and his nose was two times bigger than his face could accommodate. It was a face only a mother could love, he teased. But when he looked at his wife or his kids, the sweet, intense love that filled his entire expression made every female in the room swoon.

"Do you like kids?" she asked, thinking back on how he'd acted with Lia or, more importantly, how his niece had acted with him. She clearly adored her uncle, which said a lot for him.

"They're fine." He paused before adding, "I like them best when they're old enough to be charged as adults."

The response was unexpected. It startled her into a snort, then she caught herself, then she laughed out loud. Quint Foster could be funny.

Who ever would have suspected it?

* * *

The sky was dark with scud when they headed back to the station. Quint liked a good snow once every year or two, but Oklahoma almost always got sleet first. Those days were among the rare times everyone in the department worked traffic, including Sam. They didn't write many tickets, but they helped get dozens of stuck cars moving again and investigated a lot of accidents. Cedar Creek had a shortage of street-clearing equipment and a surplus of people who thought they could drive in hazardous conditions.

When he radioed in that he was back in service, JJ gave him a look. "Baker 201, huh? You seem such a cozy bunch that I imagined you using your names instead of call signs. What's Sam's?"

"Adam 101. The detectives are David 301, 302, etc., and patrol officers are divided into east and west districts, so they're Edward 401 and so on or William 501." He kept his gaze on the street, his fingers gripping the steering wheel just a little tighter. Would she notice that he was in patrol but had a different call prefix? Would she wonder why he had an identifier all his own? His call sign was the only thing left of his crashed-and-burned career as assistant chief. He'd suggested changing it, but Sam had said no. Everyone knew him as Baker 201. Changing it would just be a hassle.

And keeping it reminded Quint every day of how he'd screwed up.

Before she could give it any thought, he changed the subject. "What are your plans?"

"Check in with the lawyer. Find out if Mel might be a relative. Interview Maura's neighbors. Get whatever financial records I can." She shifted her gaze outside. "Pray it doesn't snow." Without missing a beat, she went on. "It's going to snow, isn't it?"

"Probably."

"I checked the forecasts before I came. Sixties and sunny for the next week."

"Forecasts lie." He turned into the parking lot. "If it snows, don't drive anywhere. You'll just be one more accident we have to work."

She sat straighter, somehow scowling down at her nose at him, indignance radiating from her. "I'll have you know..." Then she softened. "I've never driven on snow in my life. Please, God, I never will."

Soft was a good look for her.

He parked near her car, giving her the shortest distance to travel between the vehicles. After shifting into Reverse, he rested his hands on the wheel and gazed ahead, watching a piece of newspaper float and twirl on the wind. A sudden gust swept it four feet into the air, then it drifted down to snag on a light pole for just a moment before flying away again.

The paper's journey was a good semblance of his life since Linny died. All his life, he had been grounded, secure, but only two words from the surgeon had cut him loose. He'd tumbled like a leaf on a raging river, thrown every way but free. Lately, the river had calmed. There wasn't so much battering, but he still couldn't get his feet back under him.

I'm sorry. Words Quint had said a million time and had rarely meant. He had a whole vocabulary of phrases like that. *It'll be okay. Things happen for a reason. I know how you feel. With all due respect...*

He tasted the sourness stirring in his stomach as he realized JJ was looking at him expectantly. Had she said something? He turned his head to meet her gaze, his eyebrow arching in silent question.

"I said thanks for your time." She left it at that, but her smile suggested what she left unsaid. *Though it wasn't your choice.*

"Not a problem." Another of those annoying phrases. When had people stopped saying, *You're welcome*? He couldn't recall.

She dug out her car keys and used the remote to unlock the Challenger before she opened the truck door. He watched her slide to the ground, a fluid movement of heavy brown coat and snug-fitting denim. When she moved to close the door, he hastily spoke.

"If you have any trouble with the neighbors..."

Now why had he gone and said that? He was done. He'd followed Sam's orders—had gone beyond them by going shopping and having lunch with her. Why give her even the faintest idea that he might be willing to do it again?

But he couldn't take back the words, and when that naughty-little-girl grin lit up her face, he wasn't sure he wanted to. "I'll call."

She closed the door hard and disappeared into her car. Quint waited until he heard the rumble of the sports car's engine, then backed up and drove slowly out of the parking lot. He made a right turn, took the next left and drove aimlessly through one of the town's older neighborhoods. The streets ran stick straight, the blocks exactly the same length, the corner signs giving names like Oak, Elm and Maple. The lots were smallish, as were the houses, and three entire blocks were taken up by churches.

His parents' neighborhood was a lot like this one, slightly newer with slightly bigger houses. They'd sold their house to his brother Paul and resettled on five acres outside town. His mother had always loved gardening, and there she had room to grow big. It was one of the interests she and Linny had had in common. They'd planned and planted and weeded and harvested the acres together. With all the work there, Linny had never gotten around to planting even one flower at the house she and Quint had shared.

The house where he lived alone.

Grimly, he set his jaw. He was tired, and an ache was starting behind his eyes, probably from all the human contact he'd had today. Generally, he got by with minimal interaction—with Sam, his fellow officers, the people he wrote tickets to or took reports from—and generally, if anyone showed concern, he ignored it or brushed it off.

It was hard to ignore Sam fobbing off their visiting detective on him. Or Georgie squeezing his hands with pity shadowing her gaze. Or Lia, so surprised to see him and, there at the end, pulling his hand from where he'd rubbed at the ache, all too aware at her young age of what he'd been thinking.

Talking to people was hard. Being with them was harder. At first, being alone had been the only way to survive, wrapping up inside himself, pushing everyone away. Silence and solitude had become comfortable. It would have been easier to get through the day if he didn't have to pretend interest in anything else, if he didn't have to uphold his end of a conversation, if he didn't have to acknowledge the sorrow, the worry and the compassion.

In the beginning, his family and friends had understood that. Everyone grieved differently, his mother had said. Just give him time, Sam had said. After six or eight months, they'd started trying to nudge him back into a normal life. He had responsibilities, his father had reminded him. He was still alive, Ben had told him.

More meaningless platitudes. This *was* his normal life now. Him. Alone. The one person he'd loved best gone forever. He hadn't tried to explain it. He hadn't cared whether anyone understood. He'd just plodded on, one miserable, lonely, bitter day at a time. It had become routine, being alone, and after a while, everyone had gone back to leaving him that way.

He doubted JJ Logan had ever left anyone alone in her life.

As if that brief thought of her was some sort of signal, his cell phone rang. He glanced at the screen, saw Sam's name and answered without the smallest hint of disappointment. Really, truly, he hadn't thought it might be JJ. Hadn't wanted it to be.

"Since your shift's almost over, why don't you come by the office and fill me in? I'm sure Georgie sent good wishes and warm hugs to all of us down here at thug central."

"More like sneers and head thumps all around." Quint glanced at the clock on the dash, surprised to see the time was 2:46 p.m. He always returned to the station at three, finished whatever reports he had to do and got out by three thirty. Spending half the day babysitting JJ had at least made the day go faster. "I'll be in soon."

One of the nice things about Cedar Creek was that with lights and siren, he could travel the farthest distance in the city in a matter of minutes. Without running code, it took only a few extra moments to get back to the station. The wind buffeted him as he crossed the parking lot, several times gusting hard enough to make him stagger a few steps before catching himself. Rodgers and Hammerstein had famously written about the wind sweeping down the plain, and it did. Sometimes. There were also times when it thundered, howled and raged. Its iciness cut through his clothes and would have stolen his hat if he didn't have one hand clamped to it.

This would be a good night to stay home with a cozy fire, a pot of savory beef stew, fresh corn bread and, just before bed, a steaming mug of hot cocoa. It could be a perfect evening. If a person had someone to spend it with.

His jaw clenched, he jogged the last twenty yards and opened the heavy door. Ordinarily, it swung back under its own power, but it was struggling against the wind, so he shoved it shut.

"Brrr." Morwenna hugged herself as she crossed the room to the coffee machine. "I'm going to need two electric blankets to stay warm tonight."

"If you'd settle down with a boyfriend, you wouldn't need any blankets at all." That came from Cheryl, Sam's secretary and department snoop. She was nosy, gossipy and found great fun in harassing one employee or another, and she often stomped on Quint's last nerve, but she did her job for far less money than it deserved, so Sam cut her some slack. A lot of it.

Quint couldn't complain. Sam cut him a lot of slack, too.

Behind Cheryl's back, Morwenna was rolling her eyes, then she smiled. "Where is Detective JJ?"

"She was heading to the hotel last I saw of her."

"I like her. We need a female detective around here. I love my guys, but come on, a town the size of Cedar Creek should have a whole lot of female cops, and JJ's proof that they're out there. They're just not here."

She moved aside, and Quint brewed a cup of dark Italian roast for himself. "You can only hire from the people who apply." The department wasn't overly big, and except for Daniel Harper and Cullen Simpson, every cop in it had been born and raised in Cedar Creek. When Sam needed a new officer, he had more than enough locals to choose from. "Is the boss in his office?"

Morwenna gestured to Cheryl, who'd been eavesdropping from her desk. Now the woman pretended to be busy on the computer. "How should I know?"

"Because you're his secretary," Morwenna and Daniel said at the same time.

"It's your job," Ben added in concert with Morwenna.

Cheryl gave them a long look over her glasses, spun her chair around and hollered, "Sam, you over there?"

After a moment of ringing silence, Sam's voice, exaggeratedly patient, sounded. "Yes, Cheryl. I'm here."

She turned back, smiled tightly and said, "He's in."

The hiss of the coffeemaker signaled Quint's brew was ready. He grabbed a wooden stirrer, a packet of sugar and the cup and headed for Sam's office.

* * *

JJ was comfortable with old things. Her parents'
house had been built in the 1840s. The crib she'd slept
in as an infant had held more Logans than any family tree could support. Her mom's good dishes had fed
great-great-blah-grand relatives, and her first car was a
Volkswagen passed down from aunt to cousin to Kylie
to Elle to JJ, then back to more cousins. At least half
the buildings in Evanston and dozens of the stately live
oak trees were well into their second or third century.

She liked old, so she felt right at home in her room
on the third floor of the Prairie Sun Hotel, with its iron
bedstead, antique wardrobe and desk and pressed-tin
ceiling. It reminded her of home—newer by a hundred
years or so, but still homey.

The drive from the police station parking lot to the
hotel lot had been too short for the car to even bother
with warming up. Shivering, she'd dashed inside the
hotel, wrestled the door shut and heaved a great sigh
of appreciation for the heated air and the sweet scents
carried on it. Vanilla, coffee, hazelnut, chocolate. Yum.

Now she'd traded her boots for fuzzy slippers. Her
new coat had taken the place of the quilt on the bed's
footboard, and the heating unit near the window was
humming steadily as it chased out chill air with warm.
She sat cross-legged on the bed, laptop open on one
side, cell phone on the other, and sipped appreciatively
from the hot tea she'd made downstairs.

She had a call in to Mr. Winchester, another to the
Wilhelmina Evans Memorial Library, and had sent texts
to both of her sisters. JJ knew an awful lot about the
criminally inclined population of Evanston, but Kylie

and Elle knew more about the law abiders. Less than an hour after walking into the room, she had responses from three of the four. Neither Kylie nor Elle knew anyone named Mel or any variation thereof in town in the right age group, and a librarian had confirmed that the Evans family tree, dating back to the 1600s, didn't have so much as a leaflet by that name. Since she managed the extensive Evans archives, there was little doubt she was right.

With her favorite music playing on her cell, JJ turned back to Lois Gideon's notes. Miss Georgie had explained that she owned the house and twelve acres surrounding it. That included an empty lot to the south and wooded areas on the other three sides, enough to build a dozen cookie-cutter houses if she chose. She'd owned the property for sixty years now and, so far, hadn't chosen to.

Funny that Mr. Madison hadn't wanted noisy neighbors around his big house. Now the neighbors had to deal with the noisy big house, instead.

There were five other houses on the stretch of street. The nearest, according to Lois, was rented to a couple in their midtwenties with four kids under the age of five. A shudder of sympathy mixed with revulsion rippled through JJ. Like Quint, she liked kids fine, but the thought of actually having any made her queasy. Having four little ones all at once would have put the fear of God into her if her parents hadn't already done so.

Next door to Toddlerville lived three sisters in their seventies. Two were widows, the third a spinster. Yes, Lois had actually written *spinster*. On the opposite side of the street were three houses. One had stood empty since its owner died last year, one was home to two twentysomethings who worked in town and took classes at the OSU campus in downtown Tulsa and the third housed the assistant fire marshal. *Hot, hot, single and hot. Want to meet him?*

All of the neighbors except the fire marshal had made complaints to the police about Maura and her friends. Loud parties made sleep impossible at Toddlerville. The sisters thought everyone who lived at or visited the Madison house was a menace behind the wheel, and the students had been disturbed on several occasions by intoxicated guests who'd wandered off and knocked on the girls' door instead.

None of them had spoken to Maura or caught more than a glimpse of her as she drove past their houses.

The phone rang, and JJ answered without glancing at the caller ID. She'd given the number only to people she wanted to talk to, and with robots or salespeople, she was perfectly capable of hanging up.

"Have you seen Maura?" Travis Winchester didn't bother with formalities, a sign of how worried he was about his goddaughter. Being a lawyer and a Southern gentleman, he was usually the epitome of proper.

"Not yet. I plan to go to her house tomorrow morning." She'd just this minute reached the decision. She wasn't going to call and give the girl the chance to avoid her. She intended to show up on her doorstep, politely coerce her way inside and conduct a genial interview with the woman she used to babysit. Winchester had thought Maura might be more open with someone she was acquainted with but didn't know well and wouldn't expect judgment from.

Loosely translated, Maura Evans wouldn't give a damn about JJ or her opinions, so she shouldn't be overly hostile. She wouldn't be embarrassed by her actions the way she might be with her godparents.

He was probably right. Her nieces would much prefer to confess their misdeeds to JJ than to their mothers, and JJ herself had been much more willing to disappoint a neighbor or a teacher than her parents. Anger and irritation were bearable. Disappointing folks wasn't.

"Have you learned anything?" the lawyer asked.

She gave him a rundown of her conversations at the police station and with Georgie Madison. She told him about Maura's run-ins with the local cops and asked about Mel Smith/Jones. He drew a blank on Mel.

"Maura's life was pretty insular," he explained. "Here in town, her parents were friends with her friends' parents, friends of mine. In college, her sorority sisters were the daughters of her mother's sorority sisters. The frat boys she dated were sons of her father's frat brothers. Valerie and Stephen Evans knew every old-money, old-South family in the region. They went to the same parties, supported the same causes, served on the same boards and shared the same interests. Sure, she met people at college that were from the outside, but she stuck with what or who was familiar. It's a small world." He hesitated. "Was a small world."

Until her parents' deaths, when she'd run away from loss and discovered the real world. Before the deaths, she'd left the US once, for a high school spring break trip to Belize. After, she'd traveled her way around the globe two or three times.

"What does this Mel person matter? You said she's no longer a part of Maura's life."

"Apparently not. She left three months ago. Maura changed three months ago, so the ending of their relationship might have been the trigger for the change. Maybe she's grieving again."

To his credit, Winchester didn't argue that the loss of a friend wouldn't be such a great trauma. Stephen Evans had been *his* best friend, and he was still dealing with that loss every day.

And maybe it had been worse for Maura this time around. Her parents hadn't voluntarily left her. They had been murdered But it seemed Mel had just walked out the door. *Thanks, it's been nice, I'm outta here.*

Leaving was always easier than being the one left, or so they said. The only person who'd ever left JJ was Ryan, and that had really been more of an eye-opener than anything else. Sure, she'd missed him on occasion, but she hadn't wept or mourned or sworn off men, relationships and sex for the rest of her life.

Gazing up at the tin ceiling, she wondered if that was sad: to be thirty-seven and never have suffered a broken heart. To never have known that kind of passion and commitment.

Then she thought of her sisters and friends with all their ugly breakups, and she did mean *ugly*. Lots of crying and wailing, splotchy faces, swollen eyes, snotty red noses. The air around them had crackled with sadness, pity, anger, insecurity, despair and hopelessness. When Elle and Kylie had gotten dumped by their college boyfriends at the same time, their dad had claimed that every time he walked in the front door, the hormone-fueled mood swings made the hairs all over his body stand on end. It had been like waiting for lightning to strike.

Nah, JJ was lucky to have missed out on all that. She wasn't a pretty crier, self-pity gave her indigestion and Rudolph's red nose wasn't a good look for her.

Winchester had been quiet a long time. Finally he cleared his throat. "Detective—JJ, my wife and I never had children. Four miscarriages were four more than she could bear. We doted on Maura. Her parents were our best friends. We were—are her godparents. We worried when she left town. We wanted her to stay here, to take care of her, to help her heal, but the psychologist said it would be good for her to get away, to have no expectations placed on her, to go where she wanted, do what she wanted and experience life. The worst things in our lives were losing our babies, burying Stephen and Valerie, and letting Maura go. It almost killed us."

The distance between them and the telephone did nothing to diminish the intensity of his voice. JJ understood that sort of love better than romantic love. She loved her parents like that, her sisters and nieces. She couldn't imagine if one day, one of them simply said, *I don't want you in my life anymore.* That would break her heart.

And not knowing if the person was all right or why she'd cut you off, why you no longer mattered to her, why she'd stopped loving you…tough.

"I'll see her tomorrow, Mr. Winchester. I can't promise I'll have answers to your questions. I'll have to play it however she wants. But at least I can see her, talk to her and tell you that she's physically all right."

Not that it was Maura's physical condition that worried the lawyer. He hadn't detailed his fears, but JJ could figure it out from what she was told. Maura had been emotionally fragile and psychologically exhausted when she left Evanston. She'd chosen off-the-beaten-path destinations on her trips. Had she found she liked a challenge, or had she been courting danger? Had she been growing stronger or getting lost in her grief? Her small, insular world had grown into a great big one; the protection her family had given was gone. She'd met people of all types, all religions, all races, none of them vetted through their association with her parents or their friends. Though she'd never been a slacker in the spending area, she'd suddenly developed a new and greedy affection for buying, wanting not just more money but all of it. Right now.

How big a shock had it been to Mr. Winchester when she'd threatened to sue him?

A heavy sigh came from the other end of the connection. "I know you'll do your best, JJ. I'm just worried…"

That maybe her best wasn't enough. Maybe it was too late to bring back the Maura he and his wife loved as their own daughter.

But before JJ went back to South Carolina, one way or another, he would know.

This time, the forecast hadn't lied. Quint sat in his truck, engine running, wearing his duty jacket zipped up high, thick leather gloves and a knitted watch cap. A travel mug of coffee steamed the air around it in the console holder, scenting the air faintly with chocolate and spices.

He didn't particularly like chocolate-spiced coffee. It had been Linny's favorite, though, and the aromas reminded him of her. When all her fragrances had been washed out of the laundry and faded from the unworn clothing in the closets, when her perfume no longer lingered on bed pillows or sofa cushions, he'd found a few pods of the coffee in the cabinet and brewed one just for the smell. Now he started every day with a cup.

How pathetic was that?

The defrosters were blasting the cold windows, melting the snow accumulated there into thin rivulets. He'd scraped the side and rear windows, his breath puffing in white clouds, but had left the defroster to clear the windshield. In another minute, he could turn on the wipers, and a minute after that, the heat should start warming his hands and feet.

For those moments, he continued to stare out the window. Daffodils the color of lemons poked through the snow, leftovers from the retired couple he and Linny had bought the house from. Every fall, she'd said she was going to dig them up and divide them so they would make even more flowers, but she'd never managed to actually do it. Maybe this fall he would. It wasn't as if there was anything else to do with his free time.

Or maybe he wouldn't. He didn't give a damn about daffodils.

Other than the daffodils, there was nothing remarkable about the house. It was two stories, with a big front porch and a smaller one out back. The wood siding was white, the shutters and doors dark green, the porch floor gray and its ceiling light blue. About as traditional as house-paint colors could get. The garage was detached with room for two vehicles, but it stored only tools and a dual-fuel grill. They'd laid a patio in front of it one summer, all their families helping, and had cooked out every weekend it was warm enough and plenty when it wasn't. This morning he couldn't remember the last time he'd thought about grilling or having friends over or even just sitting out there on a quiet evening.

Grimly, he shook his head to clear it. *It's not good to live so much in your head,* someone had told him. Probably Mrs. Little Bear, Ben's mother. She gave everyone advice and usually accompanied it with good food, and she had been advising and feeding Quint since before Ben was born.

But in your head was the only place things could be the way you wanted. Sometimes it was the only safe place to be.

His cell phone vibrated on the console where it sat. A quick glance showed the caller was Sam. Quint had radioed in that he was in service after he'd cleaned the windows, so if he didn't answer the phone, Sam would just call him on the radio. He picked up.

"Can you come by my office before you head out on patrol?" his boss asked.

"Sure. How are the streets?"

"The usual. Sand trucks are out. People are convinced they're much better drivers than they really are. We've had five accidents in the past hour. My neighbor said, 'Oh great, school's out. We can go shopping in Tulsa.'"

Quint grunted. "My nieces have always thought snow days were for shopping and movies. They can't stand that their parents take their car keys. I'll be there... well, when I get there." His job included helping unskilled and unfortunate drivers out of ditches, pushing them when they got stuck and taking reports when they crashed. What would normally be a five-minute drive could take an hour or more.

After ending the call, he backed out of the driveway and headed toward the center of town. Sun, wind and traffic would clean the streets significantly even if the temperature didn't budge above freezing. Wouldn't it be nice if everyone whose job wasn't essential to public safety stayed in today?

Would JJ stay in? Probably. It was much easier to imagine her in shorts and a T-shirt than struggling through subfreezing snow and ice. Pull her hair back in a ponytail, trade those boots for flip-flops, give her dark shades and a glass of iced tea, and he suspected she would radiate contentment.

Not that he should be imagining her at all. There wasn't room in his head for any complications beyond the one he had to live with: himself.

It was forty minutes later when he made it into the station. He stamped snow from his boots at the door, got a cup of coffee and went to Sam's office. His boss was on the phone, but Lois, seated in front of the desk, waved him in. He sat next to her.

"School superintendent," she murmured. "Wants to

know if the streets will be clear in the morning or if he should go ahead and cancel classes for then, too."

"Does Sam look like a weatherman?" Quint and Lois asked in unison. They'd both seen this exchange plenty of times. With Oklahoma's fickle winters, the superintendent was damned if he did and damned if he didn't. Parents who'd scrambled to make other arrangements for their kids got pretty ticked if the cancellation turned out to be unnecessary, as did stay-at-home parents facing an unexpected day with their little darlings. It was amazing how many of them would risk ice and injury to get the kids to school—and out of their hair.

Quint didn't care for the sentiment *Better safe than sorry*, but it fit here.

When Sam got off the phone, he dragged his hand through his hair and glowered at them. "Seriously? What makes the man think my opinion carries more weight than the meteorologists'?"

"At least he listens to you," Quint said.

"Yeah," Lois agreed. "Ever since the time he didn't, and the school bus slid off the road and scared the snot out of twenty-seven grade-schoolers."

Sam picked up his coffee and cradled the mug in his hands. The irritation disappeared from his face, replaced with an easier look. "How did it go yesterday?"

Inside, Quint was squirming, but on the outside, he kept his body still and his expression blank. "It was fine."

"What do you think of Detective Logan?"

That question came from Lois, whose grin stretched from ear to ear. He didn't have to be a half-decent cop to know she had an ulterior motive in asking. Lois *always* had an ulterior motive. She was barely old enough to be his mother, but she acted as if she had mothering rights over everyone in the department. It was easier for all of them to let her boss them than to push back.

"She's capable."

Lois rolled her eyes. "Let me rephrase that. What do you think of JJ?"

"I wasn't aware I was supposed to think anything of her." The back of his neck grew warm. If he told too many lies, his ears would start burning red enough for any slightly observant person to notice, and Lois and Sam were both way past *slightly*.

Lois shook her finger at him. "I know how smart you are, Quinton Foster. Deliberate obtuseness won't work."

Sam took pity on him and stepped in. "Did she mention her chief at all?"

Quint shook his head. "On the way inside, she asked if you were good, bad or indifferent. I got the impression that hers wasn't much to work with."

"Yeah. That's my impression, too. When he called yesterday, he asked me to help her out. Implied that she wasn't his choice for this job and he wasn't sure she could handle it."

Lois gaped at him. Quint was surprised by the information, but he let Lois respond. "A detective who can't handle a welfare check? How could that possibly be? How has she kept her job? How she'd get it in the first place?"

"He said he inherited her when he took over the department last year. As far as keeping her, all he said was, 'Politics. You understand.'" Sam's put-on Southern accent was exaggerated enough to annoy a true Southerner. He broke off a piece of chocolate-glazed doughnut and gestured with it. "I would never send one of my officers out of town on a job, then tell the local chief he or she can't do the job without help. It reflects worse on Chadwick than it does on JJ."

"That's because you're an intelligent man who understands the value of your female officers." Lois's turquoise hair fluttered with the emphatic bob of her head. She'd been with the department longer than Quint and Sam combined, and she'd done her gender proud. She'd turned down promotions so she could stay on the street, but she would have been an outstanding detective. She would have been—still would be—an outstanding assistant chief.

And she could probably kick Chief Chadwick's ass.

"I looked him up." Sam pointed to the computer with the doughnut, then finally ate it. "He retired as chief from a small department in North Carolina, then took this job. A newspaper article said the last department didn't hire a single woman during his fifteen-year tenure. I'm thinking he might have a few old-fashioned ideas about a woman's place."

Lois snorted, then patted her sidearm. "Don't tell a woman carrying a gun where her place is. She's likely to put you in yours."

Deservedly so. Quint was no fool. He knew the strongest people in his life were the women: Linny, his mother, his grandmothers, his sisters. Not a man in the Foster family doubted that the women were in charge or that they deserved to be.

He hadn't seen enough of JJ at work to wholeheart-edly vouch for her, the way he could with Lois, Little Bear or Harper. He could say she seemed competent. Capable. Intelligent. She thought like a cop. She was looking at the situation with Maura the way a cop would. He could say one thing for sure, though.

"Georgie invited her back for a visit."

Sam's brows lifted, and Lois grimaced. "That old witch. I've known her my whole life, and she still treats me like something nasty scraped from her shoe."

"Maybe you don't insult her enough," Quint murmured.

Before Lois could question him, Morwenna appeared in the doorway. She was dressed unusually brightly today and seemed unusually stressed. She overlooked the fact that everyone in the room outranked her and snapped her fingers at them. "Come on, guys, we need you on the street. Calls are stacking up."

"We're coming." Sam stood, shrugging into his jacket before reaching for his Stetson. "On the chance that her chief isn't just a jerk and has actual reasons to be concerned, keep in touch with her, Quint, would you? Tag along. Drive her places. Tell her I'm covering our bases since she's in our jurisdiction."

Sam looked as if he'd just given a perfectly normal order, but Lois smirked on her way out of the office. Quint could practically read the delight dancing in her brain, that he was going to be forced to spend more time with someone who didn't suffer silence gladly. Some-one who was pretty. Who looked damn good in snug jeans and a tight-fitting shirt. Someone who made him remember—only for as long as it took him to quash it—that he was still living.

He should have told Sam he had unequivocal faith in JJ's ability to do her job. He should have described her as Superwoman with a badge. He should have done whatever it took to get back to his usual—solo—routine. Why hadn't he?

The scary thing about it, though... He wasn't nearly as put out by Sam's order as he should have been.

That couldn't possibly be a good thing.

Chapter 4

JJ might never be a winter aficionado, but she had to admit, there was something intriguingly clean and fresh and invigorating about the cold, sharp air that filled her lungs and cleared every last cobweb from her brain. She felt as though she could run an easy five miles, then solve a crime before lunch. After inhaling a lot of steaming-hot comfort food, she could then solve another before the workday ended.

Of course, running five miles depended on keeping her feet underneath her when an inch of ice hid beneath two inches of snow. She wasn't likely to make any head-way on determining Maura's status when she couldn't go any farther from the hotel than she could walk. And much as she loved her new coat, hat and gloves, she had gone only a few blocks down First Street and couldn't feel her toes or fingertips anymore.

She'd had breakfast at the diner across from the courthouse. Far from her usual milk, coffee and protein bar, she'd indulged in fried eggs, hash browns, biscuits and gravy and bacon—hence, the cautious stroll before returning to the hotel. She comforted herself that all those carbs and fats were helping her stay warm, at least until she saw several very good reasons for her blood to pump a little harder.

A white SUV with police markings was stuck in the parking lot across the street. The exhaust from it turned white as soon as it hit the air, drifting past the men and the lone woman who stood there talking. Officer Turquoise Hair and her band of merry police officers.

JJ gauged the distance of the oncoming traffic, making sure she had plenty of time for a jog that would take only a few seconds on dry pavement. She reached the opposite sidewalk without falling on her butt, thank heavens, then trudged through snow onto the sanded but still slick parking lot.

"Is this a privileged conference, or can anyone join in?" she asked when she got near enough.

Quint looked up, his gaze coming straight to hers. Ah, yes, there was some of that warmth she'd been looking for. She would bet she'd find a lot more of it if he would just wrap one arm around her and snuggle her up to his body, but sadly, that wasn't on his agenda.

Yet.

She did get an arm around her—Lois's—but it seemed Lois was leaching warmth away from her instead of sharing it. The other woman's affectionate smile made up for it.

"How's this for a welcome?" Lois opened her other arm wide to indicate the scene around them. "Isn't it a beautiful sight?" Then she winked slyly. "And the snow doesn't look bad, either."

Lois performed quick introductions all around that JJ responded to with nods. Sam Douglas stood next to Quint, and beside him was Detective Little Bear, who was tall enough she had to tilt her head back to see his face. Detective Harper was shorter, leaner and wirier, which had its own advantages over brute strength. The three of them wore black tactical pants, boots and jackets that said Police in gold.

With their knitted caps and red faces, the other two men—Officers Simpson and Anaya—looked very young. Like Quint, they wore uniforms, but they didn't wear them as well. For them, the khaki trousers were just clothes. For Quint, they were an accessory emphasizing lean legs, muscular thighs and a nice butt. Even with the bulky jacket, there were hints of similar solidness up above. He didn't even look cold as he stood there. Instead, he wore this weathered look, like *Yeah, it's cold, but I'm tough.*

"Lois, get behind the wheel, would you?" Sam suggested.

"Who's the unlucky—" JJ's gaze shifted across the SUV to the rear quarter panel signage that clearly read Chief of Police and winced.

"Yeah," Sam agreed. "Of everyone in the entire department, I'm the one who gets stuck in the damned parking lot."

"I'm sure it could happen to anyone—well, almost anyone."

His gaze narrowed in her direction. "But not you?"

"I can truthfully say I've never gotten a car stuck on snow or ice."

The men were lining up at the rear of the truck, preparing to give their best at pushing the vehicle free, but Quint took time to respond. "That's because you've never driven on snow or ice."

"My statement stands on its own," she said with a mock frown. "No clarification required."

Acknowledging her comment with the slightest lift of his brows, he took the spot nearest her, placing his gloved hands on the vehicle. His jacket that had been spotless yesterday was dirty and splattered this morning. So were his trouser legs and boots. This wasn't the first car he'd given a push this morning.

She stepped back and watched. It took several efforts, but through a combination of the men pushing and Lois judiciously using the gas pedal, they got the vehicle moving. She drove it to a clearer spot twenty feet away, then hopped out. "There you go, Sam," she said with a flourish. "Go forth now and rescue others in need."

"Thanks, guys." Sam turned toward JJ and Quint, who stood nearby, dusting his gloves, and gave a nod before heading for his truck. The other officers dispersed as well, each striding toward their own vehicles.

They'd all driven away, leaving the air still, before Quint finally gave up on tidying his clothes. "You still want to see Maura today? We've got a lot of calls right now, but when we get them cleared, I can take you over there, then we could have lunch if you want."

A second invitation to lunch in two days. Hmm. She would like to feel flattered, even hopeful, but the cop in her realized belatedly that the little nod from Sam that she'd thought was a goodbye more likely had been a signal to Quint. What exactly had Chief Dipstick said yesterday? That she couldn't find her way out of a paper bag with a rip in its side? That the little woman needed watching so she didn't hurt her little ol' self?

The thought annoyed the hell out of her—but with Chadwick, not Sam. Certainly not Quint. She knew she didn't need any help, and so did Chadwick, but she wasn't going to turn it down just to spite him. She liked having someone to bounce ideas off, to keep her open to all possibilities, and when that someone was as handsome as Quint...

"Can I assume you'll swing by the hotel and pick me up?"

"Unless you'd rather walk. Or...if you're interested..." He paused, his gaze flicking away, and shoved his hands into his pockets. He looked in the direction of the street that ran south of the station, the blocks visible a blend of businesses and houses, then slowly returned his attention to her and finished his faltering words. "You could ride along until I'm clear, and we can check out Maura then."

JJ followed his lead, tucking her hands into her coat pockets, finding an extra layer of warmth there. "Ride-alongs at home have to be cleared by the chief four weeks in advance. Only males need apply."

"Sam won't care."

Of course he wouldn't. The invitation had been so awkwardly given that she was pretty sure Sam would be glad he'd managed to find a way to keep an eye on her even longer than just an interview with Maura.

JJ would be much happier keeping her own eye on Quint for longer than just the interview, so she flashed him her best smile. "Sounds fun. I like watching big strong men working while I stay comfy cozy."

His truck was at the other end of the lot, so they started that way. She picked careful steps over soft snow, solid ice and hard-packed slush. Hitting the ground in the course of tackling a suspect was more fun than not. Diving to avoid a punch or a gunshot was natural instinct. Smacking to the ground in front of the man she'd really like to see naked—soon—would be nothing but embarrassing.

Even if he would feel obligated to help her to her feet. If he took her hands firmly in his and lifted her weight without so much as a deep breath. If he settled his hands on her arms or shoulders for a moment to be sure she was steady and balanced. Even if he offered his arm so she could make it safely.

Still a trade-off she didn't want to make.

"I'm surprised by how many people are out this morning," she said, glancing at him. The wool cap covered every bit of his hair, reaching almost to his eyebrows, but he managed to look amazingly handsome anyway.

"You don't have people out and about when a hurricane hits?"

"Huh. Yeah." Hurricanes were common enough in her experience—dangerous, but familiar. Though Evanston got heavy rains, high winds and flooding, the city was far enough inland to escape the brunt of most storms. Snow and ice were probably just as familiar, and a lot less scary, to the locals here.

Lucky her, Quint did take her arm when she started to climb into the truck. The running board was coated with slush and ice, so there was still a good chance she was going to splat down at least once today, but not this time. He held her just above the elbow as she gingerly stepped up and inside.

Too bad it hadn't been skin to skin, so she didn't have to guess at the texture of his palm—calloused, she would bet—or the heat his body radiated. A lot, probably.

"What did you say about your chief and ride-alongs?" he asked when he slid into the driver's seat.

JJ hesitated in fastening her seat belt, took a breath and gave him an even look. "He's pissy about them, and he generally doesn't allow women to do them. Can't have a girl get hurt or see or hear somethin' not fit for a lady's fragile nature."

"He really said that?"

"To my sister, the contractor, who climbs all over roofs and carries seventy-pound bundles of shingles up ladders. She was so mad, she about broke his legs off at the knee."

"But she didn't because you don't tick off your sister's boss."

The dispatcher called before JJ could answer, assigning Quint to a car accident on the southwest edge of town. After he acknowledged it, JJ went on. "Elle wanted to slam the chief on Facebook, complain to the mayor, write to the local newspaper, notify the ACLU. With her working in a traditionally male industry, gender discrimination is a hot-button issue for her. Plus, she's a little bit of a drama princess."

"Just a little bit, huh? What about you?"

She grinned, feeling ridiculously contented right this moment. The snow was beautiful, and she was buckled into a pickup the size of a tank with an experienced and skilled driver who just happened to leave her butterflies dizzy from spinning in time to the pit-pat-pit-pat of her heart. This was a very good place to be.

In response to his question, she assumed a royal pose. "Me? A drama princess?" Then her grin turned wicked. "Sweetie, I am the queen."

He didn't laugh. Didn't smile. But his lips quirked just a tiny bit, as if they wanted to.

When they reached the scene, he eased the truck to a stop in the outside lane, a safe distance from the wreck, and turned on his emergency lights. Frigid air rushed in when he opened the door, but instead of getting out right away, he gave her a look. Long. Level. Very blue.

And *then* he almost smiled. Really. Almost. The corners of his mouth lifted, his eyes softened, his cheeks looked a little fuller. It didn't last more than a few seconds, because he turned, let his boots slide to the ground and closed the door.

Her warm, appreciative, darn-near-dazzled sigh lasted a lot longer.

Quint was cold, wet and dirty. He'd fallen to his knee and ripped his pants when the last car he'd pushed had suddenly found traction and made him lose his. The driver hadn't stopped but had continued on his way with a jaunty wave out the window. Next an elderly woman he was helping up her sidewalk had remembered her ice cream was still in the car and spun around to go get it, hitting him in the stomach with a bag full of groceries and knocking him against an ice-crusted tree with the stump of a long-gone limb at the exact height of his shoulder blade. He was going to have a bruise there.

He'd been thanked and appreciated and fussed at and cussed at, and it was barely eleven o'clock. He still had the interview with Maura to look forward to.

It was going to be a long day. But at least it didn't have to be a long wet day.

"What do you want for lunch?"

JJ was facing out the side window, using her cell to take pictures of a newly budded dogwood tree coated in ice. "A Bloody Mary on the deck of a Mississippi riverboat sounds good. Or a piña colada on a white-sand beach."

Those both sounded better than he would have expected, considering he'd never been on a Mississippi riverboat and preferred vacations to mountains and deserts over beaches. "There's an old navy sub down in Muskogee, an hour or so from here, but they aren't known for their Bloody Marys. The only beach nearby is at Cedar Creek Park, and if you had a piña colada there, I'd have to arrest you."

Her nose wrinkled. "Has anyone ever told you you're no fun?"

"My years for being fun are long past. I'm a grown-up now." *Long* past.

"Not mine. Mine won't end until I'm at least as old as Miss Georgie." Then she slid the phone into her coat pocket. "You pick. The only places I've eaten here are Ted's Doughnuts, Judge Judie's Diner and Whataburger."

Quint believed she would certainly find life fun until she was old or in the grave.

Linny had.

His stomach rumbled quietly, bringing his attention

back to the original conversation. "You have to go to the Creek Café. It's kind of a rule in Cedar Creek. The lunch special today is—" He flipped through the menus in the console, found the right one and read, "'Chicken and dumplins and a slice of pie.' In Mrs. Little Bear's restaurant, there is no *g* in dumplins."

She beamed. There was no other way to describe her big, full-wattage smile. "Not in my kitchen, either. Grandmother Raynelle made the best dumplins. I use her recipe, and mine are pretty good, but hers were still better. And don't say she made them with love. She was a grouchy old woman who did everything with a complaint and a scowl."

"And you never deserved those complaints and scowls?" He turned west onto Teel Street before glancing at her.

"Of course I did. My grandmother said I was exuberant." She distinctly pronounced all the sounds, making clear Grandma hadn't meant it as a compliment. His grandma had been more empathetic toward him.

"Mine said I had a lot of personality."

The statement sounded strange in his own ears. He hadn't let himself think about Grandma Harris in years, or his Foster grandparents. He didn't let himself remember much about being a kid who was full of ideas and not all of them good. Even now, the memories were distant, like something he'd seen happen to someone else, not him. He'd shut out everything good and nostalgic because feeling nothing was better than feeling everything.

Grandma Foster had practically snatched his hair out when she'd heard him say that. For the last two years, Grandpa Foster had been in a nursing home, his body frail and all his memories gone. His family were strangers to him, even the wife he'd loved so dearly for more than sixty years, and it was slowly, surely breaking Grandma's heart.

She'd squeezed the stuffing out of Quint with a hug afterward.

He'd been luckier than Grandma. His heart had broken quickly and completely. One instant he'd been fine, and the next he might as well have been dead.

A soft drawl came from his side. "Unless y'all do things differently here, a four-way stop means you stop, then take your turn going. Everyone's waiting for you."

He blinked, realized he was holding up traffic at the intersection because nobody wanted to go when it was a cop's turn. Slowly he depressed the accelerator, caught traction and crossed the street.

JJ didn't ask where he'd disappeared to in his head. He appreciated that she respected his privacy. A lot of people didn't. "I thought Creek Café was about a mile from the hotel."

"It is. I just need to make a stop." His house was the last piece of property within the city limits on this road. It was a corner lot, a couple of acres, fenced in and big enough to keep the goats Linny had teased about buying. Then, she'd insisted, neither of them would have to mow anymore.

But someone would have to provide food and water and care and pick up goat poop, and he'd known that would have fallen to him.

He would be happy to pick up all the goat poop in the world if she was here to watch and laugh.

Muscles knotted in his neck and stirred a small ache between his eyes. Grimly, he pulled into the driveway, shut off the engine, then immediately restarted it. Even though changing clothes wouldn't take him long, he couldn't leave JJ waiting outside without heat, and he wasn't about to invite her inside. He hadn't invited anyone into his house since the day of Linny's funeral, and then his mother had actually issued the invitations.

"Is this your place?" JJ asked.

"Yeah. I'm going to change."

She settled comfortably in her seat. "Okay. As long as you leave the keys, you can take your time." She picked up the café menu from the console. "Just try to get back before I start drooling. It's not pretty."

Relieved that she wasn't showing any real curiosity, Quint got out and navigated the sidewalk to the porch. He'd emptied a bag of ice melt on the steps before he left this morning, and it was doing its job.

Inside, the house was quiet and warm. The only scents that greeted him were antiseptic, from the cleaning he'd done last night, along with the faint aromas of coffee and an unlit candle on the coffee table. The candle smelled like cinnamon candy, Linny's favorite, one of his least favorites. He kept it out but never lit it and wondered occasionally when its smell would fade.

Framed photographs lined the walls and climbed the stairs to the bedroom on the second floor. There were three posed pictures of the two of them: one taken at Sam and Mila's wedding, another at Daniel and Natasha Harper's, one at Linny's brother's. The rest were snapshots of people, places and things that had caught their attention. Most of what had caught his attention was her.

What would JJ have thought of all the pictures of Linny if he'd invited her to wait inside? He didn't kid himself she would have stayed on the big section of tile that fronted the door. She would have wandered around, maybe not touching, but looking intently for insights into his life. It was part of the job, being observant and learning about people. Give her an hour in this house, and she would probably learn a lot about him. She would probably sympathize with him. Or pity him. Or wonder what kind of emotional cripple couldn't take even the first step in moving on.

Grimly, he pried off his boots, then removed his gun belt before shucking his trousers, socks and jacket. Within a few minutes, he was dressed in clean clothes and dry boots, and he'd hung the damp clothes over the shower rail.

As he turned away from the shower, his gaze caught on his reflection in the bathroom mirror. His cheeks were red, his exposed skin tingling. His knitted cap fit snug over his hair, which meant it would either be pressed flat to his head when he took off the hat or it would stand on end. He didn't really care, but since they were going from here to Mrs. Little Bear's, he tugged the cap away, fluffed his hair with his fingers and combed it into some semblance of normal.

Didn't want to look untidy in uniform.

Yeah, that was the reason. Sure. Everyone's hair was going to look untidy today. Most of the officers, on going to lunch, would leave the hat on, maybe rolling up the brim to uncover their ears. They wouldn't worry about fixing their hair.

They weren't having lunch with JJ Logan.

Quint combed his hair again, stuck the cap in his pocket and trotted down the stairs, grabbing a clean jacket and gloves on the way out.

Creek Café was family-owned, family-run and pure heaven. As soon as JJ took her first breath inside, she knew this was going to be one of her favorite places in town. Naturally, growing up near the coast, she loved seafood, and ethnic food never failed to delight her, but homey Southern comfort food owned her heart.

The door had barely closed behind them when a man across the room called Quint's name and gestured. She glanced that way in time to see Lois shush Ben Little Bear with a smack to his shoulder. On his other side, Morwenna elbowed him while Detective Harper and two pretty and pregnant women, one blonde and fair, the other dark and exotic, watched with amusement.

Lois scooted her chair around to the left. "Sorry, we really can't make room for more. There's some empty tables back there in the corner. Out of our sight. Out of hearing range, too."

JJ made a slight effort at restraining her smile. "Thanks," she answered, since Quint had flushed a deep bronze and was intently ignoring the scene. She led the way between tables and around a corner to a smaller dining room that was mostly empty and chose a booth next to the windows. Though cold found its way right through the glass, a heating vent directly overhead negated its effect.

"Lois isn't the soul of subtlety, is she?" she asked as she slid onto the bench.

"I don't think she ever aspired to being subtle."

"Subtlety has its advantages. So does bluntness." JJ smiled at the waiter who brought them menus and ordered a Diet Dr Pepper. She already knew what she was eating…this time. She might try the entire menu while she was in town. "Who are the two women?"

"The blonde, Natasha, is Daniel's wife. Mila is Sam's wife."

The single women of Cedar Creek must have been sad when those two men had been taken off the market. But they still had Quint and Ben Little Bear, along with several of the younger officers, if a woman didn't mind the age difference. And surely there were gorgeous civilian guys in town, too. Every woman in America knew a disproportionate number of sigh-worthy firefighters, and according to Lois, the fire marshal was hot, hot, hot.

But Quint hadn't recovered from the breaking of his heart yet. She wondered who the woman had been. Why she'd ended things with him. Where had she gone, and what was she doing, and would she ever come back?

It was easy to wish him happiness, even though she knew nothing about the relationship. Maybe the mystery woman hadn't loved him the way he'd loved her. Maybe she'd betrayed him. Maybe they'd been one of those couples who couldn't stand to be together and couldn't bear to be apart. Maybe neither of them had loved the other enough. Ryan had sworn he loved her, and he'd treated her as if he did, until he'd dumped her for being promoted quicker than him. He'd called her the light of his life…until her light had shone a little brighter than his.

Had Mystery Woman been the light of Quint's life?

The waiter returned with their drinks and took their orders: chicken and dumplings for both, with corn bread and pumpkin pie for Quint, a hot dinner roll and rhubarb pie for JJ. When the waiter was gone, she started to pull her tablet from her purse to tell him what little she'd learned about Maura the night before, but he spoke first.

"Is your chief good, bad or indifferent?"

Ah. Turning yesterday's question back on her. Damn Chief Dipstick for assigning her a simple case, then trying to muck it up for her. "I guess that depends on your perspective."

"No, it depends on *your* perspective."

She gazed out the window at the stream below. The town had taken its name from Cedar Creek, expanding along both sides of it. The water looked clear and cold, with piles of snow and fragile bits of ice built up along the edges. The park on the east side was empty, snow clumped on swings and jungle gyms, gleaming in the sun.

Finally she looked back at Quint. "He's like any boss. Some people love him, some hate him, some tolerate him."

"And you?"

She pursed her lips. "A smart cop keeps her personal opinions to herself. Casual comments get taken out of context, tattled to someone who tattles to someone else, and the first thing you know, you're looking for a new job. I like my job."

His blue eyes took on the frigid shade of the blue sky. "If you think I would tattle to your chief, then we shouldn't be having this conversation."

"You started it, bub." JJ picked up the silverware,

unwrapped a heavy paper napkin and spread it carefully over her lap. She'd changed its position three times before meeting Quint's gaze again. "Are you annoyed because I think anything I tell you would go straight to Sam, who may or may not pass it on to Chadwick, or because I suggested you might 'tattle'?"

"I don't tattle," he said stiffly. "That's a kid thing."

"You would tell Sam anything you thought he needed to know," she retorted before adding, "You get miffed easily."

It never failed to amaze her how rewording things could make such a difference. Implying he wasn't trustworthy had insulted him. Acknowledging he would pass on necessary information to his boss, as a good police officer should, faded the chill and made his resultant scowl seem more habit than lingering annoyance.

"I'm not miffed. That's a girly thing."

"I get miffed, and I'm not girly."

He looked at her then—seriously, intently, a man-seeing-woman look that started with her hair, slid down to linger on her mouth, dipped lower to the sweater that clung to her breasts, stopped regretfully at her midriff where the table blocked the view, then drifted back to her face. "You're girly enough."

His voice was raspy, hoarse, and she was truly warm for the first time in twenty-four hours. In fact, she was pretty sure steam was escaping from her pores, heating the air in her lungs and making her heart go *pit-pat-pit-pat-pit*. Mercy, it had been a long time since she'd felt quite like this. Far longer than her ego cared to remember.

She shifted nearer the window, cooling the heat climbing her neck and gathering in her face. Heat that also pooled lower, tickly and tingly. Some part of her fogged brain realized she should probably say something flirty or suggestive, but she didn't want to talk. She wanted to touch. Explore. Experiment. Do all the X-related words that might apply. She wanted to see if he was as solid and hot-blooded as he appeared to be, if his muscles were as hard as she guessed they were, if any other part of him was hard…

"I'm glad you noticed," she managed in a husky, breathless voice. "To most cops, I'm just another badge and gun."

He snorted at that but didn't elaborate as the waiter brought their meal. He didn't say anything when the young man, who bore a striking resemblance to Ben Little Bear, though much smaller, left, either. He just picked up his knife, buttered the corn bread and broke off a piece. He spoke before eating it, but not about her astonishing girlyness or his rampant desire for her or the possibility of taking her back to the hotel after lunch and ravishing her.

Drat.

"To be honest, I will tell Sam the gist of whatever you say. He's responsible for pretty much everything that goes on here, so his need to know trumps everything else. Besides, I trust him. I respect him."

Of course he did, and Sam trusted and respected him right back. She neither trusted nor respected Chadwick, and he reciprocated in full. The only thing was, at least she had given him a chance. When he'd taken over as chief a year ago, she'd fully expected the same kind of fair, professional working relationship that she'd had with each of her two previous chiefs. She hadn't judged him until he'd proved himself lacking in every way.

While he had taken one look at her, seen she was female and written her off.

She indulged in one delicious bite of dumpling, hot and steamy and tender-chewy, followed by a shiver of sheer appreciation, then tore open her dinner roll. Quint slid the butter dish across the table to her. "From the perspective of a few good ol' boys who prefer life the way it used to be, Chief Chadwick is a good administrator. For the average officer in the department, he's not bad. He was actually a decent cop himself, for the most part. But from the perspective of a female cop who has fifteen years on the job and who earned every promotion and "attaboy" she's ever gotten, he's a misogynistic bigot who's managed to keep 1950s attitudes alive in his little kingdom.

"He didn't call your chief because he was concerned about me, and you know it. That's why Sam has pushed me off on you. To keep an eye on me. To see if I'm a major screwup or just a minor one."

Quint didn't deny the truth of that. He didn't question her remarks about Dipstick, either. "Why do you stay?"

She tasted the roll—Grandmother Raynelle would have killed to make bread this good—then dabbed melted butter from her mouth. "It's home. Except for college, it's where I've always lived. My parents and sisters and their families live there. Most of my extended family is within an hour's drive. I like my job, never wanted to live in a big city and…"

He studied her, his head tilted to one side, his gaze

serious, then a knowing look came across his face. "Quitting would mean letting him win."

She grinned, relieved he'd recognized her petty goal rather than her having to admit it herself. "He's already retired from one chief's position. If I hold on awhile longer, he'll either retire again or die. And yeah, that means I win." Was it the most mature attitude she'd ever displayed? No. Was it a satisfying one? Hell, yeah.

He'd recognized one other thing about her. "And you do like to win."

"I do."

It was one of her strengths. Probably one of her weaknesses, too. In matters big or small, great or piddling, in love or war.

Especially in love or war.

The sun glinted so brightly off the snow and leftover ice that Quint's sunglasses weren't dark enough to keep an ache from starting behind his eyes. He wanted nothing more than to go home, take a couple of aspirin tablets and sleep about twelve hours, but that would only delay the inevitable. JJ had to see Maura Evans face-to-face, and Sam wanted him to be there when it happened.

Maybe she wouldn't be home. Maybe she was sleeping off a midweek drunk and wouldn't answer the door. Maybe, like her friend Mel, she'd packed up and fled town before the storm hit last night.

Or maybe she would open the door, greet her childhood babysitter like a long-lost friend, explain the last three months of her behavior to everyone's satisfaction, and JJ's case would be officially closed. She would be free to go back to South Carolina, report in to her idiot boss and jump right back into her usual routine.

An odd little spot deep inside Quint really sort of hoped that didn't happen. Not yet. Not when he hadn't…

What?

He didn't even know.

Willow Street was untraveled past the Berryhills' house, where four small kids were probably driving their mother a little more insane than usual. No tire tracks, no footprints, no one in or out. The pricey little convertible Maura drove wasn't made for bad weather, and she was probably no more experienced with these road conditions than JJ. At the gate, he turned into the driveway, parking about the same place he'd parked when he'd written Maura that last ticket.

She wasn't the first woman who'd come on to him in an effort to avoid a ticket. But she was the only one who'd actually tempted him. Her boldness. Her beauty. His loneliness. It was what shamed him: that he *had* been tempted. That he'd actually considered using her, with just as little emotion and just as little caring, as she would have used him. That he would have dishonored Linny's memory that way.

That he would have, he'd eventually realized, dishonored Maura, too.

Maybe she wouldn't remember him. To her, he'd probably just been some lowly civil servant, someone to amuse herself with for an hour or two. She'd probably forgotten everything about him the moment she'd slammed the door on him.

"Are you going to wait here?"

JJ's voice startled him from his thoughts. She'd

opened the passenger door and sat sideways in the seat, one leg already out. "Is that an option?" He hoped she didn't identify the hopeful tone faint in his voice.

"No." She glanced ahead, then asked, "Is it just me, or is this place kind of creepy?"

He looked at the house. It stood two stories, blocky and plain, built of brick so deep a red that it came close to black. The door was white, the shutters black, the windows tall and symmetrical, every one covered inside with drapes. Instead of a porch, there was a small stoop with a concrete planter on each side that held the spindly skeletons of bushes long dead.

The lawn was big, patches of newly greened grass mixed with tall yellowed weeds. The leaves not stubborn enough to evade the wind piled against the foundation from corner to corner, in the branches of the lifeless shrubs, in the corners around the door. The sidewalk hadn't been edged in so long that snakes of dead grass crept across the surface, the tall red cedar in the middle of the yard was dying and volunteer seedlings had popped up in a dozen places. Red cedars were notoriously prolific in Oklahoma. Left unchecked, they would take over the entire acreage more quickly than seemed possible.

"It's not creepy. Just neglected."

"Miss Georgie wouldn't like that."

"No. You'd think Maura would have hired someone to clean up last fall or to get ready for spring."

"I'm not sure she gets that things have to actually be done. East Oaks, the family home, makes Tara from *Gone With the Wind* look like servants' quarters. When she got up in the morning, every room in the house was spotless, the grass was manicured and the pool was sparkling fresh and clean. Meals appeared on the table, and when she dropped dirty clothes on the floor, they reappeared, magically clean, in her closet. Which, by the way, even when she was ten, was bigger than my entire condo."

It was a life he could hardly imagine. He'd been putting his dirty clothes in a hamper for as long as he could remember. Setting the table, helping in the garden, loading the dishwasher, doing his own laundry, picking up whether he'd made the mess or someone else had—that had been life in the Foster household. They'd known where food came from, how grass got mowed, how clothes got clean.

He tuned back to her last comment. "You live in a condo?"

JJ flashed a smile. "I *know* how things get done. That's why I have nine hundred square feet of low-maintenance paradise." After a pause, she slid to the ground. "Shall we?"

Do we have to? he wanted to ask, but of course they did. He cut the engine, removed his seat belt and opened his own door. Meeting at the front of the truck, they left a trail of footprints across the pristine snow of the driveway, along the sidewalk and to the entry.

JJ rang the doorbell, then stamped her feet on the cement stoop. "I never understood why people choose such solid doors, then put windows on either side. I don't want people looking inside my place before I have a chance to look out at them."

He looked in the nearest sidelight. No lights were on inside, and the covered windows left the space in shadow. The door opened into a foyer, a chandelier overhead and stairs on the right side climbing to the second floor. The front room—Georgie had never cared for words like *living room* or *parlor*—was to the left, barely visible beyond its arched double doorway, and her husband's study opened on the right.

"I didn't call ahead because I doubt she wants to see anyone from home, but it looks like maybe I should have." JJ pushed the bell again, its echoes faint.

Shadowy movement on the stairs reminded Quint he was peeping into someone else's home. He stepped back, standing squarely in the middle of the stoop, and opened his mouth to say their summons was being answered when a thin, surly voice inside bellowed, "Don't ring that damn bell again!"

"Oh good. She's already happy to see us," JJ said with a cynical grin.

The woman ignored the sidelights and jerked the door open to glare at them. "Why are you ringing my bell?"

"Because that's the usual way to let someone know they have company." JJ's smile wasn't her usual one, full of warmth and damn near oozing friendliness. This was her professional smile—polite, cordial. Her whole manner was: the way she stood a little straighter, held her head a little higher, offered her hand for a shake. "It's been a long time, Maura."

"Anything beyond last week is a long time," Maura muttered before shoving her hair back from her face. "You'll have to remind me when we met."

"Fifteen, maybe sixteen years ago. You were ten, it was summer and I apparently wasn't the most memorable babysitter you ever had. JJ Logan."

Seconds ticked past as Maura stared at her, her brows drawn together, her blue eyes narrowing. Abruptly, a look of surprise crossed her face. "JJ! Oh my God. You were probably the best babysitter I ever had." She stepped forward, grabbing JJ in a hug that struck Quint as both awkwardly given and awkwardly received, then hastily drew back from the door, a shiver running through her. "You should come inside. This old house is impossible to keep warm. It's been awful all winter, and that comes from someone who spent a whole winter in ice hotels in Switzerland."

JJ entered first, and Quint followed. So far, he didn't think Maura had even noticed him. Good.

It was warmer in the house, though not comfortably so, as Maura had said. It took a lot to heat a foyer with a twenty-five-foot ceiling, especially with a marble floor, no rugs, no furniture, nothing to help the furnace with its job. The space smelled musty, as if it hadn't been thoroughly cleaned in at least as long as the yard hadn't been properly cared for.

Maura led the way past the front room, once home to antiques and Turkish rugs and now holding a lonely couch, and the dining room, totally empty, to the single large room at the back of the house. The kitchen occupied the left side, with a space in the center for a table and chairs, and the right side had been built for low tables, cozy couches and the kind of chairs a person could curl up in. The old rocking chair he'd sat in yesterday at Georgie's apartment had always held a place of pride next to the fireplace. Now the space had one Asian rug that couldn't be more than a year old, a leather sofa and two matching chairs that looked and felt obscenely expensive when he sat in one, and that was it.

JJ took a seat on the sofa while Maura went straight to the fireplace. She pushed the button that lit the gas, turned the flames to high, then sat on the hearth, huddling as if she might never get warm.

It had been three months since the scene in the driveway. She was much prettier in his recollections, much more put together. Amazing what makeup, combed hair and a nice dress could do. Granted, they'd apparently woken her up, if her sweatpants, thin T-shirt and bedhead were anything to judge by. Her eyes were bleary, and an air of overindulgence made her less memorable. Partying, booze, sex, drugs…whatever she was getting too much of was taking its toll.

"So." She tucked her hands between her knees. "Why are you in Cedar Creek?"

JJ relaxed on the couch, one hand at her side, fingers gently testing the texture of the expensive leather. "Your godfather is worried about you."

"My—" A scowl shifted across Maura's face, drawing her mouth taut, emphasizing the hollows in her cheeks and the shadows under her eyes. She wore the expression as comfortably as Quint did, but with extra layers of surliness and disdain. That was one big difference between them: Maura felt disdain for much of the world, while the only person Quint held in true disdain was himself.

"Winchester. Nosy old bastard. I'm twenty-five years old. What I do with my life and my money is none of his business."

Her words made Quint's head throb worse. He wasn't

surprised that she showed such loathing for a man with whom she'd always been close. It was easy to love a person when he had no authority over you. Winchester and his wife had been her parents' best friends, the easygoing godparents who never told her no, never tried to control her, just loved her from the sidelines. But with her parents' deaths, he'd become the man who reined in her spending and therefore her activities, and she was in rebellion.

Money had destroyed stronger relationships too many times to count.

"He's not only your godfather, Maura, he's the executor of the estate. Your parents chose him to help you manage your inheritance and give you advice."

"My parents." Maura scoffed as she straightened. Sort of. Her spine was still rounded, her shoulders still slumped. Her knees rested together, and one socked foot sat on top of the other. "What kind of parents go off and get themselves killed, give their only child a kajillion dollars, then take it back and say, oh, you can only spend what the godfather says you can? The selfish kind, and Winchester is just like them. What good does all that money do me when I can't freaking have it? Is this some kind of punishment? Some sort of payback from the grave?"

Quint shifted his head a fraction to the left to watch the impact of the words on JJ. Her brows twitched upward, and thin, nearly invisible lines etched out from the corners of her eyes and mouth. He could see the rigid set of her jaw and the even more rigid set of her shoulders as she drew a deep breath. Though to a casual observer, she seemed hardly affected by Maura's anger, he recognized surprise in her, maybe some shock and even a dose of anger.

"They were the kind of parents who loved you dearly, Maura. You know that. They loved you enough to make sure you were taken care of for the rest of your life. Those first few years, you were grieving, stunned. You could hardly make decisions for yourself. You needed Travis Winchester's help." JJ paused, then tried another tack. "You know your friends back home all have the same sort of setup with their trusts. An allowance now, a lump-sum payment when they turn twenty-five or thirty or thirty-five, another when they turn forty or fifty. The richer they are, the longer it takes to get the entire amount, and Maura, you're the richest of all of them."

For the first time since she'd opened the door, Maura smiled. It was a smug, happy, greedy smile. "I am, aren't I? More than any of them." But like a balloon leaking air, the cheeriness seeped away, and she huddled down again, grousing, "I thought I would get it all when I turned twenty-five, but that was two months ago, and here I am, still broke."

"You get your first lump-sum payment in five more years," JJ said evenly. "But seriously, your allowance is more than a million dollars a year, and Mr. Winchester releases other monies for special purchases. What do you want that $1.2 million a year won't pay for?"

Maura's gaze dropped, and her lower lip slid into a pout. She lifted her right hand, inspecting her nails, four of them long and polished, one bitten to the quick. She picked at that nail for a moment, tearing off a strip of skin, then squeezed the finger tightly, forcing the drop of blood to well larger.

While she stared, sullen and defensive, a soft thud came from above. JJ's and Quint's gazes both went straight to the ceiling, but Maura pretended not to notice. An instant later, there was another thud.

"I'm sorry," JJ said even though it was clear to him that she wasn't. "Did we interrupt something?"

"I don't know what you're talking about," Maura muttered.

"I heard a door close upstairs. Do you have a guest waiting for you?"

"There's no one there."

"Are you sure? I'm a cop now, Maura. I'd be happy to go up and check things out."

"Would you freaking forget about it? The point is that money belongs to me. Not my grandfather—"

"Godfather."

"Whatever. Since it's mine, why can't I have it when I want it?"

"Because your parents' wills said—"

"I don't care about their damn wills!" Maura jumped to her feet and, ignoring the blood on her finger, clenched her fists and tucked her arms across her chest. "You need to go. Tell the old bastard I want more money or else. Go on, get out. Get out!"

JJ stood, dignified and controlled, though her face was a few shades paler. Quint did, too, and followed her back through the house to the front door. Maura jerked the door open wide and pointed that one blood-tipped finger toward the stoop. JJ was outside and he was one step away when Maura finally looked at him. Really looked at him. *No, no, no,* he hoped, but per usual, there was no hope.

"Officer Foster," she said in a manner that reminded him of a big hungry cat sighting its prey. The change from hostile to seductive was as quick as turning on a light, as drastic as going from deep black to midday sun. "When are you going to take me up on my offer?"

He was hot and antsy inside, feeling the wicked gleam of her gaze, the watchful curiosity of JJ's. Maura came closer, backing him against the doorjamb, so close he could identify distinct scents: sweat, the sour after note of wine, a hint of weed, an elegant but worn-out perfume. She smiled like that big hungry cat, unaware that at this moment, she looked far more down-and-out doper than million-dollar princess.

"I didn't pay that ticket," she said throatily. Instead of sounding sexy, though, he was reminded of a cat about to hack up a ball of hair. "I've been waiting for you to come back and put handcuffs on me. Then we could have some real fun."

JJ's dry voice, barely audible, came from the top step. "Ah, the ten thousand handcuff jokes we hear all the time."

The reminder of her presence turned off the sex nymph and brought back the anger. "You know what? I lied before. You were a stupid, bad babysitter. I told my parents to never hire you back, and they never did."

So there! She didn't add the juvenile taunt, but she might as well have. She gave Quint a shove on the shoulder that wouldn't have moved him half an inch if he hadn't been eager to go, then slammed the door. The lock clicked loudly an instant later.

He and JJ walked to the truck in silence. A few deep breaths of cold air cleaned away the smells of Maura and her musty, dusty house, and the pounding in his head took a respite, far too brief but long enough for him to get settled in the driver's seat.

JJ gave him a long look before he reached for the gearshift, a questioning, wondering—judging?—sort of look. "So, Quint," she said as he backed out of the drive. "Tell me about this offer."

Chapter 5

He didn't, of course. He didn't say much of anything on the drive to the hotel, grunting a time or two, not meeting JJ's gaze. Out front, he'd muttered something about being in touch, then gone off to finish his shift.

Now JJ lay in the middle of the bed in her hotel room, shoes off, feet propped carefully on the iron birds that decorated the footboard. A pillow was stuffed under her head, a stack of file folders to one side, her cell and tablet on the other. She'd intended to use the time to type notes of the interview, to devote her quick and complicated brain to figuring out Maura's juvenile and complicated behaviors, but instead, her thoughts had drifted from Maura to Quint and back like a pendulum. She'd found herself completely unable to focus on one of them for longer than a few minutes before the other beckoned her, and now, with dinnertime approaching, her empty stomach was demanding its share of attention, too.

At least that was something she could actually handle. Her choices were slim: candy, chips and pop from downstairs, Judge Judie's a few steps down the sidewalk or a cold walk to Creek Café. She'd noticed the dinner special at the café was pot roast with carrots and potatoes and all the bread a person could eat, especially if said person wasn't worried about fitting into her jeans at the end of this trip. Plus, there was banana split cake for dessert. Yum, she did love roast and rolls and bananas and cake, and God made elastic-waist pants for a reason, right?

Besides, both exercise and food would help her puzzle through Maura's actions. The only thing the girl had said that hadn't surprised JJ was the insult she'd thrown out at the end. *Oh, by the way, you were a lousy babysitter. Neener, neener.* As if that, and telling her parents not to hire JJ again, held any power fifteen years later. It had been a crappy summer job, nothing more. JJ had just graduated college, already hired by the police department, and was waiting for a start date for her academy class. The babysitting gig had paid decently, gotten her out of the house and given her access to the Evanses' pool as long as she had Maura with her.

Oh, yeah, and that remark to Quint. *When are you going to take me up on my offer?* That hadn't surprised her at all. What grown woman with functioning hormones wasn't sexually attracted to six feet of golden-blond, blue-eyed, hard-bodied, tough, stoic, big strong silent type of man? Though she couldn't for the life of her imagine Quint feeling the same sort of attraction for Maura. He was mature. She wasn't. She was rich. He wasn't. She was blown away with just how rich she was. He wasn't.

And damn it, JJ was a better match for him.

She was wiggling her toes, watching the shadows they cast on the wall, when her stomach growled and burbled. Exercise, she reminded herself as she sat up. Cold walk plus good food equaled clearer mind.

Besides, if she got to the restaurant early enough, maybe she could bring back an extra slice of banana split cake and hide it in the refrigerator downstairs with a threatening note—*Thieves Will Be Tased.*

She changed her sweater for a long-sleeved button-down and added another sweater, this one rich purple merino wool, knitted by her mom in cable and basket stitches. After tucking her jeans into knee-high boots, she slid her credit card and ID into one hip pocket, her lipstick and a packet of tissues into one coat pocket and her cell into the other coat pocket and gripped her keys. With the coat zipped to her chin, her hat covering her hair and her gloves in hand, she opened the door and came to an abrupt stop.

Quint stood inches away, right hand raised as if to knock.

Her internal thermostat went from comfy to darn near combustible in two seconds flat. His strong nose, square jaw and high cheekbones looked as if they'd been carved from stone as hard as granite but as smooth as glass. He was scowling—habit, she reminded herself— and a muscle twitched at the corner of one lovely blue eye, but she was still happy to see him.

"Where are you going?"

It wasn't *I've missed you.* Or *That color brings out the green in your eyes.* Or *You look beautiful* or *I want you* or *I need you* or *I've got to have you.* But it was something.

"Dinner. Creek Café."

"You planning to walk?"

"I checked the temperature. It's thirty-one degrees."

"With a windchill of twenty."

She wondered exactly what twenty degrees of wind felt like, then grinned. "I'm tough."

For a moment, he didn't respond, long enough for her to realize that she was standing unusually close to him. Close enough to see the ribbed neck of the shirt he wore in the opening at the top of his jacket. To notice the stubble on his jaw, as pale gold as the hair on his head, with a few gray hairs sprinkled in. To smell the cologne he wore, a subtle, spicy, grassy scent. To get a close-up view of that muscle at the corner of his eye as it twitched again. She was starting to feel just a little light-headed when his husky, raspy voice broke the quiet.

"You are tough," he agreed, and she pretty much fell into full light-headedness. Him acknowledging her toughness was better than telling her she was beautiful. "But save it for when you need it. Invite me, and I'll drive."

"Will you have dinner with me?" she asked quickly, before he could even consider changing his mind.

"Yes."

For another moment, they still stood there. The only direction she could move was backward, and that was the wrong direction for going out. After one deep, deep breath of the smells of him, she said, "I can't come out if you don't move."

A faint flush colored his face, and he took a large step back. She closed and locked the door, and he followed her down an ordinary staircase to the second floor. The staircase that took them to the first floor was grand and lovely and allowed them to walk side by side.

She liked being at his side.

When she stepped out of the hotel, she got a full-body blast of twenty-degree cold. Her jeans only slowed the chill, and her bare skin stung. Hastily, she shoved her hands into her gloves, doubly happy Quint had come along, because walking out here alone, she would have written off her refreshing walk and dashed the short distance to Judge Judie's. While the food there was good, it wasn't pot roast.

The vehicle parked on the street was a pickup truck, but that was where the similarities to his official vehicle ended. This one was from the '60s, she estimated, and probably had enough miles for two or three lifetimes on it. Its paint style was classic blue and white, and inside it held a bench seat instead of now-standard bucket seats.

This was the kind of pickup generations before them had used for making out on a pretty night in an out-of-the-way spot.

She wondered if it worked equally as well on a frigid huddle-together-for-body-heat night.

They made the drive to Creek Café in silence, but it was companionable. JJ was a talker. All the people in her family were, and most of the guys she'd dated seriously. It was nice to meet a man who spoke mostly when he had something to say. Did he think it nice that she didn't need his assistance in carrying on a conversation?

"It didn't get above freezing today," she remarked as they made their way into the restaurant, "and the sidewalks are still yucky, but the streets are mostly clear. That's weird."

"The wind." Quint opened the door and let her enter first. "Friction."

"Ah." Like water carving a hole into rock, the friction caused by the constant wind wore away the ice the same way.

An older woman sat on a stool behind the counter, glasses perched on the tip of her nose. Hair the color of old iron was pulled into a bun resting low on her neck, and lines stretched across her skin like trails on a road map. She wore a T-shirt, a fuzzy jacket, a denim skirt that fell to her ankles and a pair of yellow house slippers. She gave JJ an uninterested look before turning to Quint. "Heh. Where you been?"

"I'm always around, Great-Aunt Weezer. How are you?"

JJ looked at the woman with renewed curiosity. Nope, no family resemblance. Miss Weezer appeared to be about one hundred and eighty, cranky enough to make Miss Georgie seem pleasant and had all the cuddly warmth of a prickly pear cactus. She was Native American, tall and bony, with eyes darker than a starless night.

"What brings you out on a night like this?" Quint asked.

"My niece. Said I needed to come hang out with the family. Do I look like I need to hang out with the family? I see them every week, sometimes twice. Isn't that enough for a sane person?" She shifted on the stool, crossing one leg and bringing one feathery house shoe into closer view. It actually had a chicken's head with a red comb and a carrot-shaped beak sewn above the toes. "What she really meant is Anita called in, so they needed someone to sit here and say, 'Welcome to Creek Café. Sit wherever you want. Thank you for coming.'" The old woman scowled. "Welcome to Creek Café. Sit wherever you want. Read the specials on your way by or let the waiter tell them to you. Just go sit down."

By the time Quint signaled JJ to go on, she had her lips pressed together hard to keep from grinning. She headed for the smaller dining room, making a beeline for the same booth where they'd eaten lunch, and slid into the same seat as before. "Isn't she a ray of sunshine."

He shrugged. "Great-Aunt Weezer's what they used to call a character."

"I recognize characters when I see them. Evanston has its share. Whose great-aunt is she?"

"Ben Little Bear's. Just because we call someone by family terms doesn't mean we're blood related." He shuddered a bit at the thought.

"I know. I have aunts, uncles and cousins whose family trees don't even grow in the same universe as ours." She didn't bother to open the menu. She'd scanned the specials board on the way past, as Miss Weezer had suggested, to make sure her first choice was still listed. It was.

They spent the next few moments settling, removing their coats and gloves, unrolling the silverware, getting comfortable. She realized belatedly that he wasn't in uniform. His long-sleeved T-shirt was a thermal weave the color of oatmeal, and over that he wore a green-and-blue-plaid shirt that looked as soft as a baby's cuddle toy. How had she not noticed in time to get a good look at him in jeans that were sure to be faded and snug?

Oh well, there was always the walk back out to the truck when they were done. So far, he'd politely allowed her to go first, but she would give him the honor when they left.

After a teenage waitress took their order, with a shy, "Hello, Quint," and a lingering, yearning look for him, JJ crossed her legs, folded her hands together and met his gaze. "Now, Officer Foster, tell me about that offer."

There was something sweet about a man his age—a man with his looks and his life's experiences—blushing. He would probably prefer to blame the color in his cheeks on the cold night, but nope, that would have been redder, rawer. This was definitely a blush.

"You know she was hungover," he mumbled.

"I could smell the booze and the weed. But that wasn't an unfounded statement. You blushed then, too. Come on, confession is good for the soul, or so they say."

He shifted his gaze to the window, and the tic beside his eye started again. This time, his jaw went taut, too, and an air of tension radiated from his entire body. He was really affected by this, she realized, her humor fading. Clearly he hadn't crossed the line of professional conduct, or Maura wouldn't have said, "I've been waiting." Did he blame himself that it had happened at all? Had he given her a reason to think he wanted her?

JJ reached across the table, her palm up, then rapped her knuckles on the surface to get his attention. He stared at it a long time before slowly resting his fingers there.

She curled her own fingers loosely, savoring the heat and texture and strength of even that small part of him.

"When I'd been on the job about six months," she began conversationally, "I pulled a big ole Cadillac over for speeding one night. The guy was in his fifties, smelled like he'd bathed in moonshine, hadn't shaved in days, hadn't washed his hair in weeks. Even his cigar looked like he'd been chewing on it for a month or two. He grinned this big snaggletoothed grin and said, 'This is your lucky day, missy. You keep that ticket book where it belongs, and Daddy's gonna show you what it's like with a real man.' Then he drew my attention down, where he wiggled his thing at me."

Fifteen years, and she remembered the scene so clearly. The humidity heavy in the air. The croaking of tree frogs and hooting from nearby owls. The ticking of the big old engine as it cooled, and the unpleasant stink emanating from the cranked-down windows. And the kicker: his dark pants undone and his pale, soft, fat flesh. A huge shudder rippled through her.

"I gagged. I actually threw up a little bit in my mouth. And then I threw up a little bit on him. By the time I hustled back to my car, *I* wanted a bath in moonshine. You know, that'll kill just about any germ.

"But you know what? It worked. I didn't write him a ticket. All I wanted to do was put as much distance and clean air between us as possible. The whole thing put me off sex and men and Cadillacs and moonshine for a long time."

A bit of tension eased from his hand, but he still looked ill—guilty? repulsed?—from the memories of his own experience. Because there was something more to his experience than hers.

"You stopped Maura for a traffic offense. I'm going to guess speeding, since she thinks the faster, the better. She offered you sex if you didn't write the ticket, and judging by her behavior today, when you turned her down, she cussed you out and threw the ticket away. Am I right?"

"She tore it in little pieces first."

"She can't be the first woman who ever hit on you to avoid a ticket. Women appreciate guys who look like you." Then she shrugged. "And women who think avoiding a $150 ticket is worth having sex with a stranger have no standards, period."

"No," he admitted. "She wasn't the first."

JJ pictured a cleaned-up Maura, sober and cheery and dressed to thrill, and a wry smile tipped her mouth. "You considered it. For an instant, maybe half that, you wondered, *Why not?* She's beautiful, she's fun and willing—and we'll just ignore the fact that she's young enough to be your daughter—and for a moment, like any living, breathing man, you wanted to take her up on the offer."

That was what bothered him so much. He had been tempted. She would laugh if he weren't so damn serious.

What about the situation made the guilt such a big deal? It wasn't just the professional aspect, because he *hadn't accepted.* It wasn't the overlap of his personal/ professional lives. Claire at the hotel had told her that Sam's wife had been the target of a crazed killer and that Daniel Harper's wife had been followed to Oklahoma by a psychotic stalker. In a small town, you got overlap. JJ doubted it was the age difference. After all, Maura had offered a quick-and-dirty deed, not an on-going affair, and while JJ figured Maura would drive Quint totally mad in record time, he could surely tolerate a snotty, snobby, superficial, whiny brat long enough for an orgasm.

So that left his own relationship status at the time. Either he'd still been with Mystery Woman, or he had been mourning her, nursing the heart she'd broken. Either way, considering sex with Maura even for a moment must have seemed like a betrayal to the woman, to himself, to them as a onetime happily-ever-after couple.

That said good things about his idea of commitment. Not-so-good things about his stance on casual sex. JJ liked commitment. But she only had time for casual sex.

"Aw, Quint, where we would we be without temptation? You didn't betray your morals or ethics." *Or the foolish woman who broke your heart.* "We'd damn well better be tempted by someone or another, or humans aren't long for this world."

He met her gaze, his eyes dark and shuttered. "So you were tempted? You were tempted by Cadillac guy?"

"Oh, hell, no. But once, for about half a second. With a twenty-year-old kid. Young enough to be my son," she said ruefully. "He was just so pretty. All golden skin and big brown eyes and muscles on muscles and the most incredible dimples. Even my mom admitted to lascivious thoughts about him. I was arresting him on a drug charge, and he made the offer, and…it was a once-in-a-lifetime thing. He was so amazingly, perfectly, breathtakingly gorgeous, and if I turned him down, that chance would never, ever come again."

She couldn't overstate what a vision of sheer masculine loveliness that young man had been. He was her sisters' if-I-was-going-to-cheat fantasy guy. Their aunt Jada, the author, had written him into one of her books, where he tempted her fortysomething protagonist almost beyond bearing. He was God's gift to a beauty-appreciating world.

"Then the kid, whose intelligence will never be a threat to his beauty, said, 'You're awfully old, you know. But, hey, if it keeps me out of jail…'" Her grimace was part amused, part still annoyed. "*Old.* That was last year. I ratcheted down those handcuffs and hauled his ass off to a marked unit so quick that he tumbled into the back seat."

She sighed as the waitress served their meals, gave their touching hands an anxious look, then disappeared without a word. "Of course, his lawyer met us at the jail, so he didn't even set foot in a cell, and his only punishment was a slap on the wrist. He deserved at least a month on a county work crew for calling me old."

Quint used the waitress's look and the food as a reason to pull his hand from hers. For a long time, he kept his attention on the plate of meat loaf, mashed potatoes, mushroom gravy and green beans. It all looked and smelled wonderful, but her own meal looked and smelled even better. Instead of a plate, it was served in a large, flat bowl: chunks of beef, wedges of potatoes, large rounds of carrots and slices of onion and celery, bathed with gravy made with homemade stock and red wine. The basket of hot yeast rolls was the final fragrance needed to complete her culinary ecstasy.

She was eating the absolute best pot roast in the world. Now she could die happy.

Then she looked across the table at Quint.

Well, not quite yet.

The table had been cleared of dishes except for coffee cups, saucers and spoons. A plastic bag held a container with JJ's dessert. The checks had been paid, and Nalria, Ben's cousin who'd waited on them, had collected her tip, then gone home to catch up on schoolwork. The main dining room was busy, but with half a dozen empty tables in the smaller one, no one was rushing them to leave.

For the first time in a very long time, Quint was in no hurry to go. He didn't linger over meals, didn't draw out visits beyond minimum social or parental requirements. He'd left the family's Christmas Eve gift opening and buffet after one hour, one minute, and had skipped out on Christmas Day dinner after two hours. He did what had to be done, he finished, he left.

But not tonight. All that awaited him at home was an empty bed in a lonely house. Here, there was JJ. Her expressions could change lightning quick, from grim to grinning to somber to ridiculous. Being happy and funny and friendly came naturally to her, the way it used to be for him. She didn't know about Linny or his demotion, so there was no tiptoeing around like everyone else did.

He envied her. Felt more normal with her than he had in a long time.

That empty bed in that lonely house… It was his bed. His house. It hadn't always been empty or lonely. He had tons of memories there, good ones, funny ones, sad ones, of Linny and himself, their families, their friends. Happy ones, sexy ones, breath-stealing ones.

Angry ones, boring ones, just plain old normal ones. He missed normal.

Grieving was hard. Carrying anger and loss and bitterness and guilt were hard. They were easy ruts to fall into, but damned if they didn't require a whole lot of energy to stay there. Wouldn't it be easier to wake up some morning and think, *This is going to be a good day*? Wouldn't it be better if he reached a point where he could remember the happiness of life without concentrating so hard on the sorrow? Did things have to be so damn bleak forever, or could he change them?

Was he sure he wanted to?

After the talk about Maura's offer, JJ had taken responsibility for most of the conversation. She'd told stories about her parents, her sisters and her nieces, who made his own nieces seem like mature, rational human beings in comparison. She'd talked about her days in the academy and how many times she'd wanted to give up but was just too damn stubborn, and she'd also told him about her ex-fiancé.

It struck him as too important that there hadn't been regret, longing or grief in her voice. Once Ryan had been part of her life. Now he wasn't. She was fine with that. Quint was totally fine with it. Obviously, the guy hadn't deserved her, hadn't respected or truly loved her. He didn't deserve any long-lasting place in her heart. She deserved someone much better.

She'd fallen into silence a few minutes ago. He didn't kid himself for a second that she'd run out of things to talk about. Maybe she was getting her thoughts in order for the main subject they hadn't talked about. Maura. He decided to broach it first.

"What was your impression of Maura this afternoon?"

She fingered one of the large buttons on her sweater. It was her favorite garment ever, and the color really did bring out the reds in her hair and the greens in the her eyes. It was called a boyfriend cardigan, she'd told him, and her mother had knitted one for each of her single daughters. Not long after, first Kylie, then Elle had gotten married. They now teasingly referred to them as their husband cardigans, and their mother lamented that JJ would never be part of the joke.

"It wasn't what I expected," she said at last. "I saw her with her parents more times than I can count. My family's not rich by any means, but my dad's a surgeon. Our parents belonged to the same country club, went to the same church, a lot of the same parties. Maura and her parents were *close*. A blind man could see that she loved them dearly. She respected them. They and her godparents may have been the only people in the world she ever did respect. And now she's calling Mr. Winchester a nosy old bastard? Calling her parents selfish for getting murdered?"

"Maybe she's just angry and doesn't know to deal with it." Quint chose his words carefully. "Losing someone you love is never easy, especially when it's unexpected. With old age or disease, at least you have a warning. You have time to prepare. But a car crash, a home invasion, a cop or a doctor saying, *I'm sorry...*" His breath caught, the pain as raw for an instant as it had been that long-ago day. He raised his hand instinctively to his chest, closed his eyes tightly and wished he was someplace other than here. Maybe nowhere.

But he'd been nowhere a very long time, and it wasn't as comfortable as it used to be.

Acutely aware of the curiosity JJ was directing his way, he opened his eyes and shrugged as if he'd just gotten off track for a moment. He kept his gaze, though, focused somewhere around her mouth. "Based on what you've said, Maura doesn't have the skills to cope with the violent murders of the two people she loved most in the world. She was a kid when it happened. She didn't try to cope; she just took off running. And she was a spoiled kid with endless amounts of money and zero responsibilities. Now her parents have left her to deal on her own, her godfather's refusing to give her endless amounts of her own money, she's disappointed about not receiving the trust on her last birthday..."

When he did finally let himself look into her eyes, he saw the curiosity he'd felt a moment ago. He saw sympathy, too, gentle and sincere. She was a detective. Of course she'd realized he was speaking in part from personal experience. His face heated, his jaw setting grimly. He should be better about keeping things hidden from strangers who would be leaving his life as quickly as they'd come into it.

Especially ones who didn't feel very much like strangers after such a short time.

"You're right—" JJ cleared her throat to erase the emotion that made her voice husky. "You're right about the shock and the coping and all that. And blaming her parents for not being here when she needs them most—I can see that, too. But as far as thinking she would get the entire estate when she turned twenty-five? Evanston has quite a few trust fund kids. They all know who's getting paid how much and when. 'Oh, I get this amount when I turn eighteen, this when I'm thirty, that when I'm forty.' Maura knew she would have only the allowance until her thirtieth birthday. It became a tradition in her family after a great-uncle received $15 million at twenty-five and blew through it before he hit twenty-eight. Being angry about that with her parents and blaming Mr. Winchester just doesn't make sense."

"Remember? Spoiled rich kid," he said drily. "Doesn't get that things have to actually be done."

The reminder of their earlier discussion made JJ smile, and that somehow made it easier for him to breathe. To ignore the ache in his chest. To push the sorrow away and just let go of it for a time.

"Right. Why am I expecting sense from someone who thought, when she graduated from high school, that flying her fifty closest friends to Fiji for a party couldn't possibly cost much more than having said party around the backyard pool?"

"Seriously?" Quint wasn't sure which he was confirming: a teenager who thought flying fifty people anywhere was reasonable or one so clueless about money that she truly didn't understand its value.

"Scout's honor. This is a girl who never in her life had to ask how much something cost. If she wanted it, she got it, and someone, possibly the money fairies, paid the bill. The summer I babysat her, she thought I was teasing when I said I couldn't afford something. She knew how buying worked. You put that little plastic card in the machine, and *snap!* Cash appeared in your hand. Or you gave it to a peon and dinner, a movie ticket, smartphone, new car—it was yours." JJ picked up her coffee cup, looked at the liquid inside, then set it down again. "Her parents didn't do her any favors. Of course, they didn't expect to die so young, but they didn't even try to teach her self-sufficiency. They assumed, with their fortune, that there would always be someone around to take care of her, to know the things she doesn't, to make sure she doesn't follow in the footsteps of her great-uncle and go broke. They didn't realize that the money they left to take care of her makes her an incredibly easy target for the wrong someone."

Hence the lawyer's professional concern. "Do you think that's what the money issues are about? That she's hooked up with someone who's manipulating her? Maybe the person upstairs today that she lied about. Maybe he or she thought Maura would get all the money on her last birthday and that was why she asked Winchester for it."

JJ reached for the dessert bag pushed to one side, ran her fingertip along the folded edge, then pushed it away. She'd insisted she was too full to eat it when she ordered it, but she was starting to look a little tempted. "Do you think it could be Zander Benson?"

Though Zander's upbringing had been 180-degrees different from Maura's, they did share some traits. Though he lacked the means to excel at entitlement, like she did, he still expected someone else to provide. Neither of them gave a damn about anyone who didn't make their lives easier. Neither saw any reason to work or make a contribution to society or do anything productive. Maura would cling to her privileged status with her dying breath, and Zander would give his left nut to share that privileged status.

"It could be. If not, he may know who. We can go

and talk to him tomorrow." Tracking down a Benson was usually frustrating, sometimes interesting and on occasion an exercise in futility. And Quint knew that from his own experience in trying to question or arrest every damn one of them. "What are you going to tell Mr. Winchester in the meantime?"

"I'd like to say that Maura's fine and just going through a phase, as usual." Then JJ's brows drew together. "I don't think she's fine, but I don't have anything concrete to base it on. She was rude to us, but that's part of who she is. She looks underfed and overindulged, but I wasn't sent here to evaluate her eating, drinking and sleeping habits. She lied about her guest, but she's twenty-five and pays the rent. It's not my business who she lets stay over. But…"

"You don't feel comfortable telling Mr. Winchester that everything's okay."

"No, I don't."

Quint's gut instinct agreed that Maura's situation deserved further investigating. It agreed that JJ should dig a little deeper.

It especially agreed that she should stay longer, and it had nothing concrete to base that on, either.

Just that it didn't have a damn thing to do with the job.

When JJ's phone rang on Wednesday morning, she groaned into her pillow before flinging a hand out to search blindly for the cell on the night table. It rang again, somewhere closer, forcing her to actually open her eyes and lift her head.

Ugh, she'd snuggled in bed last night to review Maura's financial records and to savor every last bite of her dessert, and apparently, after licking the container clean, she'd fallen asleep. The plastic spoon sat on top of the phone, vibrating slightly with the next ring.

"Hullo," she grumbled, pressing it to her ear with one hand, shoving her hair from her face with the other. A faintly icky feel to her skin reminded her she hadn't removed her makeup before getting in bed last night. She'd meant to. And to brush her teeth and put on her pajamas and pick up her clothes and make neat notes of any pertinent information she found in the records. Judging by the blank pad near the empty file folders, she hadn't done that, either.

"Are you asleep?"

"Not anymore." She looked at the window, but with the drapes closed, it was impossible to guess at the time. She checked the clock, but it was turned away from the bed and she couldn't reach it. "What time is it?"

"Seven fifteen." The voice was annoyingly male, irascibly Southern and irritatingly familiar. "I'd expect you at work any minute now if you were here, but apparently you don't feel the need to maintain a schedule when you're out of my sight."

"Chief Chadwick. It's an hour earlier here."

"Huh. I get up at five thirty every day."

Of course he did. He needed an early start to get in all the belittling, nitpicking and fault finding that occupied his day.

Of course, she didn't say that. She didn't say anything. Chadwick didn't like silence. Whenever he picked on someone, he wanted them to fall all over themselves in apology, explanation, information. So she waited. Sure, she was sociable, but when circumstances required, she could also be passive-aggressive. Or even aggressive-aggressive.

No noise came from Chadwick's end of the call. She imagined him sitting at his big desk in his big office, waiting for his subordinates to coordinate his day for him. He would be tilted back in the leather chair— oversize for an oversize man—and he would face the windows that looked out over the central hub of the station. Taking out the solid wall and replacing it with glass had been one of his first acts. How could he correct his employees if he couldn't see them?

And the glass was bulletproof, of course. The chief of police couldn't take too many precautions, now could he?

Yeah, it seemed likely to JJ that the biggest threat to the idiot came from inside his own station.

"Well?" he finally demanded. "What's going on out there? Are you actually getting any work done or are you just enjoying your little holiday on the city's dime?"

Still ticked about him forbidding her to contact the local police, then doing so himself, she politely corrected him. "Actually, it's Mr. Winchester's dime."

Chadwick mumbled something probably impolite, certainly unprofessional. "Have you found out anything about the girl? If she's there, what she's doing, if Travis is right to be concerned."

She couldn't imagine the formal and proper Mr. Winchester inviting Chadwick to call him Travis. Dipstick thought his position as police chief and his gender entitled him to liberties he hadn't been offered, and he took them as if he owned them.

"I can cc you on the report I'm sending Mr. Winchester later this week."

A moment of surprised silence came over the line, then he said stiffly, "You can cc *him* on the report you send *me*. Better yet, you just send that report to me, and I'll decide whether he needs to see it. You remember, you work for me. For the time being."

He was seventy-two and unhealthy, she reminded herself, and she was stubborn as hell. She could outlast him. She *would*, damn it.

"Why, of course, Chief," she said as innocently as she could manage when her face was screwed into a snarl and ugly images of dancing on graves were filling her head. Let him think she was agreeing to cut Mr. Winchester out of the loop. Let him believe she was giving him another chance to make her look bad on the job, or that she cared about that warning *for the time being*.

Seventy-two and unhealthy. He couldn't dog her forever.

"I'll expect it by noon."

"I'll send it when it's finished. Tomorrow, possibly Friday."

Another silence. This time she imagined *his* face screwed into a snarl. If he didn't put her in her place, as soon as he hung up, he would go looking for some other poor soul to unleash on.

She sent silent apologies to the folks in the station, reached across and knocked three times on the night table, and said, "Sorry, Chief, I've got to go. You have a good day." She was pulling her phone away before she got the last words out and disconnected the call before dropping the cell. It landed with a crinkle on the container that had held dessert. She picked it up, hoping for a single slice of banana or a spoonful of custard, but, woefully, it was empty. Very cleanly empty.

Settling back under the covers, she gazed at the patterned ceiling. She'd had a nice time last night. There had been a few times when things had been so comfortable that she'd almost caught herself thinking of it as a date. Quint may not have actually asked her to dinner, but that had been the point of his visit to the hotel, so she could count it if she wanted. They'd shared their backgrounds and experiences and worldviews. Though, as with most cops, those sharings had tended to revolve around cop stuff.

Such as the times during their training that they'd both gotten tased. The first naked person they had each arrested. Their most memorable time up and close and personal with a sick-as-a-dog drunk. The assaults they'd been subjected to or had successfully evaded. Their most ridiculous calls and the silliest situations they'd intervened in.

He had come as close to laughing as she'd ever seen when she'd told him about her probationary period, straight out of the academy but not yet allowed on the street alone, when a jerk weighing a hundred pounds more than her had taken a swing at her. She'd ducked, and the guy had broken his hand on her six-four training officer. Sadly, the next time someone had swung on her, her training officer had been on the other side of the room.

She needed to stay in Cedar Creek long enough to see Quint really, truly laugh. She could tell he'd done it a lot in the past. Those weren't scowl lines at the corners of his eyes and mouth, or hadn't been originally. She wanted to hear him do it again. She wanted to see how breathtakingly gorgeous he was when he was happy.

She'd seen how heartbreakingly sad he'd been last night. *Losing someone you love is never easy...a car crash, a home invasion, a cop or a doctor saying* I'm sorry...

Her own heart had hurt at the grief that etched his face, at the trembling hand he'd placed on his chest, at the exquisite sorrow in his eyes the instant before he closed them. She was convinced that Mystery Woman hadn't left him, not in the traditional sense. Their romance hadn't been a love/hate sort of thing. It hadn't been that they couldn't stand to be together and couldn't bear to be apart.

She had died unexpectedly, with no time for either of them to prepare. That was the only explanation that felt right. One day, going about their lives as usual, everyday normal in every way, and *poof.* The next thing he knew, a cop or likely a doctor was telling him, *I'm sorry.* He'd probably been thinking about dinner, how they would spend the evening, what they would do with the upcoming weekend, never even imagining that the vibrancy and life and love he needed so much was seeping away.

He grieved hard. It was a given that he'd also loved hard.

JJ had pushed the matter to the back of her mind last night and wished she could stuff it back there again. That kind of sorrow should be reserved for people her grandparents' age, when they'd had an entire life together, when they'd had time to accept that the end was

coming. She was like a teenager in that she didn't like
to contemplate death. She was too young, right? Not
yet forty. Had her entire life ahead of her. Even though
she investigated other people's deaths, she hadn't come
to peace with the notion of her own or her loved ones'
deaths.

And Quint hadn't come to peace with the reality of
his loved one's death.

Just as Maura hadn't come to peace with hers.

Feeling unusually grim for a fresh new morning full
of promise, JJ slid out of bed and walked to the bathroom in her socks, underwear and button-down shirt.
Her hair stood on end, her eye makeup was smudged
and her morning breath could strip varnish from a door.
It was a scary thing for so early in the morning.

A hot shower with lots of soap, suds and shampoo made her feel much better. She dressed, reapplied
makeup, tidied the room and moved the files to the
desk beside the windows. Traffic passed regularly on
First Street, occasionally a voice called to another, and
water dripped steadily from the roof edge, trickling to
the sidewalk below.

She had two sets of files from Mr. Winchester, sent
as digital copies before she left home. Though both
were on her tablet, she'd brought paper copies, too.
She luxuriated in the digital world, but when it came
to cookbooks and evidence, she liked books she could
handle, paper she could write on, files she could spread
out and see all once. In some old-fashioned part of her,
it made details more knowable.

The first set of files were condensed versions of
Maura's monthly expenses, covering the year before

she'd arrived in Cedar Creek. The second set were credit card and bank records for the past six months. JJ felt naked without cash in her pocket, even if for nothing more than an emergency Pepsi, but not so Maura. Her withdrawals for cash were rare and minimal.

She glanced through some of the pre-Oklahoma expenses. Seven hundred fifty dollars for a haircut and color. Twelve thousand dollars and change for clothing. Just under $18,000 for meals and drinks. Another $10,000 for jewelry. Fifteen thousand for shoes. In *one* freaking month. For *one* freaking person who already had closets filled with clothes and shoes that she never wore.

She could have bought her own hotel for the money she'd spent on rooms, her own restaurant for the price of meals out. Her entertainment costs, translating to clubs and parties, averaged twenty to thirty thousand a month, depending on her location.

What could JJ do with an extra hundred grand a month? Pay off her condo and her sisters' houses. Give freely to every charity she supported. Fund her nieces' college educations. She could send her parents on a luxury cruise. Support an animal shelter. She could buy a wicked-expensive pair of boots, take a few vacations, beef up her retirement account and...

She couldn't think of anything else.

She liked working, once she removed the Dipstick factor from the equation. Liked traveling so seldom that it was special. Liked cooking her own meals and cleaning up after herself. Liked knowing what was in her closet and where she would be next month and that her friends loved her for herself because she had nothing to give them but herself.

"Don't ever get rich, sweetie," she murmured. "You would fail spectacularly at it."

When her cell rang, she reached automatically to answer it, thought of her unpleasant awakening and checked caller ID. It was Quint, calling as he'd said he would. "Have you ever spent $700 on a haircut," she began, skipping the greeting, "or $49,000 on your own birthday party?"

There was a moment of silence before he mentally caught up. "My barber charges eight bucks. I pay her twelve because she's my sister-in-law and she lets me sit at the kitchen table instead of making me go to the shop. And my entire family would never spend $49,000 on birthday parties in forty-nine years." He paused, the radio audible in the background. "Are you seeing how the other half—more like half of half a percent—live?"

"Yeah. It's pretty astonishing. In the past six months, Maura's spent $11,000 on facials and cosmetics. She's twenty-five. How much help can she possibly need to look good?"

"She *was* a little scary yesterday."

He was right about that. She'd been a pale reflection of the beautiful girl JJ had seen at the Evanses' funerals five years ago. Losing weight, drinking and spending millions of dollars with little to show for it was evidently harder than it looked.

And grieving, she reminded herself, feeling guilty that she'd left out the biggest factor in Maura's downfall.

"I would dearly appreciate a raise of ten or twenty thousand dollars. Hell, I'd be happy with five. It would be awfully nice to have a bit of a cushion in the budget. But there's not a soul alive who could sell me a $9,500 pair of jeans. Or an $800 pair of sweatpants. Or a ninety-dollar lipstick. Maura bought eight of them at the same time."

"And yet you manage to look beautiful at a fraction of the price."

JJ's breath caught, a hitch in her chest that came with a moment's sharp throb. She wished he was sitting across from her so she could see his face, his eyes. Was he teasing, the way her fellow officers at home so often did, or just tossing a careless comment into the conversation, the way her mom and sisters did?

Or did he, maybe, really think she was pretty? No, not pretty. Beautiful.

She would really like for him to think she was beautiful. She certainly thought he was.

When she drew a breath, it was unsteady, but her voice sounded totally normal. "Just think how good I could look if I didn't buy my cosmetics at the drugstore."

There was another moment's silence—did he regret the remark?—then he quietly said, "I don't believe there are degrees of beautiful."

It was a good thing she was sitting, because sweet, warm heat washed over her, weakening her muscles, making her nerves quiver. She was glad he wasn't sitting across from her, because she was fairly sure he never would have made the remark to her face. He was taciturn. Scowly and growly. Grieving.

Not ready to move on? Or maybe thinking ever so slightly about it?

Before the quiet became awkward, he changed subjects with relief evident in his voice. "If we want to talk to Zander today, we should head over to his house soon. He stays out late, sleeps in late. He doesn't always sleep in his own bed, but it's a place to start."

"I can be ready in five minutes."

"I'm sitting out front."

Leaning forward, she parted the blinds so she could see out and rolled her eyes at the sight of his truck. "I'll be right down."

Chapter 6

Beautiful? Quint scrubbed his hands over his face. Where had that come from? Sure, he'd been thinking it, but he hadn't meant to say it. He wasn't the sort to give compliments like that to people. He'd never told anyone that but Linny, and with her it had been so obviously true that there'd been no point in not saying it.

But JJ was cute. Pretty, even. And okay, he'd woken up this morning with her image in his head. When he'd taken her back to the hotel after dinner, he had walked upstairs to her room with her, waited while she unlocked the door, set down her bag and took off her coat. She had come back, still wearing that orange hat and that broad, bright smile that came so naturally to her and lit up her entire face, and he'd been...

Words and emotions had come more naturally to him before Linny died. Not communicating had become a habit. Not feeling. It was how he'd survived. Now, after so many months of isolating himself, sometimes he had to stop and think to find the right thing to say, to recognize the proper emotion. It had become his default behavior.

Even now, after far too much thinking, he really wasn't sure what he felt for JJ. Drawn to her? She was pretty. Confident. Sexy. Forthright. And who wouldn't be drawn to that bright smile when their own smiles had disappeared?

Tempted by her? Maura had proved he could be tempted. Then, in that situation, he'd *had* to resist. Giving in to her would have been the lowest point of his life without Linny. But giving in to JJ would be...

She suddenly appeared at the passenger door, smiling, lively, brimming with energy. In deference to the warmer weather, her coat wasn't done up to her neck, and the hat and gloves were missing from her outfit. She wore jeans again, a light blue shirt and a darker blue pullover, and she brought with her a cloud of sweet fragrance and cool air when she climbed into the seat. She tossed her bag on the back floorboard, belted up and focused her gaze on him. "I could get used to being chauffeured around."

I could get used to doing it. Hell, he'd gotten used to things a whole lot less pleasant. Of course, he didn't say that out loud. "What? Your chief won't assign you a driver? Doesn't he believe life was better when the little woman didn't drive?"

"Or vote. Or have an opinion." She screwed up her face as she rubbed her nose. "He called this morning. Told me to report back to him instead of Winchester and he would decide what to pass on. Reminded me that I work for him. For the moment."

Quint shook his head as he pulled away from the

curb. He understood her reasons for staying in Evanston. They were the same reasons he stayed in Cedar Creek. He could have gone to any city in the state, to any state in the union, and done more exciting work for more money and better benefits. But Cedar Creek was home. What it lacked in opportunities, it made up for in comforts. Linny had felt the same way.

"At least you're out of his reach for the moment. Experiencing cool weather. Eating great food."

"Hanging out with good people." She fumbled in her pocket and came up with a pair of sunglasses.

Not being able to see her eyes didn't lessen the intensity of her gaze one bit.

"Is there anything I should know about Zander before we get there?"

"You've seen the highlights of his record. He chooses family over cops every time. He probably won't be there. Hank probably will. He collects disability from a bad back that keeps him from working but hasn't stopped him from playing basketball with his buddies—put one of them through a plate glass window last summer—or spending hunting season in the woods. Zander's got a sister, Zoey, and a brother, Zeke. Zeke's in jail over in Norman, but Zoey's been a guest of the city almost as often as Zander has. She's tough."

"What about Mom?"

An image of Marisa the last time he'd seen her formed in Quint's mind: thin, weary, looking a bad ten years older than she was. "Works twelve-hour shifts five or six days a week at the nursing home over on Aspen. Tries to be a calming influence, or used to, but raising hell is what the rest of the family does best."

"Wow. Sounds like the poster family for birth control. I'm guessing there are no grandkids yet?"

That was a thought that would scare all the official types who had to deal with the family. "Please, God, no."

Odd. He hadn't said that in a long time. God had let him down. He'd figured he would return the favor. But there it was, without even thinking.

He turned toward the north side of town. The Bensons' neighborhood, a single street two blocks long and halfway up the big hill, had never been a good one. When Hank and Marisa got married, he hadn't moved out of his mother's house; he'd just moved his wife in. Before Mrs. Benson had gone to the same nursing home where her daughter-in-law worked, she'd signed the property over to Hank, and the endless cycle of neglect and disrepair had continued.

It wasn't just that the house was old. It wasn't that it had been cheaply built by relatives who hadn't known what they were doing. It was a total lack of desire on anyone's part to actually do anything with it. When a screen fell off, it stayed where it landed. When a window was broken by one of the kids, they taped a piece of cardboard over it. The only paint on the siding was sprayed on by Hank to cover up obscenities sprayed there by Zoey. The grass never got mowed, not even when the city levied fines against them, and the trash they threw down never got picked up.

No wonder Marisa worked so many hours away and Hank and the kids didn't object to spending time in jail. There was nothing homey about this place.

"Sometimes I forget that every town has its less desirable areas." JJ's head swiveled from left to right, from one ramshackle house to another. All of them were better maintained than the Benson house, but they were still sad. The residents were elderly, having lived their entire lives on that street, or poor. They had nowhere else to go.

The Bensons were just too damn lazy to care. Five adults, each with a regular income, could afford so much better than this. But only one of the adults had that regular income, he reminded himself.

The street was still covered with snow and ice. Overhead, tree branches blocked the sun, and the hill rising up to the west rerouted the winds elsewhere. The Benson yard was patchy with new weeds and snow that partially covered their garbage. A half-buried hot water tank here, an old tire there, the chassis of an ancient pickup over there, two three-legged chairs nearby.

There were two vehicles in the driveway: Hank's battered Chevy and Zoey's equally battered Mustang. Quint assumed Zeke's car was wherever he'd been arrested this time and that Marisa's was at her job. Zander had a motorcycle, which meant he often sneaked out with whoever's car he could find the keys to when the weather was bad.

Quint shut off the engine, took a breath and climbed out. JJ would have gone first up to the porch with its sagging support posts and broken steps, but he laid his hand on her arm. "You were a kid when you ducked that punch you told me about. You might want to stay behind me until it's clear."

"Are you implying I'm old?" she asked, brows raised as if she was certain he couldn't have actually said that. Before she could go further, the front door opened with a scrape and a groan. Hank Benson, six foot two and gone soft, stood there in sweatpants, a dirty T-shirt and socks. It was early for both the beer and the cigarette he held.

"Hey, Quint, you seen Zeke lately?"

"Last I checked, he was in lockup over in Cleveland County."

"Huh. Yeah, I seem to remember he was going over there to Norman for something. Dumb kid." Hank scratched his jaw with the hand that held the cigarette. "Zander ain't here, either, so that leaves me and Zoey, and I ain't been outta the house in a week. Had a cold." He coughed a few times for effect.

Quint hid his grimace. If he considered how many germs he was exposed to in the daily course of his duties, he'd hole up in his bedroom and never come out. "Can we come in, Hank?"

"Sure."

Hank stepped away from the door, and Quint grasped the metal handle of the wood-frame screen door. Considering the top half of the screen had been ripped loose and dragged across the porch floor, it wasn't exactly functional, but he'd bet it hadn't occurred to anyone to fix it or take it down.

"Hey, Hank, don't tell—"

"Zoey! Police here for you!" Hank bellowed down the hall.

The missile came from that direction, an opened bottle, spewing beer all along its trail. Quint reached behind him, catching JJ's arm, and backed her up and to the right as the bottle slammed into the door frame, inches from his shoulder, then clunked to the floor.

"What the hell—" JJ's muscles were tight beneath his hand, her voice tipping somewhere between curiosity and anger.

"She usually throws it hard enough to break," he murmured, then raised his voice. "Come out where I can see you, Zoey."

After a moment, the girl—woman— stepped into view in the kitchen. Like her father, she wore sweatpants, a T-shirt and socks. Unlike him, she wasn't the least bit soft. She was an inch taller than JJ and fifteen pounds lighter, and she swore, drank and fought like her brothers. Linny had been convinced Zoey was full of potential to bring men to their knees with nothing more than a seductive smile. Quint knew men went weak around her because they were scared to death of her. They found it hard to notice how pretty and sexy a woman might be when she was threatening to beat the tar out of them.

"Let me see your hands," he directed, and she obeyed with a sardonic smile. "We're coming in to talk, okay?"

"We?" she echoed. Her gaze dropped to the floor—apparently, most of JJ was hidden behind his bulk, but her feet must have been visible—then she lifted onto her toes and leaned to one side. He released his hold on JJ, and she stepped out to his right, as anxious to see as Zoey was.

With Hank bringing up the rear, they walked the short hall and into the kitchen. A wobbly table sat to the left, a mess of wrappers and bottles, both empty and full. Quint didn't bother to look at the kitchen area. Dirty dishes, stale food, spills, trash. He'd seen it all before.

"Don't know why you couldn't have thrown an empty bottle," Hank muttered as he slid into a chair. "You're gonna have to clean that up before your mother gets home."

Zoey ignored him and Quint and walked right up to JJ. The need to put himself between them niggled along Quint's spine, but JJ wouldn't appreciate it, and Zoey... Hell, no one knew how Zoey might take it.

"I don't know you," she said flatly. "I know all the cops in town. I know all the cops in the county. Hell, I probably know all the state cops in Troop B. Who are you?"

"JJ Logan." JJ drew her hand from her pocket, showing her ID.

"South Carolina. You can't be after me, then. I've never been any farther east than Arkansas." Zoey crossed her arms over her chest. "I heard you say Zeke's in jail—idiot—so that means you're here about Zander. Or his South Carolina girlfriend. Tell me what you want to know, and what I get for telling you, and maybe we can make a deal."

Ten minutes later, JJ found herself in Zoey's bedroom. It reminded her of descriptions she'd read of nuns' rooms at convents: tiny, sparsely furnished, severely undecorated. There was a twin bed that fit so tightly between the walls that it must be hell to change the sheets, a small bureau and a half dozen wooden cubes stacked together. Only the exterior wall had Sheetrock. The other three had been framed to create the room, then left unfinished, studs exposed and used for shelving.

She sat on one of the storage cubes while Zoey

dropped onto the bed. Zoey had decided she would talk only to JJ, but now that they were alone, she slumped against the wall, rubbing at a worn area on her sweats above her right knee, and stole occasional looks at JJ that were part hostility, part curiosity.

"So you're a detective," Zoey said at last. "How'd you get to do that?"

"I worked my ass off for it." JJ crossed her legs and saw the woman give her leather boots an appreciative look. "Back in the day, my department required a college degree. I got that, went to the academy and went into uniform. I spent seven years proving I could do as good as or better than the men, and I eventually got promoted up the chain to where I am now."

"Do you still have to prove you're as good as or better than the men?"

"Every day. Do you?"

A wry expression crossed Zoey's face. "Not so much anymore. You beat up enough people, word gets around."

JJ had no problem imagining her in a physical confrontation—and handling it quite well. She wasn't big, but she was strong, wiry and savvy. She'd probably learned to fight dirty when she was still in diapers, and she had attitude enough to keep her skills honed.

She was also very pretty: red haired, porcelain skinned and green eyed. Her muscles had curves, and for a woman about JJ's own height, her legs seemed a heck of a lot longer. With a little refinement and polish, she could walk into a room and make men tremble, and not from fear.

"Do you know Maura Evans?"

"I've met her. Don't like her. Rich bitch."

"But she's Zander's girlfriend."

"She's slumming. Women like her do it all the time."

"Do you see her very often?"

Zoey finally stopped picking at the spot on her sweats and met JJ's gaze directly. "I've been to a few of her parties. Me and Zander, we each got our own friends. His are hoods. Mine are punks."

Hoods. There was a word JJ hadn't heard in a long time. She figured Zander's friends were all probably hoodlums. *Like likes like*, Grandmother Raynelle used to say. *Birds of a feather*, Kylie used to translate.

"Have you met Maura's friend Mel?"

"A couple times. She was like a little puppy dog, wanted to dress like Maura, look like Maura. She didn't have the money to be Maura, but the bitch spent a lot on her. Dressed her up like a doll, got her hair and nails done, taught her how to walk and talk and not be so low-class."

Bitterness colored her voice at the end. A little jealousy? Was there a part of her that wished Maura had chosen to make *her* over instead of Mel? Hell, there was a part of JJ that wouldn't mind a makeover from someone with limitless funds. She loved expensive clothes when she could afford them, and there was no denying pricey cosmetics felt and looked better than bargain brands. When a woman had had nothing, the prevailing opinion of Mel pre-Maura, how dizzying would it be to suddenly be given not just everything, but the best of it?

"They were good friends?"

"Yeah, I guess. As long as Mel didn't mind turning into a Maura clone, and she was brainless enough to like it."

"Do you know why Mel left?"

She lifted one shoulder. "I think it had something to do with Zander. He likes attention, and he don't play nice with others. I think he weaseled his way into Maura's life and kinda pushed Mel out. At least, that's what he said. 'Course, he didn't like Mel. Thought she took advantage of Maura."

More likely, he thought that every dollar Maura spent on her friend was a dollar she couldn't spend on him. It could be true that Mel had gotten bored and moved on, or maybe Zander's dislike had been mutual. His ego might have claimed credit for getting rid of her, or he truly might have driven a wedge between the two friends.

"Is Zander in love with Maura or just taking what he can get?"

JJ expected a disbelieving snort for the first half of the question or a defense spurred by the second, but Zoey was thoughtful instead. "Zander's never loved anything but himself. And money. But he's been with her five months. Longer than anyone else ever. And he's not antsy yet about moving on. Maybe…"

Maybe he did love her.

Or maybe he was just in a long-term con. As long as there was money in her bank, there would be love in his heart.

It was a depressing thought to consider.

Zoey was watching JJ, a restless air about her. She didn't sit still for long, JJ suspected. Didn't play nice for long. Or cooperate with the police, or talk with someone who, apparently, if Zoey's growing twitchiness was anything to judge by, intimidated her in some way.

JJ rose, bowed her spine a little to ease the stiffness from sitting on the wooden cube, then asked casually, "Do you know where we can find Zander today? We'd like to talk to him."

Zoey stood, too. "Are you going to all this trouble to look in on Maura because you're friends back home?"

"I babysat her fifteen years ago, but we're not friends. I'm doing it because people are worried about her."

"You think Zander's a bad influence on her?"

JJ bit her lip for a moment, then with a shrug, ruefully answered with the truth. "I think Zander might be a bad influence on everyone he meets."

"Has he done anything illegal? Spending time with her so she gives him stuff?"

"No." In the larger scheme of things, the amount of money Maura had spent in Cedar Creek was insubstantial. There were tens of millions of dollars more where it came from.

The answer satisfied Zoey, who gave an agreeing sort of nod. "He's been pretty much living there in that big house with her since around Christmas. The downstairs is empty, but upstairs they've got furniture, TVs, electronics, games. You wanna see a picture of him?"

There must be a pocket in the ragged sweats, because she whipped her cell phone from somewhere and began scrolling through pictures. When she found the one she wanted, she offered the phone to JJ.

JJ didn't see a shred of resemblance between Zoey and her brother, unless surliness counted. His skin tone was dark, his hair was brown, his eyes appeared brown, and he was fair to middlin' in looks. His power was all in her manner, she assumed. Attitude, charm, just the right amount of don't-give-a-damn insolence, and susceptible women's hearts would start to pound.

"He looks like your father."

Zoey took the phone back. "Yeah, he's gonna be just like him in twenty years. Idiot."

"Your dad's a good-looking guy." Mentally JJ crossed her fingers to cover the lie.

Zoey scowled. "Him and Quint graduated school together. *Quint's* a good-looking guy. My dad's a bad son, a bad husband, a bad father and a lazy-ass human being who hasn't done anything but drink and smoke weed his whole adult life."

Well, yeah, when you put it that way... But JJ found it hard to compare run-of-the-mill losers to hard-bodied men who reminded her every day of all the passion and hunger and sex missing from her life. Now was not the time to think of that.

"Worst part is," Zoey continued, "that's all he ever wanted." Her head ducked, her gaze scanned the room and she added in a whisper, "Not what I want."

Hiding her sympathetic wince, JJ closed the distance between them and extended her hand. "Thank you for talking to me, Zoey. I appreciate it."

The look of discomfort suggested she didn't hear thanks very often. "Yeah, just do us a favor and take the rich bitch back to South Carolina with you. We don't need the trouble."

After collecting Quint from the kitchen, JJ picked her way carefully down the broken steps. She inhaled deeply, only then realizing how musty and stale the inside of the house had smelled. "She's a nice girl," she remarked when they reached the driveway.

"You weren't quaking in your boots the whole time you were alone with her?"

She scowled at him. "These boots aren't made for quaking. And I wouldn't have quaked, anyway. I'm not scared of her."

"Only because you have your Taser."

"There's that. And she was barefooted. I figured if I needed an advantage, I could stomp on her foot first. That might give me a half second's head start." She hesitated before making her next observation. "She's a little feral, isn't she?"

Quint hesitated, too. They'd both run across people who bragged about being wild, but there was nothing to brag about in this situation, except that Zoey had survived. "She never had any parenting. Mom's too busy trying to feed and clothe them. Dad's too lazy. Her role model was Zander, and the two of them taught Zeke everything he knows."

Not what I want, Zoey had said under her breath. She could have been so much more. Could still be so much more. There was intelligence in her green eyes, strength of will, a hint of lost little girl that betrayed her boldness. She'd learned only one way to cope—to be tough—and unfortunately, that wasn't enough to live any kind of life.

But she'd learned it. Which meant she could learn anything else she put her mind to.

Sadly, not JJ's problem. She was just a visitor here. But that didn't stop her from adding Zoey to the long list in the back of her mind of people she'd come across on the job who were better, or deserved better, than circumstances had given them.

JJ was about to get into Quint's truck when a tiny whimper caught her attention. A quick look around didn't reveal the source, but when it came again, she followed it to Hank's Chevrolet, ducking low to look beneath it. A tan fur ball lay on a bare patch of concrete, huddling in the chill, watching her with huge suspicious eyes.

"There's an animal under here."

"Likely a skunk or rabid possum."

"You grow skunks in different colors here? 'Cause this one's tan." Clutching her coat close, she bent lower. "Hey, baby. You look so cold in there. Are you okay?"

Quint's steps sloshed around to join her. He bent to look under the economy-size truck bed. "I bet he doesn't live here. Zander doesn't like dogs."

"See if you can coax him out." She straightened and retraced her steps to the front door, knocking directly on the door through the gap in the screen. Zoey answered, hands empty of weapons to throw. "Is that your dog under the truck?"

Zoey snorted. "We don't have dogs. Zander doesn't like them. Dog bit him when he was about twelve and—" Abruptly, her face went pale, flat and blank. "We don't have dogs."

That was all JJ needed to know to shove that subject to the back of her mind. Though she probably couldn't whip Zoey in a fair fight, or an unfair one, she might be able to take Zander, especially with little tidbits like that feeding her aggression. "Do you know who he belongs to?"

"Nobody. Some woman in an Escalade dumped him here a few days ago."

"None of your neighbors are feeding him?"

Zoey's gaze flickered the length of the street. "No one can afford to."

"Then I'm gonna take him. Okay?"

"Please do." She said it with a shrug, as if she didn't care either way, but JJ heard the very faint undertone. *Before Zander comes home and finds him.*

She was seriously looking forward to meeting Alexander Benson.

Quint sat in the warm cab of the pickup truck, his pants wet from knee to ankle and an oil smudge on his jacket from having to get down under Hank's old truck to reach the pup. Their assumption it was a male was wrong; the female had shaken violently when he'd first touched her, but she'd let him pull her out into the open, where JJ had scooped her quickly into her arms. Quint had donated a hoodie from the back seat to the cause of warming the dog, whose face was the only part now visible. Her wide brown eyes, hypercautious and distrusting, were fixed on him.

"Zoey said a woman in an Escalade threw her out."

The sour taste of disgust rose in his stomach. He'd worked too many neglect, abuse and abandonment cases involving animals in his career. It was so ridiculously simple: if you don't want to take care of a pet, don't get a pet. Why were people so damn stupid?

"An Escalade," she repeated. "It's not likely this little one was a financial hardship. Just a nuisance. She probably peed on the carpet or chewed up a shoe."

"I hope it was an expensive carpet or an even more expensive shoe." Quint adjusted the vents on his side to blow in the puppy's direction. A hint of dread, as sour as the disgust a moment ago, stirred in his gut. "What are you going to do with her?"

JJ bent her head to the dog's, nuzzling the top of her head. The dog was dirty, wet and smelled, but the human didn't seem to notice. He didn't need the knot growing around his dread to know how this was going to play out. He rarely hoped he was wrong, but this time, if he were still a praying man, he would pray that he was.

JJ looked up, her hazel eyes troubled and, yes, that was a little naïveté there, too. "I don't suppose you know anyone…"

The dog was probably two or three months old. Seriously underweight. Most likely not spayed. Given the warm weather before this latest front, probably had ticks, fleas or other buddies. And she was a pit bull. Pits had a serious public relations problem around Cedar Creek.

He shook his head.

"Hmm. My nieces would love her. And would fight over whose house she lived at." She ruefully wrinkled her nose. "So would my sisters. The fighting part, not the love."

"Claire has cats," he pointed out. "She's not going to like a stray pit coming into her hotel. A dirty, stray unhousebroken pit. Not with all the antique rugs and furniture and paying guests."

The animal lifted her face to the warm air, sighed and snuggled deeper into JJ's lap. Quint trusted animal instincts, and judging by the dog's blissful expression, this one knew she was safe with JJ, that she would be protected and fed and taken care of. Her worries were over.

But his weren't. Though if they traded places, the dog and him, and he was snuggled in JJ's arms, he might be feeling pretty blissful, too.

"Aw, jeez," he grumbled, turning his head away. He was in trouble on two fronts, wasn't he? And one was far more dangerous than the other.

The dangerous one smiled at him. Even though his gaze was directed at the pin oaks past the Benson house whose new buds were pushing off the few dead leaves that remained, he could feel the warmth of the smile. It was bright and happy and guilty and hopeful and manipulative, and he'd never been strong in the face of sweet-natured, kindhearted, vulnerable and tender female manipulation. No matter how much he didn't want a woman in his life or a dog in his house, he was going to end up with both. He might as well roll over and show them his belly right now.

"You like dogs, don't you?" JJ's voice sounded more feminine, more Southern, more everything good. Manipulation, he reminded himself.

A muscle clenched in his jaw as he tried to find some resistance deep inside. "I like 'em fine. Outside. At a distance. Belonging to someone else."

"Aw, come on, you crawled under a vehicle in the snow and melt to get her. Look at her little face. Look how grateful she is."

He did look, focusing hard on the dog's face rather than hers. "That's not gratitude. It's entitlement." She resembled canine royalty whose Prince Charming had, of course, rescued her and whose Princess Charming would, of course, pamper away her discomforts. Or con someone else into doing it.

"She's so sweet."

"Have you not noticed that she's a pit bull? She's lulling you into complacency before she takes over the world." *JJ's* world. Not his.

"I promise I'll take her with me when I go. I just need a place to leave her until then."

Finally realizing they still sat in the Bensons' driveway, Quint backed out and turned onto Main Street once again. "You don't know how long that will be."

"Neither do you."

He scowled her way, but he was too cowardly to make eye contact. She was expert at what she was doing, and his defenses these past few days weren't as good as they should have been. "It'll be long enough for me to have to make sure she's not sick, put some weight on her, get started socializing her and house-train her. Do you even want a dog?"

"Of course I do. I love dogs. I had a sheepdog when I was a kid. I loved him better than my boyfriend."

"Did you want one before ten minutes ago?"

Her cheeks turned a delicate pink, and like so many people he'd known, she looked away in a sure sign of duplicity. "I always planned to get one. Someday. Maybe when I make captain or chief of detectives."

As a delaying tactic, he let her answer distract him. "You want to be in management? Overseeing people like yourself?"

"I'd be a damn good chief of Ds. And I'd be very

hands-on and in the field most of the time." She gave him an arch look. "And there are no people like me."

Then her nose wrinkled again. It was a cute look on her, even though its purpose was to convey disappointment. In him. "Maybe we should contact a rescue group."

We? He wasn't part of this. He was just along for the ride. If she chose to contact a rescue group, it didn't matter to him. Not that it would help. "Like their resources aren't strained to the limits."

He hadn't meant to say that out loud.

"Put up flyers? *Free Dog.*"

"There are plenty of free dogs around. And if you put up *Free Pit Bull*, you'll scare off the possibly decent owners and attract the possibly bad ones."

She wasn't accepting defeat yet. Her gaze was distant, noticing nothing as they drove, but thoughts were running through that brain of hers. He could practically see them, like a breaking-news scroll across the bottom of a TV screen.

He turned into the Walmart parking lot without fully acknowledging that had been his destination, because that meant admitting *his* defeat. He shut off the engine and faced her with his usual scowl. He tried one last time to find the most important word in his vocabulary at the moment—*No*, times ten—but it had disappeared as thoroughly as if he'd never known it.

Grinding his jaw, he growled out the words he did find. "Cleaning carpets is your job. And she has to have a crate. And you can't give her a silly name that makes her sound like a poodle. I won't stand outside and yell for Chou-Chou or Bitsy-Poo or anything like that. She's a pit. She deserves respect."

JJ's eyes widened as his words sank in. So did his. Hell, he was surrendering. Agreeing to take the dog so she and the pup would both be comfortable until it was time to leave. Offering to feed her, play with her and house-train her. Offering to let JJ into his house to do any necessary disaster recovery.

"I owe you for this," she said.

"Yeah?" he asked grudgingly. "What am I gonna get?"

"Anything you want." This time her smile was warm and wicked and full of promise. Even though she immediately slid to the ground, dog still in her arms, and closed the door, the heat lingered. So did the promise. And the wickedness.

Damn, he'd missed wickedness.

They took the dog inside with them—who was going to complain about a cop in uniform doing a good deed for a pathetic-looking pup?—and headed to the pet aisles with a shopping cart while Quint wondered when he had officially lost his mind. He'd only ever had one indoor dog, when Linny had moved in with him and brought her elderly spaniel with her. Brutus—the most brutal thing he ever did was pee on his own foot when he got excited—had been sweet and creaky and had absolutely devastated Linny when he passed.

But you're not taking this dog to raise. You won't have her long. You won't get attached, you won't miss her when she's gone and you won't even know when she passes.

And he *had* gotten something out of the deal. *I owe you...anything you want.* Damn, he could think of some things. Sweet things, hot things, intimate things, naughty things, things that might make him blush. Things that might make *her* blush.

He'd been without *things* for so very long, and he felt so very lonely.

But how much lonelier would he feel when both pesky females were gone?

You won't have her long, the voice in his head repeated. *You won't get attached. You won't miss her when she's gone.*

He wasn't sure he believed the voice.

"Look—jail cells for puppies." She pointed at a collapsible wire cage. "And collars and beds and automatic feeders and toys and outfits. Wow!"

"No outfits," he added to his earlier list.

With a guilty look on her face, her hand froze an inch above the hanger holding a pink ballerina-looking thing, utterly ridiculous, especially the glittery headband that came with it.

"You have better taste than that, don't you, chica?" he asked the dog, who lifted her head from JJ's chest. He held up the garment, let the dog sniff it and was rewarded with a small growl and a show of teeth. *Good girl.*

"Chica," JJ repeated thoughtfully. "Would you be embarrassed to go out and yell for Chica?"

He returned the hanger to the rack and reached instead for a black nylon leash and a matching collar. "I have a cousin named Chica. Short for Chiquita." He shrugged. Everyone had weird names in their family trees. "The only time I was embarrassed yelling her name was when she had me in a headlock and wouldn't let go until I yelled, 'Chica rules.'"

JJ laughed. He kept to himself the fact that he'd been fifteen and had reached his full height the last time Chica had bested him, though thinking about it almost made him smile. He could have taken her, he'd always insisted. He just hadn't wanted to risk hurting her. Chica, now forty-one, rounder and lazier and still not above putting one of her teenage sons in a head-lock, didn't agree.

He'd had a life of good times with good people, he acknowledged as he lifted down the boxed kennel JJ pointed out. He'd shoved that out of his mind for too long. He needed to remind himself until it became sec-ond nature again: no matter how much life took from him, he would always have his memories.

Glancing at JJ, holding two doggie beds and debating between hot-pink fuzz and a subdued navy blue fabric that was less of a hair magnet, he extended that thought.

And he could always make new ones.

It wasn't far from Walmart to Quint's house. JJ car-ried Chica and the bagged smaller items onto the porch and waited while he unlocked the door, then she hesi-tated.

This was a big deal, his inviting her inside. This was his personal space, his private space, and she ap-preciated that. Like she appreciated his taking in the dog, and the help he'd given with Maura, and, hell, ev-erything about him. She was anxious to see where he lived. Anxious to see the colors he preferred, the styles of furniture, the mementos he kept on display.

She was anxious to see signs of *her*. The mystery woman. His love. His sorrow.

The door opened into a small foyer that, in turn, opened into the living/dining room. Large windows let in sunlight, and a rock fireplace centered the wall on the left. Stairs, stained dark with white balusters, made a straight shot to the second floor on the right side, and a doorway opened into a hall on the right that extended to the back of the house.

As soon as JJ dried her boots on the rug, then stepped from the tile onto the hardwood floor, Chica leaped from her arms, her claws scrabbling as she began a careful check of the room. JJ said a silent plea to the animal to not scratch, pee or worse while Quint deposited his load—the kennel in its box, the dog bed and a bag of puppy kibble—on the dining table.

He didn't watch Chica explore, or JJ, either, but took off his jacket, laid down his keys and mumbled, "I'll be back."

Inviting her in was a big deal for him, too.

After he'd disappeared upstairs, JJ took off her own coat and drew in a deep breath of cinnamon-scented air while slowly taking in every detail of the room. The furniture was overstuffed and easy-to-clean leather: a couch, a love seat and two chairs. The wood floor was on the dark side, as was the trim, gleaming against the pale green walls. A chandelier of colored bits of glass hung over the dining table, casting rainbow prisms around the room. They glinted off the polished surfaces and reflected off the glass in picture frames, and for a moment, one of them held Chica mesmerized.

For much longer than a moment, JJ was mesmerized, too, by the face that appeared in most of the photos. The woman was beautiful, her skin as delicate as porcelain, her hair black and long and straight. It was impossible to tell in the casual shots, but JJ figured gray eyes would go perfectly with the face, and she *was* otherwise perfect. She was cool and serene, very happy with her life, and just looking at her made JJ's heart hurt.

"Her name was Belinda."

JJ didn't startle. Somewhere inside, she'd registered the sound of Quint's footsteps on the stairs. She'd just been too sorrowful to turn around. He had loved this woman very much, and he'd lost her, and that made her unbearably sad.

"Your wife?" She had asked him at lunch the first day if he was married. Somehow, she'd taken his negative response to mean he never had been, but at his age, being madly in love with Belinda, marriage would have been the traditional route. Compared to the younger people she knew, he and she were both very traditional.

"We talked about it." He came down the last few steps from where he'd stopped and crossed over to the dining table. He wore dry trousers and had left a clean jacket hanging on the banister. "We were just happy enough where we were that we never did anything to change it."

Listening to a blade slicing through tape, JJ studied the photos a moment longer. She was jealous, in a good way, of people who found that kind of connection with another human being. She never wished them ill; she just wanted to experience it herself. She knew it didn't come easily, knew it required giving and taking and bending and standing strong and that some people never found it, no matter how hard they searched.

She wanted to be one of the lucky ones.

But deep love also meant deep pain. Unless a couple died together, one would always leave and the other would always be left behind. If they were incredibly lucky, they would share decades before that happened. If they weren't...

Quint had been spectacularly lucky in finding Belinda when he did. And spectacularly unlucky in losing her when he did. He would spend far more years mourning her than he'd had with her. That was so sad.

"Can you hold the box here?"

Giving herself a shake and forcing a more upbeat expression onto her face, she joined him at the table. She grabbed hold of the box, and he pulled the wire panels and the plastic bottom tray from its tight confines. The page of instructions fell to the floor. By the time she picked it up and smoothed it out, he'd unfolded the bottom panel and assembled two of the remaining five.

Chica watched from a distance, showing no curiosity whatsoever. Had she already experienced life inside a cell? Would she like her new quarters or hate them? *Please don't be difficult*, she warned the pup. *He's doing us a huge favor.*

Within ten minutes, the crate was put together and slid against the wall beneath the stairs, giving a good view of all parts of the space. It sat on an old blanket Quint had gotten from somewhere through the dining room door, to protect the wood floor, and the blue bed was tucked inside while the gate was propped open.

Chica sniffed the perimeter of the kennel, made sure JJ and Quint were too far away to try something stupid like closing the door on her, then walked inside, smelling everything so thoroughly and quickly that JJ felt light-headed just watching.

"Get used to it, Chica," Quint said as he stuffed the packing back into the box. "You live in this house, you don't get to roam free when you're alone."

The dog trotted back out and over to the couch where JJ had laid her coat and the hoodie. She clamped her teeth on the dangling sleeve of the hoodie, pulled it to the floor and dragged it into the kennel. After arranging it on the bed in as prissy a manner as JJ had ever seen, she plopped down on top of it with a sigh.

JJ sighed, too. It made Quint look at her, his blue eyes knowing. "You thought she was going to be difficult."

"Of course not," she lied. "Look at that sweet face. How could you expect anything but sterling behavior from her?"

He snorted, picked up the dog food and headed for the dining room door. This time JJ followed him.

The feeling of the other room was farmhouse cozy. She'd expected the kitchen to be the same, and it was, just decades newer and cozier. The soapstone countertops were dark and finely veined. Cream-colored cabinets with glass fronts up top, a big deep sink and windows stretching entirely the width of the sink wall were the highlights, with dark-fronted appliances and an island-centered six-burner gas cooktop close behind. A black table and four chairs sat in a nook to the right, with more storage space framing the windows there.

"Wow. Belinda liked to cook, huh?"

Quint pulled a large storage container from a cabinet before slanting her a look. "No, actually, I do. Did." He shrugged. "Do."

The rattle of dog nuggets emptying into the plastic bin brought Chica in to investigate. He poured a small serving into a bowl and barely managed to set it on the floor before she dived in, face in the bowl, butt in the air, tail quivering.

"I chose all the cooking stuff," he went on as he filled another bowl with water, "and Linny put it together so it looked good. The windows were her idea. All she ever did in here was dishes, so she wanted a nice view while she did them."

Ugh. JJ hated doing dishes. And she had no decorating skills to speak of. Her idea of redoing a room was slapping a coat of white paint on it and calling it done.

No, that wasn't even true. She would call her mother or Elle and be happy with whatever they suggested.

It wasn't a competition, a relatively sane portion of her brain pointed out. She and Belinda were different people. Belinda was beautiful and utterly feminine, and JJ was cute, maybe pretty, but the closest she got to beautiful was when the guys had had a few beers. In every one of her pictures, Belinda had this calm, cool, serene air about her. JJ could be calm. And cool. And chaos walking. To get anywhere near serene, though, she would have to be comatose.

But that was okay. Belinda had her attributes, and JJ had hers. Belinda surely had had a failing or two, and JJ had…well, more than a few. The world needed women like Belinda, and it needed women like JJ, too.

She didn't want to replace Belinda. That wasn't even possible. She just wanted a little bit of what Belinda and Quint had shared.

The man in question was looking at her curiously

now. Apparently, he'd said something, and she'd been too lost in balancing insecurities and confidence to hear it. "What?"

"If you want to get her collar and leash, we can take her out before we leave."

She blinked, then remembered. Collar, leash, in the shopping bag with two sets of food and water dishes, three toys and a box of treats.

She brought the bag in from the living room and emptied it onto the island. After cutting the tags from the collar and leash, she knelt to secure both to the dog, who was now pushing her empty dish around the floor, looking for just one more bite.

"She's still hungry," she commented.

"If we give her too much, she'll throw up. Cleaning puke is your job, too." He peeled the stickers from the dishes, stacked them next to the sink with the used one, put the treats in a cabinet and stored the shopping bag in a drawer.

As JJ stood up, she suspiciously asked, "Do you have a housekeeper?"

"I live alone. What do I need with a housekeeper?"

She thought of her condo, and her idea of what constituted good housekeeping, and shook her head. She didn't need to worry about measuring up to Belinda.

She couldn't measure up to Quint, either.

Chapter 7

After a quick lunch at the Chinese buffet, Quint headed in the direction of Maura's house. The dread that had twisted him in knots yesterday was gone, both because he'd faced Maura and because he'd confided the incident to JJ. There was no way Maura could conceivably tempt him now, a glance at JJ confirmed, and judging by her behavior yesterday, no way she would want to. He was safe in that regard.

His mouth quirked at the idea that he'd confided anything in JJ. She'd teased out a dozen words and filled in all the rest herself. It was in her job description—figuring out things people didn't want to tell—and she was good at it. He appreciated it, because he certainly felt better about that winter afternoon now.

"Do you think she'll let us in?" he asked as he turned onto Willow Street.

"Who knows? Maybe I could pick the lock."

"Can you?"

"Yeah. One of my confidential informants taught me how." She grinned. "Would you let me?"

"No."

"Hmm. I might have another idea or two."

"What exactly are you hoping for?" They'd discussed it after dinner last night, and he fully understood her reluctance to call the lawyer and tell him his client was fine, just a brat, don't worry. If she *was* being taken advantage of, if she was being scammed out of her inheritance, if anything the least bit sinister was going on, JJ felt an obligation to ferret it out.

So did Quint.

But how much time could either of them or their departments spare to help someone who obviously didn't want it?

After a long silence—at least, for her — she sighed. "I'm hoping that she's grown up in the past twenty-four hours, has come to her senses and started acting reasonably. Since that's not likely, I'd settle for her convincing me that nothing untoward is going on. Or for a believable explanation for her behavior the last few months. An offer to go home with me and make things right with her godparents would delight me." She lifted a shoulder. "I'm easy to please."

Good to know.

The only tracks in the driveway at Maura's house were theirs from the day before. Most of the snow had melted to slush, but it was pristine enough slush to know. He parked near the garage, where a few stubborn icicles clung to the eaves overhead.

"Is there a side door into the garage?" JJ slid out without waiting for an answer and headed for the south side of the house. He caught up as she cupped her hands to her face and peered inside the window there.

"Her car's here. So's a motorcycle." She whistled long and low, something Quint couldn't do if his life depended on it. "Nice bike. Looks new."

He stepped closer behind her, closer than he should have. In fact, he should have nudged her to the right and made room for himself, but no, he leaned over her, blocking out the light with his own hands to see the bike in the unlit garage.

The smell of dirt on the window filled his nose, then was joined by a sweet fragrance, not floral, not spicy, just clean. It came from JJ's hair and her skin, along with the heat radiating from her body. It teased him with its simplicity: fresh air, rain, spring breezes, nature at its best. It was soothing and calming and appealing, and he wanted very much for it to become familiar.

"What do you think?" she asked, her shoulder bumping against his chest.

You smell incredibly good.

Scowling, he forced his attention to the bike. "It's not the one Zander was riding last time I stopped him." He swallowed hard, trying to forget the scent. "We were halfway to Bristow and the highway patrol and the sheriff's office had joined the chase by the time he finally pulled over. He spent three days in jail and goes to trial next month."

"His mama must be so proud of him."

She smiled up at him. Between the fragrance and her closeness, Quint thought he might never move. Never think. He might just stand there and…

Feel.

Though he was overwhelmed at the moment, JJ wasn't. She stepped back, chill air replacing the warmth between them, and moved around him to the driveway. "Maura must have bought him a faster bike so he could get away next time. Not being a cop, she doesn't know you—"

"Can't outrun that radio," he finished for her. A motorcycle was faster and more maneuverable than any patrol car, but as long as the officer got the tag number, the guy was going to get caught.

They went to the front stoop, where JJ rang the doorbell. Apparently wanting to provoke Maura, she waited mere seconds before pushing it again. And again. While its tones were fading, she pulled out her cell and dialed a number in the directory.

Maura didn't bother with a greeting. "Quit ringing the doorbell!"

Quint clearly heard the command over the phone, though as much concrete separated him from JJ as the stoop allowed.

"We want to talk to you."

"I don't want to talk to you!"

JJ pushed the bell again, then pressed redial. While it rang, she conversationally asked, "Did I tell you that once when I was babysitting her, she locked me out of the house in a thunderstorm? It was the servants' day off, and I hadn't learned to pick locks yet, so I had to climb a tree to the second-floor balcony. She was in the safe room, watching on the monitors there. By the time she realized I'd found an unlocked door, it was too late to stop me. So instead she pushed the panic button and brought the guards from the gate and half the police department rushing in, guns drawn. I was soaked to the skin, in shorts and a T-shirt and barefooted, because I couldn't climb the tree in flip-flops, and my first introduction to most of my new coworkers was from the business end of their gun barrels."

Quint's mouth twitched. "What does it say that I can easily imagine the scene?"

She gave him a stern, brow-raised look, then shrugged. "That you know me well?"

Maura's voice screeched again from the phone. "Go away or I'll call the police!"

"Officer Foster is already here. Come on, Maura, you know I'm more stubborn than this. We just want to talk to you and Zander, and then you can go back to whatever it is you're doing."

An instant later, glass shattered overhead and a sparkle-encrusted cell phone landed on the grass fifteen feet behind them.

Quint gazed at it a moment, then at the glass shards scattered across the ground, then at JJ, who was looking smug and self-satisfied. "You're going to drive your chief to his grave, aren't you?"

"I'll even give him a shove in."

Wryly shaking his head, he backed off onto the sidewalk and looked up. "Zander, it's Quint. We need to talk to you a minute about Zoey. Come on down, would you? Then I promise I'll take Detective Logan away and leave you alone for the rest of the day."

Though JJ glared at him, he hadn't lied. He would take her away and give Zander and Maura a few hours of peace and privacy. Until tomorrow, at least. Hey, he'd specified *for the rest of the day*. Nothing more.

In the silence that followed, JJ rang the bell one more time. Its peal faded, and other sounds took its place: the lock being undone, the door opening with a slight creak.

And there stood Zander Benson.

He wore jeans, a white T-shirt and a blue button-down shirt, buttons undone, tails hanging out. All three garments were similar to clothing hanging in Quint's closet, but even he could tell these were a whole lot pricier.

Zander also wore the only expression Quint had ever seen on him: sullen. He didn't glance at JJ, not even a cops-are-getting-prettier look, but fixed his gaze on Quint instead. "What about Zoey?"

JJ didn't look the least bit impressed by him, either. She pushed past him into the foyer, gazing about for signs of Maura. "She told us to kick your ass when we found you."

"For what?" He dragged his fingers through his hair, leaving it standing at odd angles about his head.

Seeing no Maura, JJ smiled at him. "There's always a reason. Is Maura upstairs? I'm going to run up and say hello while you guys get cozy." She moved forward, and so did Zander. Expecting it, she sidestepped to the right, went around him and jogged up the stairs.

"Hey. Hey!"

Quint put a hand on his shoulder when he moved toward the stairs. "Let her go. You don't want her to embarrass you in front of your girlfriend. Let's go on back and sit down."

Zander ignored his prodding until JJ turned the corner out of sight upstairs, and then he combed his hair again, pulled a pack of cigarettes from his hip pocket, lit one and started walking. No sissy e-cig for him. These were the real thing, the smell acrid and sharp. Quint made a face as he walked through the trailing cloud of smoke.

"So, did you see Zoey, or were you lying about that?"

Quint moved away from him when they reached the family room. "I didn't say we saw her. I said we wanted to talk to you about her." He waited until Zander took a seat before he chose the same chair as before. They were facing each other, rectangular coffee table between them. They were about the same distance to the hall door, though Zander had a shorter run to the rear door, if he chose to take it, and Quint excelled at flying tackles.

The things a cop had to consider with the town's less law-abiding folks.

"We did see Zoey," Quint offered. "The beer bottle she threw missed my head by this much." He held up his hand, two fingers barely apart.

"If she'd wanted to hit you, she would've." Zander absently fingered a scar on his right temple. He'd been sixteen, Zoey thirteen, when she'd given it to him in their driveway. The neighbors had called the police, and Quint had arrived with backup to find Zander lying in the grass, dazed and bleeding everywhere. He hadn't cared about the pain, the stitches soon to come or the resulting scar. He had, however, been damned impressed with his sister's throwing arm.

"When we were here yesterday, you were upstairs, weren't you?"

"So?"

"No problem. I just wondered why she lied about it."

Zander took a long drag on the cigarette, turned his head to the right and exhaled, away from Quint, then shrugged. "Maybe she was embarrassed. She's rich, you know. Usually hangs out with a different class of people."

"Different. Not better." Maura was slumming, Zoey had said. If Zander's emotions were involved, that could be a hard thing to face. If he even had emotions other than the negative ones that were all he ever exhibited.

But if Maura was just slumming, it wasn't as if Zander would walk away empty-handed. At the least, he'd had a couple months of easy living, new clothes and what looked like an expensive watch on his wrist and a large diamond stud in his left ear—plus a $25,000 bike to show for it.

"Yeah, whatever." He blew out another lungful of smoke. "I don't have any warrants. I haven't missed any court dates. You got no reason to be harassing me."

"You've seen me harass before, Zander, and this ain't it." Quint settled more comfortably in the chair. "This is just a friendly conversation."

"You're like a bad dream that won't go away."

Standing in the doorway of the master suite, JJ smiled. "I believe the word you're looking for is *nightmare*."

In front of the fireplace, where a cheery flame burned and fake logs glowed, Maura fisted her hands on her hips. "What do you want?"

"An invitation to come in?"

"Why? It hasn't stopped you yet."

JJ strolled into the room. It wasn't much smaller

than her condo and covered all the bases except for the kitchen. There was a sitting area with sofas, chairs and a television; a mammoth four-poster bed with matching dresser, chest and nightstands; an open door showing a glimpse of a marbled bathroom; and another open door that led to what closely resembled a high-end clothing store. The pitiful contents of JJ's closet wouldn't fill even a fraction of this one.

Zoey had been right. Austerity downstairs, all the comforts of home, sweet mansion upstairs.

"Why rent such a big house if you're just going to live upstairs?" JJ asked before seating herself on the couch.

Maura reluctantly sat down, too, drawing her feet into the chair at a left angle to JJ's. "It's cool. Bigger is better, don't you know?" After a moment, she hugged her arms to her middle. "Something happen to Zoey?"

"No, she's fine."

"You obviously don't know her."

"Not a fan?" JJ asked, keeping her tone cordial.

"She's jealous of Zander and me. Mostly me. He pays more attention to me than to her, and she doesn't like it."

There was probably some truth to that, but JJ knew, too, that most people who disliked Maura had valid reasons for it. She wasn't sweet and cute and cuddly—had only ever been those things on rare occasions, even as a child. She didn't project friendliness, and she didn't get it back, with or without jealousy as a component. JJ, for example, had zero jealousy of Maura, and zero warm fuzzies for her, either.

Wondering how Quint's chat with Zander was going, JJ shifted to see Maura better. "How did you two meet?"

Again Maura began picking at her broken nail. "At a club. In Tulsa. Cedar Creek only has dumps."

"And you hit it off that quickly."

"Yeah. Kinda like you and that cop. Officer Foster." Finally Maura smiled. It reminded JJ of an alligator showing all its teeth in preparation for a bone-crushing snap. "I could've had him, you know. Foster. If I'd wanted."

Surprise: there was a bit of the jealousy JJ had just claimed didn't exist. It raised its ugly little head and whispered that yanking a handful of Maura's hair seemed both reasonable and well deserved. She kept her hands folded in her lap, and she tried, for at least an instant, to bite her tongue, but yeah, she knew that wasn't going to work.

"Sure, that's why you tore up the ticket when he turned you down."

Surliness slid over Maura's face like a mask. It claimed her eyes first, shifting them to hard blue shards, then it curled her nose into a delicate sneer and thinned her mouth till her ninety-dollar lipstick almost disappeared. "I wasn't really trying. If I'd really wanted him, I would've had him."

"Zander wouldn't have liked that."

"Zander does what I say. Not the other way around."

JJ wanted to shake her head with dismay, maybe yank Maura's hair just enough to make the roots squeak in alarm. And then maybe slap her in handcuffs and haul her home so Mr. Winchester could determine her state of mind and competency. Except Chief Dipstick would gloat—*Told you she couldn't handle it*—and JJ would be back in Evanston and Quint would be here, and she and Chica would be very sad girls, indeed.

She softened her expression, her voice, her body, and focused her gaze on the other woman. "How are you, Maura? Really, seriously. I haven't seen you since your parents' funeral. How are you coping?"

A stricken look came across her face, making JJ feel a stirring of guilt. "I'm not going back there. Me and my friend, we talked about it. She said it was just a house and that a house needed to be lived in. She said it would show everyone how strong I am if I went back. But my parents *died* there. And every time I think of it, all I see is—" She swiped her hand across her eyes, then stared off into the distance. "I'm not going back."

JJ knew exactly what Maura saw, because she'd seen it first. The instant she'd walked through the door, she'd felt the silence. The eerie disturbance of nothingness. The skin-crawling chill of violence. Next had come the smell as she followed the housekeeper through the foyer—thick, sour, heavy and getting worse the nearer she got. Then the blood.

So damn much blood.

She had felt loss before. Had smelled death. Had seen that stark frozen shock of last moments lived. Sometimes she had recognized victims. A few times, she'd had dealings with them. But she'd *known* Mr. and Mrs. Evans. Had seen them all over town. Chatted with them. Sat down to meals with them. Been trusted one summer with the care of their precious daughter.

She would never forget a single detail of the ugly scene, and apparently, Maura remembered it all, too.

Hence the booze and the weed. Who wouldn't need a little help after something like that?

"I don't think anyone expects you to go back there to stay," she said gently. "But your godparents and your friends there miss you."

Maura sniffed. "Those people aren't friends. They're just kids I grew up with. I bet they never think about what happened to my parents or wonder about me. They liked me because I was an Evans, because we had even more money than all of them. But friends? They don't know what the word means."

JJ would have given even odds that Maura didn't, either. But if she could recognize the difference between a friend and a hanger-on, she'd matured at least a little, hadn't she? The comment about her boyfriend—*Zander does what I say*—suggested she still had a lot to learn, but this was some progress.

"I understand you came here with a friend named Mel."

From stricken to dismissive to a blunt affect. Maura had a broader emotional range than Zander. "She's gone."

"Where to?"

"Don't know."

"Where did you meet her?"

Maura shifted into the lotus position in the oversize chair with an ease that made JJ's joints creak. "Memphis. She needed a ride, and I wanted company. We had a lot in common, except..." Tilting her head to one side, she said, "I had money, and she didn't. But she was a better friend than any of those kids at home ever were."

A better friend. Someone to ease her loneliness.

Someone to spend money on, do things for. A distraction from the horrors she was running from. "But she left?"

Impatience surged through Maura, though she remained in the yoga pose. "She didn't like it here. Didn't like the cold. I asked her to stay, but she wanted to go someplace warmer." She shrugged. "She had to go."

"It must have been sad, her leaving right before Christmas."

Another shrug. "I gave her a first-class ticket to New Orleans. My Christmas gift to her. And I wasn't sad. She was fun while she was here, and I still have Zander."

The closest JJ had gotten to first class had been traipsing through on her way to join the unwashed masses in coach, who, by the way, arrived at their destination at the same time as first class for a whole lot less money. But flying first class on someone else's tab would be fun. Someone else chartering a jet for her—one of Maura's frequent means of transportation—would be decadently fun.

Add Quint, and it would be heavenly.

Knowing that would never happen—also knowing she didn't need to leave the ground to be in heaven with Quint—JJ softly asked, "Can we talk about your godparents?"

Before the word finished, Maura's lip curled. "I don't want to fight with him, but I will. I want my money."

Because Zander wanted it? She'd been satisfied with her allowance until he'd come into her life. What did he want that $100,000 a month couldn't cover? Maybe he was tired of the monthly dole. Maybe he was tired of

Maura but wanted to get his hands on as much of her money as he could before he cut himself loose.

"You've known since you were a kid that you wouldn't get the first payment until you're thirty," JJ reminded her. At the blank look she received, she went on. "The Hamilton rule? That's what your family called it. Because your great-uncle Hamilton blew his millions in no time."

After another empty moment, Maura waved one hand dismissively. "Oh yeah, that. But I'm not him. If they'd given me such a dumb name, I might have spent all the money, too, just to spite them."

If she thought wasting her too many millions to count would negatively impact someone else and not herself, she hadn't grown up as much as JJ had hoped. Did she even truly understand that when the money was gone, it was gone? That the family businesses had been sold, that there were no parents generating more income for her? Did she know it was even possible to spend her entire inheritance, or was the money limitless in her mind? She was less suited to being broke than anyone JJ had ever met. Also more likely to be taken advantage of.

"What do you need more money for, Maura? Maybe I could talk to Mr. Winchester."

"Things."

"Like clothes? Trips? You want to buy a house? A new car?"

Her petulant response reminded JJ of a commercial she saw far too much of when she was too lazy to switch channels. "It's my money, and I want it now."

"But what would you do with it?"

"I dunno. Put it in the bank." Almost immediately,

her face turned pink as if she realized the silliness of showing up at a bank with $50-plus million to open a simple savings account. "I would invest it."

"How would you know what to invest in?"

She rolled her eyes. "There are people for that."

"Where do you find them?"

"I don't know. I'm sure there are people for that, too."

"What if you hire someone who's not as trustworthy as Mr. Winchester? Someone who invests badly, maybe someone who embezzles your fortune then disappears?"

"Then you'd have a real crime to investigate, and you could leave me alone." Then she ran her hands through her hair, a dozen shades of artful blond that managed to look unique and natural and totally cool all at once. "I'm tired of being treated like a kid. I'm not ten anymore! My parents didn't trust me, Winchester doesn't trust me, you don't trust me! I'm an adult who happens to have a hell of a lot of money and who also happens to want everybody who knew little Maura Evans to get the hell out of my life!"

It wasn't a totally unreasonable request. People grew up and away from their family and friends. It happened all the time. Not to JJ, of course, but others. Sometimes the family got to know why; sometimes they didn't. Sometimes, like now, maybe the kid couldn't even verbalize why.

As long as she was doing it of her own volition, as long as JJ was comfortable that there was no coercion involved and that Maura was as stable as she'd ever been, it was okay. Her choice. A bad one, but still hers.

But JJ wasn't comfortable with anything, most of all Maura's sudden insistence that she needed all her money *now*, when she'd grown up knowing the terms, and her anger toward Mr. Winchester. JJ knew he and his wife were good people. She knew how close they'd been to the Evanses, all three of them. She'd heard the pain in his voice, deep and abiding…*letting Maura go… almost killed us.*

Travis and Kate Winchester deserved more than a perfunctory *She's okay, leave her alone.*

Hearing footsteps on the stairs, JJ got to her feet. "Listen, I feel bad about upsetting you. Let me take you to lunch tomorrow. We'll have a girls' afternoon out." Because the steps were getting closer and Maura was looking reluctant, she rushed on. "I'll pick you up at eleven. Sound good?"

After a sigh and a roll of her eyes, Maura said, "You can meet me here at twelve. I'll drive."

"Good. I'll see you then." JJ met Zander at the door, ducked around him and headed down the stairs.

Quint walked into his house after work Wednesday half expecting a disaster scene. Chica could have managed to undo the simple latch and opened the door, or she could have squeezed out between the bars. She was awfully scrawny. Brutus had once turned his kennel, minus the plastic tray, upside down, then wiggled out through the larger squares the tray was supposed to conceal. Another time sans tray, he'd turned the kennel over and walked/carried it to a sunny section of the floor for a cozy nap.

Quint never underestimated the intelligence of dogs. People, yes. Canines, no.

The house was quiet, though, and the only new sound

was the deep rhythmic breathing of a sleepy dog. Chica curled in the middle of her bed, the hoodie scooped up to form a pillow, her paws pressed together.

Breathing a sigh of relief, he closed the door quietly and headed upstairs. After a shower and shave, he dressed in jeans and a T-shirt, pulled on a well-worn pair of boots, and returned to the stairs. Halfway down, he became aware of an intense gaze locked on him. "You're awake."

Chica lay in the same position, but there was no avoiding her sharp look. Only her eyes moved as he continued down the stairs, then stopped at the front of the kennel. When he bent, the muscles in her jaw, shoulders and chest tightened, and her stare took on a razor edge.

Cautiously he slid the latch loose and pulled the door open an inch. Then he went on to the kitchen, trusting she would come out when she was ready.

He had invited JJ over for dinner. Standing in front of the refrigerator, both doors open, he wondered how that had happened. He didn't invite people to his house. Not anymore. But somehow her concern and desire for a thrown-away pup had gotten inside his head, and he'd let her bring Chica here, and he couldn't very well refuse to let her visit her own dog. Especially since there might be cleaning and definitely would be bathing and leash walking and probably snuggling.

But only with the dog, damn it.

He'd told JJ that he cooked, and he did, though not every day, like he used to, or even every week. Once in a while, he spent an entire day shopping, peeling, chopping and cooking, then freezing all of it. If he was going to eat alone, he was going to eat good food.

He'd had three lunches and tonight would make two dinners with JJ in the days since she'd arrived. It was a routine that had become familiar and comfortable really fast. And really easy.

Really hopeful.

Becoming aware of the chill radiating from the freezer and the refrigerator, he grabbed a gallon bag of Italian sausage and bean soup and left it on the island to thaw. He filled a cup with warm water, stirred in sugar and yeast, and while the yeast fed, he measured the rest of the ingredients for a rustic loaf of bread.

Little claws clicked across the wood, stopped in the doorway, then trotted over to where he stood. Chica tilted her head back and gave him a long, solemn look.

"Okay, Chica." He gave her a small portion of nuggets, maybe a third what she would normally get, and she wolfed them down while he refilled her water dish. She needed a bath, and who knew? She might be that rare dog who sat serenely like the princess she thought she was while the lesser human attended her.

But he had no intention of depriving JJ of the experience. Instead, he got the leash and half coaxed, half dragged Chica through the laundry room and down the back steps.

She walked stiffly across the yard, as if she had no intention of loosening up. Recognizing a bit of himself in her actions, Quint wavered between empathy and playing the firm alpha. Before he had to admit that empathy would win out, his cell rang.

A glance at caller ID tempted him to let it go to voice mail. Rhonda, Linny's mother, had moved to south Texas last summer, but she kept in touch with him.

Once, he'd asked if it bothered her, seeing and talking to him when Linny was gone, and she'd given him a tight hug. *You're family*, she'd said. *With or without her.*

Now, interrupting preparations for dinner with another woman to take out that woman's dog made him feel like guilty family. Rhonda would never put that kind of burden on him; she'd told him a dozen times that Linny wouldn't want him to be alone forever. Still, that had been his intent. His expectation. The reality of his new life.

Chica had stopped moving and was staring at him, seeking the source of the noise. With a sigh, he pulled out the phone and greeted his almost mother-in-law. "Hey, Rhonda, how are you?"

"I thought I was freezing until I saw online that it snowed in Cedar Creek. I'm good now. How about you?"

"I'm okay." He said it a lot when it wasn't true, but this afternoon, standing in the yard where patches of green were interspersed with slushy snow, where weeds were already starting to thrive and where a puppy whose luck had turned was giving him a calculated, searching look far too old for her few months on this earth, he found a little truth in the words. *Okay* wasn't *good* or *fine*, but it was better than *lost*, *hopeless* or *filled with despair*. It promised that things had improved and that there was room for even more improvement. It suggested that he might actually reach *good* or *fine*.

"How's Darryl?" he asked. Linny's stepfather was from the Texas coast, so when Rhonda had decided she needed to get away, his home had seemed the natural choice. Linny's brother and his wife had followed a few months later. They'd done their best to persuade Rhonda's mother—the resident of room 318 at the assisted-living facility—to move, too, but NeNe Caulfield had insisted she was going to die in Cedar Creek, where she'd been born.

A new source of guilt pricked at him, that he hadn't stopped in to see NeNe when he and JJ visited Georgie. He saw her every weekend, so it wasn't as if he was past due. But if the old lady knew he'd sneaked right past her door without even saying hello…

"Darryl's good. The kids are good. We're coming up to see Mom for Easter. Can we see you then, too?"

"Sure." They hadn't been in town since Christmas, and he realized, possibly for the first time, that he missed them. Even if he hadn't genuinely liked them, being Linny's family had made them a constant in his life practically forever, and then they weren't.

"Hey, Quint—"

The new voice startled him, his muscles twitching as he turned to face JJ. He hadn't heard her pull into the driveway, hadn't heard her car door close or any sound at all as she'd made her way across the sodden ground, until she was practically close enough to touch. When she saw his cell, she mouthed, *Sorry*, then gestured for Chica's leash.

His fingers clenched tighter on the phone as he handed the black nylon to her. With a few words of encouragement, she got the dog moving again, walking toward the distant fence to give him privacy.

There was a moment's silence on the other end. When Rhonda broke it, her tone was careful, measured. "You have company."

"Yeah. She, uh, just got here."

Another silence. He could imagine her trying on the idea for size: he'd invited a woman to his house. He, who had zealously avoided a social life since Linny died, who had wished he could avoid life, period, had invited a woman who wasn't Rhonda's daughter into the home he'd shared with her daughter.

"Oh, Quint, I'm glad. Tell me about her."

She didn't sound glad—or suspicious, accusatory, hostile or even regretful. She sounded the way his own mother would. Stunned. Relieved. A little cautious.

He, who had become the master of one-, two- or three-word responses over the last sixteen months, took a deep breath. "Her name is JJ. She's a cop from South Carolina, and she's here on a case. Sam assigned me to help out, to introduce her to folks and drive her around. She's never driven on snow before. And she adopted a puppy this morning that someone threw out."

And she's funny. Bubbling over with life. Pretty. She reminds me that there were good times in the past and there can be good ones in the future, and she makes me want to smile and laugh and touch her and kiss her and connect with her and be a real person again and not just a sulking lump of sorrow.

Watching the woman's and the dog's halting movements across the yard, he wasn't sure Chica understood yet that she was JJ's dog. The puppy dragged and scuffed, turning every few feet to give him a reproving look.

"Oh well, that makes her one of God's gifts, doesn't it?" Rhonda said. "Darryl and I are fostering a mama collie and her four puppies. Just got them over the weekend. The chaos twins went to their new home Friday. I'll miss them, but I'm ready for some peace."

"With four new puppies in the house?"

Rhonda snorted. "That's how chaotic the twins were. I sent you pictures. You saw the gleam in their eyes."

He had seen the gleam. He'd also seen that one twin was a full-grown shepherd and the other a young terrier.

"So, tell me more. What are you fixing her for dinner?"

"Italian sausage soup and peasant bre— Who said I'm fixing dinner?"

"Because that's what you do when you invite a woman to your house around dinnertime. You have dinner and dessert, and if it's a cold night, you light a fire, and you talk, and you get to know all the important things about each other, and you… Well, you know where it goes from there."

There was a hiccup at the end, with her head turned away or her hand clamped over her mouth, but he heard it, and it sent a flutter of panic through him. "Rhonda—"

"It's okay, Quint. Honey, it's okay." Her laugh was mostly forced, but it held the promise of real laughter. *As long as I can laugh*, she'd say, *I'll know I'm alive.*

He hadn't laughed in a very long time, but he knew he was alive. He had suspected it before he'd met JJ, but he knew it for a fact now.

"Sweetie, Belinda is gone, and you and me doing nothing but missing her is disrespectful to her. No one loved life more than she did, and no one hated wasting it more than her. If you love anyone half as well as you did Belinda, she'll be a very lucky woman. Every day

I've prayed that you would meet that woman and that your heart would heal and that you would find pleasure in life again. Do I wish Belinda was still here? You bet. Do I want you to be happy even if it's with someone else's daughter? Absolutely. I'll dance with joy and love her like she's my own. You got that?"

JJ and Chica had reached the fence and were now turning back. At least, JJ was turning back. Chica, her interest caught by something on the other side, dug her feet in and refused to move. JJ appeared to be talking to the dog, who appeared to have suddenly gone deaf. After a moment, JJ tugged on the leash. Tugged harder. And harder. Then Chica leaped into the air, twisting while all four feet were off the ground, and came running toward him at top speed, little more than a tan blur while her new owner—he snorted silently—chased after her. They both looked so exuberant and full of delight and sheer pleasure at racing across the grass in the twilight that it hurt his heart.

A new set of chaos twins. Running to him.

"I got it, Rhonda," he said quietly. Healing heart, pleasure, dancing with joy. He got every word.

Chapter 8

"Bath time is not fun time."

JJ muttered the words from behind the towel Quint had handed over without a single smirk or smart-ass remark. Trust Chica to feel a sudden surge of emotion for JJ that must be expressed at that very moment, while she was dripping wet and covered with doggie shampoo. The dog had plastered herself to JJ's front and enthusiastically licked most of her face before Quint wrestled her back into the laundry room's utility sink.

When she lowered the towel, Quint still wasn't smirking, but only because he'd curled his lips in so tightly that they'd almost disappeared. Chica, on the other hand, was very openly smirking.

"I thought rescue dogs were supposed to be grateful."

"She's grateful. She's filled with gratitude."

"She's filled with attitude."

"So you two are a good match." He picked up the sprayer and tested the temperature before directing it to the now perfectly well-behaved pup. "Why don't you grab something dry from my closet?"

She eyed him a moment. Granted, she couldn't sit around in a shirt that was soaked all the way to the skin, but he made the suggestion so casually, when it was anything but casual to her. Being invited to the house he'd shared with Belinda seemed a big deal. Being given free rein to go into his bedroom, the room he'd most intimately shared with Belinda, and to rummage through his closet for something to wear seemed a very big deal. Maybe he could run up and grab her a T-shirt and she could change in the bathroom down the hall.

While she watched Princess Chica. The schemer would probably give Quint time to get upstairs, then leap out of the tub and race through the house, shaking water everywhere.

Tako the sheepdog, the only canine JJ had ever owned entirely by herself, had been a lazy, loving sweetheart. Being his mama had been so easy, even a teenager could do it. She wasn't sure she was prepared for a bitch with an attitude. Which was funny, considering that some people considered *her* a bitch with an attitude.

"I'll be right back."

She hurried up the stairs, though the photographs there were so tempting that she had to avert her eyes. There were three doors on the second level, but only one was open. She went inside, flipping the light switch, and stopped short.

She hadn't imagined Quint in any bedroom but the room she was currently occupying at the inn, but if she'd given any thought to where he spent much of his life, she was pretty sure this never would have crossed her mind.

It was large, spacious, airy and bright, even though night had fallen outside the big windows on three walls. Like downstairs, the hardwood floor was dark, but that and the wood furniture were the only things. The rest—walls, ceiling, bedding, chairs, curtains—were shades of cream and white. It was a room that made her think of islands, from the coast of Maine all the way down to the Caribbean. The woven rugs on the floor were soft in texture and subdued in color, with the only real hue present a sapphire-blue throw on each chair and a couple of small pillows to match on the bed.

It was peaceful. Serene. Quiet. Calm.

It was Belinda.

JJ hovered there, just inside the door, before inhaling for courage and walking purposefully across the room to the closet door. She expected a normal closet, something like the long narrow slot her condo people called a walk-in, but the door opened to a large space. More than half the rods and shelves were empty; the rest contained men's clothing. Quint's clothing.

She hated to admit relief that Belinda's things weren't still occupying all that empty space. None of her business, right? A person never knew how they would react to the death of a loved one until it actually happened, and if it had given Quint comfort to keep Belinda's clothes hanging with his own, where he could see them and touch them and smell her perfume on them every day, that was totally his right.

But she felt less guilty for wanting to have steamy

sex with the woman's fiancé in the woman's house in her own bed with the clothes gone.

Grabbing a T-shirt from the stack on a shelf, she tugged off her shirt and bra, shivered in the sudden chill of bare skin, and pulled on his shirt. It was old and soft, a mottled shade of well-washed black, and even though it smelled of laundry products, she fancied she could catch a faint whiff of him on it.

Back downstairs, she got a plastic bag from a kitchen drawer, stuffed her clothes inside and wandered into the laundry room. Chica was out of the tub, looking bonier than ever, her tan fur ruffled all over from the vigorous drying Quint had given her. He was crouched beside her, lifting each paw and rubbing it gently. "She smells better. Looks more pitiful."

Quint grunted. The dog, bless her heart, lifted her head and very slightly bared her teeth at JJ.

"There's an old saying. Don't adopt the puppy that even the mama and daddy are scared of. I think that's exactly what I've done here."

Quint unfolded easily to his full height and hung the wet towel over a bar with several others. "Aw, come on, look at that little face. How can you say that?"

She poked him on the upper arm. "Don't throw my words back at me. That line was for your benefit. I know better than to believe half of what I say."

"For the record, I didn't believe it, either. Letting her stay here just seemed reasonable." He slipped past her and into the kitchen, where soup bubbled on the stove and the bread she'd oohed over was cooling on a rack on the island. She breathed deeply of its aroma when she followed.

"I can't believe you made bread."

"It's easy bread. You don't knead it."

She slid onto a cushy black stool at the island. She couldn't imagine a much better way to spend an evening than with a sexy guy who cooked and thought she was worthy of even easy homemade bread.

Well, if the evening ended in that super calm bedroom, that would be better. Even if it ended with just a bit of cuddling on the couch, that would be an improvement over ninety percent of the dates she'd had.

Because Quint was a major improvement over at least ninety percent of the guys she'd dated.

Her cell phone beeped in her pocket, and she pulled it out to glance at the screen. "Chief Dipstick," she muttered, muting, then setting the phone aside.

"Does he work this late?"

She scoffed. "Are you kidding? He probably just finished dinner, so he figured it was dinnertime here now. Back home, he might see me in the station five times a day, but when he calls, it's always when I'm at lunch."

The phone signaled a message, but she wasn't tempted to listen to it. "I told you he wants to cut Mr. Winchester out of the loop and have me report directly to him? Well, he wanted that report by noon. I told him tomorrow, maybe Friday." Maybe never.

"Sounds like a fun guy."

"Yeah. No. He's a miserable old coot trying to live in the past."

Quint stirred the soup a time or two, his expression distant. "But you're not really living if you're in the past."

His stark tone made her grimace. She hadn't meant

to include anyone but Dipstick in that comment, and certainly hadn't meant to remind Quint of his own loss.

But loss of that magnitude didn't need reminders. Even if he moved thousands of miles away, changed his career, his surroundings and his very self, he would still think of Belinda and miss her every single day. Memories lived everywhere. Nowhere.

After a moment, he set down the ladle and went to a cabinet for dishes. He gestured with the bowls. "Island, kitchen table, dining table, sofa?"

She didn't ask where he and Belinda had usually eaten. Didn't care. He didn't need anything more than a glance at JJ's auburn hair and hazel eyes for a reminder that she wasn't Belinda. "Dining table. I really like that chandelier."

He carried in bowls of soup. She took bread and butter and a dish of freshly grated parmesan. He returned for drinks, and she picked up silverware and napkins. For a few moments, they quietly sat opposite each other, the glass prisms overhead swaying when the furnace came on and stirred the air. It was lovely.

Except for Chica, sitting primly a few feet from JJ, watching every bite like a hawk, prepared to swoop in, snatch the food and possibly take a few fingers in the process. Warily, JJ turned her head so she could focus on Quint but keep the pooch in her peripheral vision. "How long has it been since Belinda…?"

For an instant, he stiffened, as if he'd never been asked the question outright. As if, when he'd first mentioned Belinda, he'd never intended for JJ to presume to bring her up later. If she'd overstepped—

"Passed," he finished for her, then offered the slightest,

faintest, most barely there smile she'd ever seen. "All my life, I just said *died*. Passed on, passed away, deceased, departed…all those other words seemed pointless. Dead was dead. But I learned it depends on which side you're looking at it from. When it's a stranger, *died* is a perfectly good word. When it's someone you expected to spend the next forty years with, it's an awfully hard word."

"It's an awfully hard concept."

"Yeah." He sliced a piece of bread, buttered it, then laid it on his plate without taking a bite. "Sixteen months ago. The end of November, year before last."

After Thanksgiving, before Christmas. Hello, ruined family holiday season.

JJ bit into her own bread, barely noticing the salty tang of the crispy crust or the soft dense crumb inside. She wouldn't ask how. She wouldn't push for information. When he wanted her to know, when he felt ready to talk about it, he would tell her and until then—

"What happened?" Good Lord, did she not know herself? Of course, she was going to ask how. The man who rationed out his words a few at a time was talking, and she wanted to know what he wanted to say. She wanted to know everything.

He took another bite of soup, then finally tore the bread slice in two. "She'd been having a sore throat off and on for a year or so. Antibiotics helped, but it always came back, so her doctor suggested a tonsillectomy. It was supposed to be an outpatient procedure. No big deal. They do it on kids all the time, right? She didn't even want me to take off work to be there because it was so simple, but Sam insisted."

A tonsillectomy. JJ had hers when she was ten. She

remembered only two things about it: her big sisters being so unbelievably nice to her that she'd feared she was dying, and her mother giving her all the ice cream she wanted.

"I stayed with her in pre-op until they sent me out. She reminded me she wanted tiramisu that night, and rice pudding, and mashed potatoes. They took her to the OR, and an hour later, the doctor came out and said…"

His breath caught, and his fingers clenched his spoon so tightly that his knuckles turned white. JJ watched his fingers work, flexing, relaxing. She didn't want to see the heartache in his face that she could hear in his voice.

After a while, he went on, his tone flat now. Empty. "When they put her under anesthesia, she had a stroke. She never woke up."

JJ didn't like to think about death, particularly her own, her parents', her sisters', her nieces' and her brothers-in-law's. It made her sad and would turn her weepy if she didn't shy away from the first mention like a spooked horse. The rare times she allowed herself to wonder how her own death might occur, she always chose something job related. An arrest gone bad. An ambush. A hundred-mile-per-hour car chase. Her chief driven to strangle her.

But a stroke? Uh-uh. Natural causes for a healthy woman her age—Belinda's age—were too unnatural to accept. It was just too wrong.

"Wow," she murmured. "That sucks." Almost immediately, she tried to correct the words. "I'm sorry. I'm not good with dea—with passing. I never do death notifications because I'm not empathetic enough. I mean, I am. Empathetic. I just don't ever know what to say because I kind of get freaked out about it. But I am sorry—"

Her words dried up as Quint took the hand she'd been gesturing with in his. He removed the spoon from her grip and laid it down, then wrapped his fingers around hers. His hand was warm, calloused, comforting as hell.

"I've never had to tell anyone that story. My sister was with me at the hospital. She got the details from the doctor, and she told Mom and Sam, and they told everyone else. In all the time since, I never dealt with anyone who knew Linny but didn't know what had happened."

He squeezed her hand gently and whispered. "I never dealt with anyone. Until you." His gaze shifted to hers, damp, intense, exhausted. "I'm glad I met you, JJ."

Housework had never been a popular subject in the Foster home. It was a chore to be shared by everyone, even if his sisters did insist their parents were *so* unfair and that their *friends'* parents didn't make *their* children do forced labor. Quint couldn't say he enjoyed it, but he did like the order and cleanliness that followed. Though he supposed in a way he did kind of like it when he had help.

Disdaining the dishwasher, as he often did, JJ had decided to wash their few dishes by hand. She was filling the sink with hot soapy water while he poured another small serving of food into Chica's dish.

As far as he knew, the dog had had no vomiting or diarrhea, but he figured caution was the way to go for another day or two. The pup gulped down every bite, then sat on her haunches, looking from him to the bin that held the nuggets, then back again.

"You'd think, having been thrown out like so much garbage, she would be a little humble," JJ remarked.

"Pits don't do humble. It's not in their makeup." He gave in to Chica's steady gaze and dropped another dozen small nuggets into the dish. That done, he lowered himself to the floor beside her and watched as she hoovered the extra treats, pushed the bowl away and began sniffing him.

"You like pits."

"I respect them. They're a good dog with a bad reputation mostly caused by bad owners." He leaned against the cabinets and crossed his legs at his ankles. For a moment, water running was the only sound, then Chica climbed onto his lap and performed her hyperfast sniffing routine before lying down there with her head on his knee.

"People are the source of all our problems." JJ rinsed the dishes, left them on the drain board and dried her hands. As naturally as if it was her own kitchen, she squirted the lotion on the windowsill into one palm, then rubbed her hands together as she sat down opposite him.

"Speaking of problem people, I'm taking Maura to lunch tomorrow."

He nodded. She'd mentioned it earlier in passing. "You okay with it?" He didn't trust Maura or Zander, but JJ was almost as experienced and certainly as well trained as he was. She wore her Taser and had her gun locked away. She could handle herself.

"Yeah. I told her girls' day out, but that doesn't mean it'll be just her and me. One time her parents set her up on a date with the son of some friends who had just moved back to South Carolina from France. She didn't fuss or complain. She just happily showed up at the country club restaurant. With another date in tow. Her reasoning was if the *guy* was allowed to bring a date, why wasn't she?"

"So your girls' day out might be just you two, or include Zander, or every other woman she knows in this area. She's tough to predict." Quint was coming to appreciate unpredictability. He'd gotten out of bed Monday morning, expecting another ugly day like the previous 480-some ugly days, and instead he'd met JJ. He wasn't generally melodramatic, but three days, out of 480-some ugly ones, had changed everything. He felt it. Was afraid of it. Welcomed it. Would appreciate it, and JJ, until the day he died.

Three short days.

Life could change in an instant, people said, and he couldn't recall a time when they hadn't meant it in a bad way. Accidents, tragedies, death. Life *could* change in an instant, and sometimes that change was good. A cop stumbled, and the sniper's bullet flew harmlessly over his head. A light got stuck on red, keeping a vehicle full of kids out of the intersection when the drunk driver barreled through. A gate mix-up stopped a passenger from boarding the plane that was going to crash.

There were bad in-an-instant events. But in one instant, he hadn't known JJ Logan existed, and in the next, he did, and it was the best thing that had happened to him in a long time.

"What are your plans while we're dining?" JJ asked.

"I was thinking I could work on my surveillance skills."

"On Zander, if she leaves him at home?"

"On you." He watched her. Would she be offended? Was she thinking that if he were going out with Zander, she wouldn't even consider following him? That this was a big-strong-man-versus-frail-incompetent-woman thing?

"Good," she agreed, then nudged his foot. "You didn't expect me to whine, did you? Because I'm not that kind of cop. Backup is always good."

"I went to the academy with a hotshot who was ordered to wait for backup at a domestic dispute, but he loved being the hero, so he raced in anyway. The husband shot him in the head."

"Domestics are bad," she said sympathetically. "We had one family that we never went in to see without at least four officers. It was a mom, dad and two sons in their twenties. Their usual affectionate exchanges were closer to assault than most of us ever see. When they were pissed, they threw punches and dishes and furniture. Dad threw a son at Mom one time. Just heaved him over his shoulder, and kid and Mom both went out the window, rolled off the porch and landed at the feet of the chief before Chadwick. His only response was to remark, 'Business as usual, Mercy Ann, isn't it?' And the mom replied, 'Can't talk now, Chief. I've got to kick my old man's butt.'"

Relaxation eased over Quint. He knew exactly the kind of family she was talking about. Cedar Creek had their share. In fact, the Bensons headed the list, though Marisa stayed out of the fray. Though he and Linny had never lacked for conversational material, knowing JJ had experienced all the same things he had on the job made for a certain connection.

And he was already feeling so many connections that he damn near sizzled with them.

Providing a distraction, Chica stretched and stood up, then trotted to the back door. JJ looked proud of how much the dog had learned in half a day until Quint stood up, offered her his hand and drily said, "I'm glad cleaning floors isn't my job."

He actually saw the instant the ammonia odor of urine reached her nose, saw it twitch as her mouth thinned in a straight line. Chica stood at the door, pretending the pool behind her had just mysteriously appeared. Wow, lucky she'd already passed those tiles before the nasty got there.

Oh well, it could have been worse.

He got a spray bottle of all-purpose cleaner, a pair of vinyl gloves and a small tub filled with old rags. "Gloves, rags, spray, then toss everything icky in the trash."

JJ gave him a narrow look as she pulled on a glove, then mockingly saluted. He put on a battered jacket that was hanging next to the door, hooked on the leash and followed Chica out into the night.

Chica shivered in the cold and made quick work of finding an appropriate spot to finish her business. Even so, by the time they returned to the house, a four-foot square of tile was cleaned, sanitized and dried, and the kitchen was empty. He and Chica went into the living room to find JJ sitting at one end of the couch, the arm at her back, her knees drawn onto the cushion. She appeared to be studying the lamp on the opposite end table, a large art glass piece with a prairie arts–style shade, all subdued colors, straight lines and geometrics. The one behind her matched it, while the chandelier in the entry was similar enough to complement them.

She looked right in this house that he and Linny had done together. It was clean lined and welcoming and warm, and she fit as if she'd been part of the design. As if she belonged.

But how could she? In a few days, she would go home. All the way back to South Carolina. But she could come back. He could go there. They could email, text and video call in between. They could be together even in different places.

For a while, at least.

"You're quick and efficient," he said as he sat down at the opposite end, angled to face her.

She grinned. "Thank you. My mom says my talents shine in strange places."

"Outshooting every man in the department."

"Taking down suspects."

"I bet you're quick with the Taser or pepper spray."

She nodded. "I'm a good tree climber, toilet cleaner and pizza-crust maker. I'm a decent babysitter, and I can spot a good deal on boots from a hundred yards. I can also roll my tongue and wiggle my ears one at a time."

"You're just full of surprises, aren't you?"

Her answering smile was radiant. She wasn't merely good-natured. She looked for reason to be happy in the smallest things. He admired that. He needed to copy it. He wanted that kind of light in his life again.

"How long will they let you stay?" The question surprised him. He'd just been thinking about her leaving, but it wasn't something he wanted to focus on right this moment. Tonight was a different sort of night. An anything's-possible sort of night. Leave reality until tomorrow.

"I have no idea. Mr. Winchester says money is no obstacle, and the chief is glad to not have to see me every day." She shrugged. "I can't even make a guess. In the real world, how long is long enough on something like this? But in the real world, Chadwick would have told Mr. Winchester to contact the local police or hire a private detective. A real-world chief never would have agreed to send an officer—a detective—in the first place."

"Chica is very glad he did."

The dog, lying in front of the fireplace, lifted her head to look at him, then JJ, before resettling.

"Do you know she bares her teeth at me when you're not looking? She does not look on me as her rescuer. She does, however, like you."

He appreciated the dog's affection. He appreciated more that it kind of ticked off JJ. She was used to being adored by, if not all, most. "Females like me."

"I bet they do. Even when you were surly, I liked you. Maura liked you before you rejected her. And obviously, Belinda liked you a whole lot."

"She did. Enough to stick with me for twelve years. To live with me for ten." The more he talked about Linny, the easier it got. Not by a whole lot, granted. It still stirred all the aches and sadness inside, but it didn't feel like hot coals dancing across raw skin anymore. Not quite. That was an improvement.

It helped that talking about Linny seemed easier for JJ than most people. She apparently didn't feel threatened by Belinda's sad story or her importance in his life. She didn't avoid the subject or expect him to. She was empathetic and accepting without treating him as if he might break. A lot of people had believed he might. Including himself.

"Ryan and I were together nearly three years. We were engaged for four months, but we never lived together. I was twenty-seven and had an apartment above my parents' garage." Looking rueful, she quickly explained, "It was a detached garage at the back of the property, and I had my own driveway coming in off the alley, and I paid rent, so it wasn't really like I was living at home. Honestly. Not at twenty-seven. When he broke up with me, I spent all the money I'd saved living there and bought the condo."

"How did you date him for three years and not know he was a jerk?" Looking back, he'd known everything there was to know about Linny within the first three months. Not little things like favorite colors, pork or beef barbecue, beer or wine, but the important things. That she was an honorable person. That she was smarter than she was pretty. That she had compassion and manners and liked kids and old folks and respected everyone in between. That he wanted to spend the rest of his life with her.

Of course, Linny had been a normal person with a normal ego, and she was as open and honest as anyone he'd ever met. She'd had no secret quirks, no hidden flaws.

Like JJ.

"It wasn't that he was a jerk, so much."

Quint undid the laces on his boots, then toed them off before propping his feet on the middle cushion. "He ended your engagement because you got promoted and he didn't. That's a jerk."

"Well...yeah. I knew he always expected things to go his way, but that was because they always had. He never had to exert himself. In school, other kids spent hours studying while he got everything the first time through. Other kids practiced their passes or their pitches or their strategy, and Ryan just did them, and did them better. He was a natural at everything he tried. It never occurred to him that I could get promoted—that *anyone* could get promoted—before him. I honestly think it was the first time that he ever didn't get something he wanted. It wasn't the way his life was supposed to go."

Linny had done that sort of thing—looked for the reason someone behaved like a jackass. It wasn't Quint's job to excuse anyone's behavior. He just stopped them when they strayed too far out of line.

"So he dealt with it by pushing the woman he loved out of his life and leaving town." Quint couldn't filter out his derision for the man. "He was a jerk, and you're better off without him."

"You're right. I am. I lost someone I would have eventually had to kill and gained a brand-new home all my own. Couldn't beat a deal like that." Then she gestured around the room. "Though compared to this place, my condo falls more in the sparse, spare, spartan style of living. It's a place to spend time. This is a place to live."

It was, Quint agreed. He and Linny had done a lot of living here, just like the couple they'd bought it from. He'd thought for a long time that living was over, but he'd been wrong. There was a lot more to be done, and it was up to him how he did it: full of misery and self-pity or choosing to live again. Sinking deeper into the bleakness or moving forward.

It was scary, and it was hard, but he wanted to move forward. He'd been afraid before. He'd taken up residence in hard. Now...

He took a long look at JJ, curled on the sofa, relaxed and easy and pretty and tempting. Now, he wanted more.

When her yawns started making her eyes water, JJ sighed deeply, stood up and stretched her arms high above her head. In her own shirt, the move would have exposed her flat, pale stomach. In Quint's T-shirt, it didn't bare anything at all. She wondered how much he valued the shirt. It had been one of a half dozen in various shades of dark fabric folded on that closet shelf. The brand stamped inside the neckline was faded, but it was a common, inexpensive one. It was, in fact, probably one from that five-year-old six-pack his niece Lia had teased him about. That made her feel a little better about her plans to not return it tomorrow. Or ever. She wanted a souvenir that reminded her of how he felt and looked and smelled, and what better than a scruffy shirt?

"I should go." She glanced around for Chica and found her curled in a tiny ball behind the sofa, eyes closed. "Let sleeping dogs lie," she murmured, heading toward the door in a route that didn't take her past the dog. "I learned that lesson with Tako, my sheepdog. His alertness factor when he was wide-awake was somewhere close to comatose for human beings, but he had a startle reflex when he was sleeping that was impressive. Given that he weighed about ninety pounds, and his most favorite place in the world when he was scared was in my arms, I never, ever disturbed his sleep if I could avoid it."

"Tako's not a respectable name for a sheepdog," Quint chided, taking her coat from the front closet and holding it while she slipped her arms into it.

"No, Shep is not a respectable name for a sheepdog. That's what his original owner named him." She rolled her eyes. "I called him Tako, which is Japanese for octopus, because when he got hold of something he wasn't supposed to have, he held on like he had eight arms with suction cups. His original owner sold him because the only creatures he ever wanted to herd were kids. I discovered that, oddly, city moms didn't like their kids being herded by a dog two to three times their size."

"Not his fault the herding instinct was wonky."

She smiled at the memory of the big fuzzy baby. "One day he got out of the yard and came home with four of the neighbors' kids. Another time, during the summer of Maura, she and I were taking a walk, so we stopped by the house and got him. Maura loved dogs and thought he was the coolest thing ever. She had his leash, and everything was fine until we got to the edge of the park. He heard the kids on the playground, shot off and yanked Maura off her feet. Her fingers got caught in the leash, and two of them were broken, and the mothers were screaming because Tako had gathered the kids in the middle of the playground and wouldn't let them go.

"I was horrified. Mr. and Mrs. Evans had trusted me with their daughter, and my dog had broken her and traumatized half the young kids in town along with their mothers." She heaved a dramatic sigh. "I just wanted to climb high into the nearest oak and hide until it was all over."

"But the Evanses didn't have you shot, Maura recovered, Tako went on to herd other small humans and you survived." He reached out then, to tuck a strand of hair behind her ear. It was an easy movement, but she would bet he hadn't done it or anything similar in sixteen months. Bet he hadn't touched anyone in any way that might even hint of intimacy.

And she would have won that bet, because his hand, when he drew it back, was trembling the tiniest bit. Inside, she was trembling a whole lot. She was suddenly warm and fluttery, and her lungs were getting tight and her heart was *pat*ting only once for every two *pit*s.

What if she touched him back? Brushed her hand through his hair? Rubbed the backs of her fingers across the beard stubble that darkened his cheek? Cupped his face in both her hands and pulled him down and planted a greedy hungry kiss right on his oh-so-very-kissable mouth? Would he be tempted, the way he'd been with Maura, or appalled that JJ had somehow gotten the wrong idea?

His blue eyes were serious, intense—the norm for him. Their depths were too shadowy to identify anything else. Desire, arousal. Surprise, revulsion. Embarrassment. Delight. She did see a muscle twitch at the corner of his mouth. She felt the tension humming in the air between them, a big, warm, indecisive, nerves-on-edge sort of tension.

She really wanted to grab him anyway.

But she also really wanted a sign from him, like maybe *him* grabbing *her* and planting one on her. She needed him to want her as much as she wanted him.

With an inward sigh of regret, she wrapped her fingers around the doorknob and opened the door. Cold air raced inside, backed by a wind from the south. Behind them, Chica gave a tiny whimper, but she didn't waken. "Thank you for dinner. And for taking Chica. I really, really do appreciate it."

She was poised to go outside and hustle to her car, but at the last instant, she swung back, rose onto her toes and pressed as innocent a kiss as she could summon to his jaw. A flush rolled across his face, and his breath caught, and for just a moment she felt downright giddy with sensation. A smile bubbled up and spread across her face as she darted back and turned to walk outside.

Just as suddenly as the door had swung open, it shut with a decisive click. Quint's hand rested flat on the wood above JJ's head as he reached around her and secured the lock with his other hand. She stood frozen, all the nerves in her body doing fancy zips and twirls, her breath shallow and rapid, a puny accompaniment to his slow, steady, even breathing a few inches behind her.

She huddled there for five or twenty or sixty seconds, unsure what to do next, and then his body pressed against hers from behind, solid and warm, and his mouth brushed her temple, soft and wicked. Her hair stirred. Her heart stirred, gaining strength and speed with each beat. Instinctively, she tilted her head to the left, exposing more of her face to him, and then she closed her eyes so she could concentrate her whole being on this moment.

Quint was taller, broader, sturdier, the kind of guy who made her feel a hundred percent safe, the kind of guy who would protect her or help her out if she needed it. She rarely needed it, but she still appreciated that he could. That he would. After so many years of being the one who did the protecting and the serving and the helping, it was a lovely feeling to know she could abdicate the responsibility if she wanted.

On rare occasions, when she was feeling really girly, she wanted. For a bit.

He was in no rush, finally reaching her ear and making her shiver with delight. She loved discovering erogenous zones, hers and his, like a new experience every time, and she delighted again when his teeth lightly nipped the lobe of her ear before he continued moving lower, lower.

At this pace, it might take all night to reach the bits of her that were really erogenous. Hours and hours of pure sensual pleasure…

She shifted restlessly, torn between staying exactly as she was and savoring every single muscle-tightening second of his exploration, and turning to face him so she could do some exploration of her own. Savoring lost to need. She twisted in the small space between his body and the door, wrapped her arms around his neck and kissed him again.

This time it didn't involve his jaw. It didn't exist in the same universe as innocence. This time it was eager and demanding and so needy that it sent tremors through her. She rose onto her toes, pushed harder, held him tighter, tried to fuse her body to his so she could have a part of him, be a part of him, forever.

From somewhere came a whimper. Chica? JJ thought

blankly, then felt rather than heard the sound again. It came from her, deep in her throat, a wordless plea for more heat, more sensation, more needing, more wanting, more everything and now, right now.

And an answer, deeper in tone, nearly a growl, from Quint, too. She pulled free of his mouth and opened her eyes and saw him staring at her, the same stark look she was sure was on her face, and she wondered—no, prayed—he hadn't suddenly decided she was too poor a substitute for Belinda.

The fear stirred by the possibility was small but very real. Before it had time to coalesce into insecurity and rejection, he brushed his lips across hers, then stayed so close that she felt each movement, each tiny puff of air, as he whispered, "You are so…" Trailing off, he nuzzled her cheek with bristly beard and soft lips, then finished the thought. "Bright."

Bright. Another tremor flirted through her, this time making her eyes damp. She'd been called a lot of things at times like this: pretty, beautiful, sexy, hot, even gorgeous. But bright almost brought her to her knees. He had mourned so deeply. He'd immersed himself in such a dark lonely place, spiritually and emotionally, that he'd lost touch with everything that was good and light.

And she was *bright*.

It was the sweetest compliment she'd ever been given. And the sexiest. And she was torn in that moment between how much she wanted him and how very much she didn't want to hurt him. A fling…that was all she'd been after when she met him. A night or three of great sex, no strings attached, no emotions attached, and some excellent memories for the future.

But she hadn't known his story then. Hadn't known *him*. She hadn't known how quickly she would fall for him. She didn't want just a fling anymore. She wanted strings and emotions and complications and great sex and more, endless hours more, of those slow lazy kisses, and she hoped—thought—he did, too, and she didn't want the fact that she was leaving soon to hurt him in any way. He'd had too much hurt already.

The intensity in his gaze sharpened, and he bent his head until their foreheads touched, until the tip of his nose touched the tip of hers. "Don't you dare."

The places where their skin was in contact sizzled, and she briefly wished he'd left the door open to let the cold in. She was positive steam would rise from her entire body if he had. "Don't what?"

"Decide what's best for me. That I can't handle this. That I'm still not over Linny, that I'm not ready, that I can't have you. I'll never be over Linny. I'll always love her. But that doesn't mean I can't want you. I've been broken a long time, JJ, and you make me feel…" His eyes closed, and he dragged in a raspy breath. "You give me hope, and if that's all I come out of this with, it's still a hell of a lot more than I had before. I want you. Tonight. Tomorrow. For as long as I can have you. Don't break my heart for my own good."

Her heart hurt. Her lungs refused to expand, and her muscles felt as if she'd just finished a twenty-mile run in sand: weak, quivery, jerky. She hadn't expected how quickly she'd fallen for Quint, nor had she guessed how deeply until that very moment. Who'd have known words could affect her so thoroughly?

She summoned a smile, unsure if it was a mischievous or naughty one, seductive or just damned happy, and she pressed a kiss to his mouth before shrugging out of her coat, taking his hand and turning toward the stairs. The sight of Chica, sprawled on her back, snoring with her legs propped against the sofa, stopped her. "Better put Chica in her cell."

This time she knew her smile was the wicked one. "We don't want to traumatize the baby."

Though he hadn't chosen anything in the bedroom, it had always been Quint's favorite room in the house. Walking through the door was pretty much guaranteed to lower his blood pressure, ease the tension in his muscles and quiet the chaos outside its four walls. Most nights.

Tonight, watching chaos on two legs stroll into the room, the first two benefits flip-flopped. His heart was pounding, and his muscles were strung tight enough to hum, but it was still easy to put everything else in the world out of his mind. Tonight—for a few nights—the only things that mattered were in this room: JJ and him.

The only light came from the moon, nearly full in the sky, and the hall light. Standing in the doorway, he considered flipping the switch beside him so he could see every detail, but he decided he preferred the intimacy of the shadows. She was bright enough all on her own to dispel the dark.

She stood near the bed. Balancing gracefully, she bent one knee, undid the zip on her boot and pulled it off, then switched positions and removed the other. Instead of dropping them, the way he would if he hadn't taken off his own boots earlier, she set them side by side against the wall, out of the way of virtually anything that might happen in the room.

"I've always found undressing to be the least romantic part of sex," she said, her hands sliding underneath the baggy shirt of his that she wore. Her tone was casual, but there was nothing casual about the huskiness in her voice. Regardless of the words she was saying, that voice was an invitation all on its own. "Unless I've dressed for that specific moment. You know, like a formal event where I wear a dress and very little, if anything, else. But regular clothes...buttons, belts, zippers, shoes, jeans... There's just so many opportunities for awkwardness and clumsiness, and I really prefer most of the time to just cut to the chase."

She pushed, bent, did a little wiggle, and removed her jeans. She handled them carefully, the belt still in its loops, the Taser and her pistol holstered on either side of the waistband. She folded the jeans with the weapons on top and set them on the chair in the corner, tossed her socks there, too, then barefooted, bare-legged, she slowly approached him.

"Those are my thoughts on undressing," she said as she came nearer. "You, of course, are entitled to your own preferences." Stopping so near he felt the heat radiating from her, she toyed with the hem of his shirt. "I can undress you. I can help you undress yourself. I can lie back and enjoy the view while you undress yourself, or you can—"

He tugged the fabric gently from her fingers, then pulled the shirt over his head. "Make that offer again in a few hours." His own voice was husky, his throat closing off just from looking at her in the too-big shirt that ended mid–muscular thighs, that led to muscular calves, that led to delicately arched feet. She looked innocent and tempting and teasing and sultry. Put her in a dress that was fitted and sexy with very little underneath, and damn, his heart would stop. It was already stuttering in his chest.

His weapons were already on the nightstand, so there were no holsters to dally with. He shucked his jeans in a couple seconds flat, taking his boxers with them, peeling off his socks at the same time. He was nothing if not efficient.

He stood there naked in the room he'd shared so many nights with Linny, erection straining, heart thudding, nerves quivering, all for another woman. For JJ. He waited for some sense of shame, guilt, some little whisper that this was wrong, but none came, and he knew why: because it wasn't wrong. It was the rightest thing he'd done in far too long.

He stepped forward, invading her space but not yet touching her. He could hear her breathing, feel the soft puffs, see the rise and fall of her chest. Her offer a moment ago had been careless, but there was nothing casual or easy about her now. Her heart was pounding, too. Her skin was also feverish. Her arousal was throbbing, rising, and anticipation danced like a wild spirit along her veins, making standing still impossible.

For a long time, he stared at her, imprinting every detail, every freckle, every shiver, every tiny emotion that crowded her hazel eyes. Had he honestly thought only a few days ago that there was nothing special about the way she looked? He'd been stupid blind. She was gorgeous. Amazing. She made him want and need and feel.

He hadn't felt in so damn long.

In the dim light, her eyes widened, and her lips parted, just a little, a small exhalation of *oh*. Soft. Awed. She raised her trembling fingers to his mouth, and he realized he was smiling.

He hadn't smiled in so damn long.

"You're beautiful when you smile," she whispered, cupping her hands to his face.

Before her last word disappeared into the air, he kissed her, hard and hungry, backing her to the bed, hastily pulling the shirt over her head. In the instant between her lying back on the mattress and his moving over her, he saw that she was naked, too. Like him, she'd efficiently removed her underwear with her jeans.

Naked and gorgeous and his.

There was a time that bright day, standing in the driveway of the Madison house with Maura, that he'd missed this—being with a woman, skin to skin, blood boiling like crazy—so much that he'd almost, *almost* been willing to take it from anyone. He'd craved the physical part badly enough that he could have forgotten about the emotional part, but some small sane part of him had known he would regret it.

He would never regret this.

He could lie there, his body pressed to hers, kissing her, exploring her mouth with his tongue and everywhere else with his hands, for hours. Forever. Then he mentally snorted. In another minute or two, he would explode into a seething mess of nothing but need, hunger and plain old wanting.

Her fingers brushed across his flesh, dragging from him a guttural noise and stiffening him even more.

Breathing in shallow, desperate pants, she said, "I…forgot…condom…"

Sweat dotted his forehead, and hers, too, and heat came off them both in waves, even though in his mind, he knew the room was cool. He admired that she was coherent enough to think of protection and was grateful that the incident with Maura had prompted him, for the first time in more than a decade, to buy a box of condoms. "I have some."

She grinned. "Thank you, Maura."

He leaned across to reach the top drawer of the night table, to snag a condom from the unused box there, then returned to her. Before he could free his other hand to open the package, she grinned again, grabbed the edge and ripped. He caught it before it slipped from his fingers, and the wrapper separated neatly.

So many opportunities for awkwardness and clumsiness, JJ had mentioned earlier. At this moment, he decided, hers were the most talented fingers in the world. They had the condom in place in seconds, and then she pulled *him* into place, tugging, thrusting upward to meet him, and when he was sheathed deeply inside her, he felt a minute of utter peace and comfort and belonging.

Followed instantly by utter chaos.

It was incredible.

Chapter 9

JJ had some experience with waking up and not knowing where she was, but that didn't happen this time. The instant her brain struggled up to awareness, she knew exactly where she was: in Quint's bed. In his arms. She thought she might stay there forever.

She lay on her left side, facing the southern windows. Even though it was the middle of the night, the room practically glowed in the pale light, as if it had absorbed all the quiet of the day and reflected it back during the night.

Her body was warmed in back by Quint's, but her front side was cool and goose bumpy. Should she try to maneuver under the covers without waking him, or just turn over and let him warm that side next? She debated the question for a while, but in the end she decided she was too lazy—too comfortable—to move. Cool was bearable. If she got cold, she might change her mind.

From downstairs came a whimper. Was Chica having bad dreams? Was she lonely, afraid or unsure about her new home? Did she think her humans had abandoned her again?

When she barked once, loud and sharp, JJ figured the disturbance was more along the lines of my-puppy-bladder-is-full. Quint stirred beside her, golden in the thin light, looking tired and wickedly handsome and easy.

He did *easy* so well.

"Baby needs to go out," he murmured.

"I'll take her." She started to wriggle out from beneath his arm, but it tightened across her middle. Glancing over her shoulder, she saw his eyes were open now, his look so intense she could feel it in a sweet, intimate way caressing her body.

Chica barked again, and he released her. "I'll go. It's dark."

She sniffed disdainfully as she pulled on his shirt, then stepped into her jeans. "I'm not afraid of the dark. My Taser has a flashlight, and Herr Glock keeps me safe." She patted both weapons, shoved her feet into her boots, then bent over to kiss his cheek. "Go back to sleep. I've got plans for you later."

He grunted, closed his eyes and resumed his deep breathing. With a light from below for illumination, she made her way down the hall and the stairs, grabbed her jacket and released Chica from the kennel. The puppy dashed to the back door, doing an impatient little dance while JJ hooked on the leash, unlocked the door and then hustled down the steps with her.

While Chica searched for the most appropriate blades of grass, JJ unholstered the Taser and turned on the flashlight. Her feet felt icky in her boots without socks, her, um, other parts felt strangely airy without panties and it was a good thirty degrees colder outside than in. "This isn't going to be a thing, is it?" she asked the dog, who was head down, quivering butt up a few feet away.

Chica pretended not to hear.

"Because I get really cranky being woken up in the middle of the night so someone can pee. I mean, I didn't have kids for a reason, right?" She rubbed her nose with the hand that held the Taser, making the light bob crazily. "Of course, that's not the only reason. And I was actually already awake, so you didn't really wake me up. But come on, you have all day long to pee, and Quint took you out after we, uh, well, you don't need details."

She'd been too sated to move anything but her gaze then, studying the long line of his spine when he sat up, and the curve of his butt when he stood, and the lean muscular legs as he walked into the closet. He came back out in sweatpants, but knowing what they covered, she found that view pretty damn nice, too.

It seemed like Chica had taken care of business much more quickly with him. Frost was starting to form on parts of JJ's body that normally didn't get that cold, and the dog was still stalking across the ground, burying her nose into every tuft of grass.

But the night was gorgeous. Quiet. Soft. The sky spread overhead like velvet, the stars glittering like randomly scattered jewels and the air smelled fresh and springlike. New, clean, full of promise.

Oh, she did love promise.

Finally Chica settled on a spot, then they jogged back to the house. JJ reholstered her Taser, rekenneled the baby, dropped her coat on the couch and made a semi-frozen rush back to the bedroom. Quint had slid under the covers while she was gone, and as soon as she undressed, he opened his arms, holding the linens high enough for her to dive in next to him.

"Next time I offer to take her out, maybe you'll agree and stay warm." He wrapped his arms around her, snuggled her tightly to his overly warm body and shifted one leg to rest on her hip and legs.

"Maybe." But being held like this was so worth a few minutes of frigid air.

"Just for the record…" He nuzzled her hair back and kissed her forehead. "This going out in the middle of the night might very well be a thing."

She tilted her head back to give him a narrow look. "Were you making sure I was qualified to take Chica out?"

Her scowl didn't perturb him at all. "I just checked out the window to make sure she wasn't taking you for a wild dash around the property. I could carry her back if she got worn out. You, I'm not so sure about."

She was an adult, serious and responsible. She wouldn't do anything as juvenile as seeing if he was ticklish or poking him in the chest—which was so solid it would probably just hurt her fingertip. Instead, like a thoroughly mature woman, she rolled on top of him, pinning his arms to the bed and straddling his hips, sliding ever so slowly over his penis, back and forth, as his erection sprang to life.

"I'm a cop. I'm strong. My sister's a firefighter, and I dated several firefighters. I could carry *you* back."

As she continued rubbing her pelvis against his, he

lifted his head to kiss her. Laughing, she drew back out of reach.

"You know, I could flip you over without even trying," he pointed out, his tone even, his voice just the slightest bit breathless.

"I know, but remember I said I had plans for you later?" She released his arms then, sitting straighter, and guided his hands to her breasts. The simple sensation of his fingers against her nipples made her gasp and sent a jolt of pure pleasure through her. "Well, sweetie, it's later."

Mornings were different when Quint wasn't alone in the house.

He hadn't forgotten that. He'd just become so accustomed to the freaking emptiness that hovered everywhere. No one hurrying him through a shower. No one to offer a cup of coffee. No one to discuss the upcoming day or how well they had or hadn't slept or about the dream they couldn't escape.

This morning, JJ didn't harry him about the shower. She just climbed into the big tub with him. Chica greeted them with excited yips and barks when they finally made it downstairs. Both females went outside with him, both too perky given that it was still mostly dark outside, both tempting him to relax and even smile when they faced off at one point, each menacing in her own way.

"What time is lunch with Maura?" he asked as Chica finally did what she had to and they headed back inside.

"I suggested eleven. She said twelve, so it'll probably be closer to one."

"Any idea where you're going?"

"Nope. I'm hoping for someplace here in town, but I doubt anything's pricey enough to make her happy. I'll probably spend a hundred bucks on a sliver of beef, two slices of blue potato and three baby green beans, and I'll still be starving when I walk out the door."

He nudged her inside, then cut Chica loose from her leash. "I'll fix a big dinner."

JJ grinned. "I'll eat it." In a quick change of topic, she asked, "You know anyone in the local FBI office?"

"I do." He checked the clock. He'd intended to cook breakfast this morning—it had been a long time since he'd hauled out his cast-iron skillet for bacon and eggs—but the shower interruption had put him behind schedule. It was the type of disruption he could happily embrace.

"Could you check on any female Mels who flew from Tulsa to New Orleans in December? Any fed worth his badge will cringe at the idea of searching for only a partial first name, no last name, no Social Security number and no date of birth, but surely there's a limited number of names that Mel's a reasonable nickname for."

"I'll call when I get into the station." He cut four thick slices from the leftover bread, buttered them, popped them into the toaster oven and took a tub of cream cheese from the refrigerator while they browned. "You want to come over?"

"Yeah, after I go to the hotel and change. I'd better call Mr. Winchester, too, and maybe even Dipstick. Why don't you text me when you're ready?" She slid onto a stool, legs crossed, spine straight. With her makeup mostly gone, her hair in a ponytail and her weapons not visible thanks to the island, she looked half his age and twice as innocent.

But after last night he knew for a fact that she wasn't innocent at all.

As he started the coffee, he wondered why he didn't feel more…*something* this morning. Awkward, maybe. Nervous. Guilty. Just as Linny had been removed from his life, so had any hint of intimacy. He had never imagined he would feel it again. Hadn't even hoped. Yet here was JJ. A gift from the God he'd stopped praying to.

And he hadn't lied last night. For the first time in months, he'd awakened with the calm comfort of hope. Even if this thing between them didn't go anywhere, he would always have that.

They ate quietly, Chica munching on her nuggets while casting longing looks at their toast. With that done, and one last trip around the yard with the pup, he and JJ left in separate vehicles. He wondered if any of his neighbors had noticed the strange car in the driveway. He knew everyone who lived within a half mile of him. Linny had been big on neighborhood cookouts, and they had all come to her funeral. He hadn't seen much of them since then. Not because they hadn't tried. He just couldn't.

After a couple hours of patrol around the school complexes and on the main route to Tulsa, Quint went into the station. He got a cup of coffee, then stopped by Sam's office, standing in the open door. His boss was on the phone, but he motioned to him to wait.

The phone calls were one thing Quint didn't miss about the assistant chief's job. He'd spent most of his time communicating in some way with someone—calls, emails, faxes, letters, meetings—and very little time on the actual police work that had drawn him to the job in the first place. Though he was ashamed of the actions that had led to his demotion, he was glad he was out of the position. He didn't want to go back.

When Sam hung up, he gestured to a stack of messages on his desk. "JJ's chief. Is she not keeping him informed?"

"She talked to him yesterday morning." Quint didn't mention that she'd ignored a call from Chadwick last night. That would mean explaining everything. It didn't matter how determined a person was to not tell all, Sam still managed to find it out.

Not that it was a secret. Not that he even wanted it to be a secret. Besides, Rhonda knew, and she would surely tell his mother or sisters soon, if not already, and then Lois would find out, and that meant no hope for privacy ever again.

Sam's narrowed gaze made Quint offer more of an explanation. "The chief's running the department, but the lawyer's running this sideshow. The chief's decided he wants to cut the lawyer out of the loop. He wants to control whatever information JJ comes up with, and he'll probably use it to undermine her."

"So the chief and the lawyer are about to get in a pissing contest with JJ in the mid—" Sam broke off and grimaced. "Damn. Forget I said that. That would explain why Chadwick is wanting a moment-by-moment update. Not on the case, on her."

"Should I keep a log?" Quint asked drily. *3:00 p.m. Noticed for the hundredth time how pretty she is. 5:00 p.m. Thought about kissing her. 5:10 p.m. Wanted to kiss her. 6:00 p.m. Saw her in wet shirt and* really *wanted to kiss her. 8:49 p.m. Kissed her. Had good sex with her. Had great sex with her. Slept beside her. Found out "later" is a very good thing.*

Yep, that would just delight Chief Dipstick.

Sam shook his head. "I'll call him later. Maybe I can get him to back off a little. So... I'm guessing she's not satisfied with whatever she's learned."

"She babysat Maura one entire summer. She wants to be sure the kid really is okay. She doesn't want to just go with the popular conclusion that Maura's a spoiled brat if there really is something going on." Quint shifted his weight. "Zander Benson's living there with her. She bought him a new motorcycle."

"Mila and I are looking for new wheels, too," Sam said wistfully.

"Yeah, yours will be attached to a baby carriage."

Sam nodded, but he didn't look for one second like he regretted that. He was so ready to be a father, and better suited for the job than just about anyone Quint knew.

"Anytime Zander's involved, there's trouble." The desk phone rang, and Sam glanced at it. "Best-case scenario, he's seduced himself into her bank account. It's her right to be a sucker for a good-looking guy. But worst case..."

"He might be planning to take every million she's got. Even the best case is a problem if she's not competent and he's taking advantage of it." Quint backed up. "I'll be in the conference room for a while if you need anything."

Sam nodded, already speaking into the phone.

Everything about Maura's behavior shift traced back

to mid-December, the time of Mel's leaving. One more loss than Maura could bear? With no more of a name to go by, their chances of finding the woman on their own were between nil and none. But as JJ had suggested, the FBI could do an indices search and give them a list of airline passengers traveling during the proper time frame. It might or might not be a daunting list, but he and JJ had the time for the grunt work of narrowing it down. From there, focusing on particular passengers on specific flights, they could view the surveillance footage from the Tulsa airport and, at least, confirm that Mel got on the plane.

It wasn't much. Just one small part of Maura's story they could prove.

Before he picked up the phone, he texted JJ. Her response came quickly. Be there soon.

A warm, comforting kind of feeling went through him. It was still lingering while he waited on hold for his FBI agent friend when his cell beeped again.

Who is this woman you cooked dinner for last night? His sister Diane. I can't believe you told Rhonda about her before us. Usually, her texts were long and rambling, but this morning she must be hitting Send with the completion of every thought, which suggested she was excited or upset.

What is her name?
Where is she from?
Why would you introduce her to Lia before your favorite sister?

He loved Diane, and their sister Emily, and their

brother Dean, and especially his parents, but he had no intention of making a big production out of this. With JJ's time in town so limited, he didn't want to share any of it with anyone else.

Rather than ignore her—an impossible task, he'd learned when they were kids—he took the coward's way out. Busy. Will talk to you later. Rhonda and Lia right place, right time. I thought Emily was my favorite.

He'd just sent the message when the agent came on the phone. He'd met Chrissie at a bank robbery a few years earlier, and they'd traded information a few times since. Her British accent lent the agency some class, Morwenna, also British, said with pride, and she was unfazed by his request.

"You've heard of the needle in the haystack?" she asked, her keyboard clicking quietly in the background.

"I have, but my next option is to search the entire city of Memphis for a woman named Mel who was there for an unknown period of time six months ago."

"I see your point. Besides, how many Mels could there be?" she asked optimistically.

The door opened, and JJ slipped inside. She wore a gray-and-purple-plaid shirt underneath the purple boyfriend sweater. A delicate gray stone, polished to a high sheen, rested at the base of her throat on a silver chain, and snug-fitting gray trousers and boots finished the outfit. She looked incredible. Sensual. Womanly. Blissful.

The coming-home warmth eased through him again. Last night had been about as close to perfect as real life ever came, but with that one look, he knew it would never be enough. He would always want more.

She smiled at him as she set her bag in a chair. He found it harder than he expected to smile back. Some things were easier in a moonlit room, without clothing and distance and defenses to hide behind. He managed, though. Just an uptick at the corners of his mouth that faded the instant Chrissie began speaking in his ear.

Eleven was the answer to her earlier question. Eleven female versions of Mel had traveled from Tulsa to New Orleans during that time period. Six of them were over the age of forty and one was nine, which left four in the right age range. Though Chrissie said she would email the information to him, she gave him the names over the phone, and he scrawled them onto a notepad.

While he thanked her, JJ came around the table and leaned over his shoulder, bringing her fresh, sweet, unforgettable scent with her. She didn't kiss him—he wished she would, even if they were in the station, even if someone might walk in the door any moment—but she laid her hand on his shoulder, and her hair, worn loose now, gently brushed his cheek.

Intimacy.

"'Melinda Andrews, Melanie Britton, Melanie Jackson, Melody Smithfield,'" she read. In his peripheral vision, her nose wrinkled. "Morwenna said her last name was common, like Smith or Jones. Can you call up DMV photos?"

Quint traded the ink pen for the laptop. The first three searches yielded photographs of women who bore not the slightest resemblance to Maura. There was no hit on Melody Smithfield, reasonable considering—if she was the one—she'd lived in Oklahoma only three months. If she was as transient as Maura had been the last five years, odds were good that she didn't have a license anywhere, especially as disadvantaged as people thought she'd been.

That done, he slid the computer to JJ while he made arrangements to get airport surveillance footage. She Googled and Facebooked and Instagrammed and found nothing. Along with her personality and, apparently, her emotional stability, Maura's social media presence had suffered during her time in Cedar Creek.

Just how emotionally unstable might she be?

And how was he going to hide how much he hated the idea of JJ going off alone with her?

Nearly an hour passed before the emailed airport footage arrived. This particular video was from the security gates. A steady line of people streamed through—personal belongings, belts and shoes in tubs, passing through the metal detector, some directed to the side for wanding, others reclaiming their property from the conveyor belt.

JJ spotted a blonde in line, but as the woman slowly moved forward, placing a leather bag and a pair of heels in a tub, her face was obscured by the shifting people and the equipment around her. If someone moved this way, she went that; if a structure hid her from the camera, she stood squarely behind it. Almost as if she was avoiding it.

Then, abruptly, she looked straight at it.

Quint stopped the video, and they both stared at it for a long time. Finally, JJ sank back in her chair. "Wow."

Brown hair and brown eyes, Georgie Madison had said of Mel, but both hair and eye color were easy to change. Blond and blue, both Morwenna and Lois had said. Strong resemblance, all three of them had said. That was an understatement. The woman frozen on the video looked enough like Maura Evans to be her twin.

"Zoey said Maura dressed Mel up like a doll." JJ's voice was quiet. She managed to keep it level, but distaste for the situation still darkened it. "She said she was turning her into a clone of herself."

She must have liked the idea of taking someone she considered less than herself and creating her own mini me. The notion was egotistical and arrogant, even for someone like Maura. Worse, it was flat-out creepy. JJ couldn't imagine thinking herself so perfect that anyone else should aspire to be like her, or anyone thinking she was so perfect that they wanted to be like her. It was just icky.

"Miss Georgie said Mel had a hunger about her, as if she'd never had anything. She must have been desperate, thinking she was just so much nothing." Quint's solemn features were marked with sympathy for a woman he'd never met. He was a good guy that way. He was a good guy in all ways. "She must have thought she'd landed in the middle of a fairy tale when she met Maura. The beautiful princess taking in the poor peasant, feeding and clothing her, giving her everything her heart desires, and all the peasant has to do is stop being. Become nothing but the princess's mirror image."

JJ's hand was a little shaky when she gestured to the screen. "By this time, there was no Mel. It was just Maura and Maura 2.0. Maybe that's why she left. Maybe she realized she couldn't be Maura 2.0 for the rest of her life."

"Or not," he quietly disagreed.

JJ studied the image again, backed the video up to the point where Mel first came into view, then let it run all the way through, to where she walked out of the camera's range. She wore a royal purple dress that looked as if it had been designed and sewn with her in mind, along with a pair of incredible heels. Sizable diamonds studded her earlobes, with others sparkling in two necklaces, two bracelets and a watch. JJ didn't know brands once the price exceeded not-even-in-her-dreams, but she recognized the signature fabric of the purse as Burberry, only because Elle's husband had given her one to celebrate the tenth anniversary of her contracting business.

The woman in the video didn't look as if she'd lost herself, as if she was escaping a bizarre situation in order to reclaim her identity. She looked, simply, like a pretty, wealthy young woman. The clothes were expensive, the haircut obscenely so, the color job so skillfully done that it looked natural. She walked, even stood, with grace and elegance, and her air of boredom was over-the-top perfect. Everyone around was beneath her notice: the man in front of her who held up the line to retrieve personal belongings, the kids behind her who were bouncing with excitement, the screening employee who handed her bag to her. They weren't people. They were obstructions keeping her from her destination, and they were way too close for the princess's comfort.

No, this definitely was not a young woman running away from something.

"Tell me I'm a cynic," JJ said, propping her left hand under her cheek. "But the first thing I think, looking at her, on her way to New Orleans, is that there are a lot of rich men in New Orleans. That Mel is probably thinking she's learned all she needs from Maura, so she's heading off to a warmer climate to find another rich person to support her in the style she's become accustomed to. She's probably thinking a man this time. The odds of Maura losing patience with or interest in Mel and kicking her out are pretty good, but a man who likes a pretty face and a pretty body is so much easier to manipulate. To hold on to."

"If you're a cynic, so am I." Quint shifted in his chair, giving her a better view of his sinfully handsome face. "When a friend drops you, it's hard to make a claim for money. When a rich man drops you, it's pretty much a given that he's going to have to pay."

Judging by Mel's demeanor on the video, something they confirmed by speeding ahead to the camera at the gate and watching her while she waited to board, there was no great drama in her leaving, at least not on her part. It seemed safe to assume that Maura had happily waved goodbye to her with Zander at her side, that there had been no hearts broken on either part. Mel had simply gone off to find her own fairy tale to star in.

JJ wasn't aware she was twisting the ring on her finger until Quint stilled the motion, then drew her hand close to study the stone. "What is this?"

"Mexican fire opal." She gazed fondly at it. "It's supposed to be a symbol of hope and innocence. My mother gave it to me when I graduated from the police academy. She wanted it to keep me in the light."

"It must be working."

It was, because last night he'd called her *bright*. The memory sent warm whispers curling through her, easing tension here, tightening it there, stirring the butterflies in her stomach from their nap into lazy swoops and twirls of pleasure.

He clasped her hand in his, and it fit. Though his hand was larger and her fingers were shorter, they matched perfectly. There was something totally reassuring about looking at them. No wonder wedding photographers came up with a standard shot of brides and grooms holding hands. The symbolism was powerful.

But a glance at the time swirled a different kind of tension. "We'd better be going. I assume you're picking up your personal vehicle or borrowing one?"

"I'm taking mine. I'm not sure Maura recognizes something that old as a vehicle. I'll park at the fast-food place at the end of the street. You'll have to pass me to get out."

"And you're only a short run away if things go south at the house." JJ stood but didn't move out of the way as he also stood. "Not that I have any intention of letting things go south."

"We never do. The problem is bad guys don't ask our permission before they throw the first punch or fire the first shot or make a run for it." He took one step forward, all the space she'd allowed him, and smiled down at her. The smile still wasn't smooth; it was as if instinct started it, brain interrupted, then let it finish. "That's what you've got me for."

The warmth of his body, though they weren't actually touching, was palpable, intense. A glance at his eyes, a glance lower, and she knew it wouldn't take any effort at all to fan the heat into a blaze fueling one impressive hard-on. If only they could go to her hotel instead of Maura's house…

Sighing regretfully, she backed away and wove around chairs and cast-off furniture to the doorway. As they walked down the hallway, a scuffle of noise came from the bullpen. Not a struggle but people jumping and rushing out. They turned the corner by the counter in time to see Ben Little Bear and Lois disappearing in the back, where stairs led to the sally port below and the exit there. The thundering sound of footsteps suggested that other officers were ahead of them.

"What's up, Morwenna?" Quint asked the dispatcher, standing in the doorway of the shack.

"Hey, JJ. I didn't see you come in." She shifted her attention to Quint. "You know Mr. Latham, lives out by Two-Mile Park? His dog Angel was out exploring, and she brought him home a present. Part of a human leg, apparently. Most of the tissue's gone. Simpson got the call, and he is totally grossed out. This isn't even his first dead body, though it may be his first body part. That boy's got to develop a stronger stomach or stick to writing speeding tickets."

They called goodbye to her and continued to the main entrance, where JJ pushed the heavy door open. "I hate body parts. Chica had better never bring home anything that used to be attached to a person. I don't think there's enough doggy mouthwash in the world to make me okay with that."

As they stepped outside, the temperature was in the low seventies, and the sun was shining brightly. This was the kind of weather she'd been expecting when she'd packed for the trip. She fished shades out of her bag and slid them on. "You wish you were out with them instead of babysitting me?"

He slid on his own dark glasses, looking—just like the first time she'd seen him—like a golden god in khaki. "I hate body parts, too, and..."

When she would have started toward the hotel the next street over, he steered her toward his truck. Facing each other over the bed, he said, "I saw my share of them when I was a detective. I don't care to see any more."

He got into the truck, and JJ stood there, her brows arched to meet her hairline. Hastily, she climbed inside. "You were a detective?"

He started the engine and fastened his seat belt with more care than needed, then sat motionless a moment. Clearly, he'd decided to confide something in her. Just as clearly, he was having second thoughts.

So, clearly, her response had to be just right. Not too much surprise, no censure, no disappointment.

Finally he fixed a rueful look on her. "Did you think I stayed in patrol twenty years because I wasn't good enough to promote or bad enough to fire?"

She'd run into that attitude, both with cops and civilians. As a brand-new cop, she'd kept an eye on the calendar, eager for that first chance to move up the food chain. It had always been her intent to do minimal time on the street, then advance, advance, advance. But that was her, not everyone, and she knew it. "I thought you stayed in patrol because you liked it there. A lot of people do."

"I made detective when I was twenty-seven. Five years ago, I became assistant chief. Four months ago, I was drowning my sorrow in a bottle. I showed up at a domestic violence case, and I—" He drew a deep breath and forced the rest out on his exhale. "I punched the handcuffed suspect."

He looked at her, awaiting judgment, and she steadily looked back, her brain working furiously. The flippant part of her wanted to ask, *Did he deserve it?* The protect-and-serve part of her was stunned. The cop part of her wanted to say, *Good job*, and the woman part of her who had comforted far too many victims of abuse wanted to applaud. Justice in domestic violence cases could be swift, it could be fleeting or it could be non-existent. She figured this was one suspect who would never forget the time he'd received swift justice.

Grimly, he looked away. "We're supposed to be better than the people we arrest."

"We are. But God knows, we're not perfect. The Quint before Linny passed never would have showed up drunk or laid an unnecessary hand on a suspect. You were grieving. You'd had your emotional footing kicked out from under you."

He started to speak, but she raised her hand. "I'm not making excuses for you. I'm just stating the facts. You made a mistake. You accepted the consequences of that mistake, and you're coping with them." She laid her hand over his, knotted on the steering wheel. "I'm sorry you're not God, but that position's been unavailable for a long time."

For a long moment, he stared ahead, a tiny muscle in his jaw working. JJ watched him, catching sight peripherally of three department vehicles passing on the street behind him. No lights, no siren. After all, unless

Mr. Latham's dog got hold of it again, that leg wasn't going anywhere.

Inside, she winced at the thought. It sounded callous, and she wasn't that way at all. Well, no more than was necessary to do the job. People expected cops to be good and nice and always polite, to never make a mistake, to be all compassionate, all wise and all knowing at all times. But good cops saw things a civilian never did, witnessed pain and suffering on an unimaginable scale, faced danger and sorrow and grief and cruelty and despair and disgust and disrespect, and sometimes, yeah, they were human. They made mistakes. They paid for them.

Finally, she gave in to her flippant side. "Did the guy deserve it?"

He tilted his head to slant his gaze her way. "He hit his pregnant wife in the stomach." Another few somber moments passed before he went on. "Hell, yeah, he deserved it."

At the Prairie Sun, JJ ran upstairs to her room to get a jacket and make one last check of her appearance. Her outfit was dressy for her, though not for most high-end restaurants. Being with Maura would stop anyone from questioning her, though they might lift eyebrows behind Maura's back.

That was okay. JJ had raised eyebrows before.

She sprayed on perfume and touched up her lipstick. With a jacket folded over her arm, she went to the back parking lot, climbed in the Challenger and pulled out of the alley. It was six minutes to twelve when she left, one minute till when she turned onto Maura's street. Quint was sitting in the back corner of the fast-food place there. He lifted his fingers in a wave when she drove by, and she grinned broadly, waving back.

A minute later, her smile was gone. She shut off the engine in Maura's driveway, scanned the house and blew out a breath. The place looked as dreary as before— even more so now, with the addition of a piece of beat-up plywood over the second-floor window Maura had pitched her phone through.

JJ hadn't been looking forward to this meal in the first place, but watching the video of Mel had dampened her enthusiasm even more. Had Maura lulled Mel into the scheme, seducing her with the money she'd never had? Had Mel's previous life been deprived enough that she'd welcomed being made into someone else? Had she even been given a choice in the matter?

Wishing Quint was at her side, she got out and strode to the sidewalk. When she climbed the steps to the stoop, she found a note taped to the door. "Don't ring the freaking doorbell." Horrible penmanship for a girl who'd gone to the best schools money could afford. Rolling her eyes, she tried the knob, found it unlocked and stepped inside. "Maura? It's JJ."

Her voice echoed faintly in the empty rooms. After a beat, Maura answered. "Back here."

JJ's boots echoed, too, as she followed the hall into the kitchen. Maura was standing next to the island, an e-cigarette dangling between her lips, her gaze fixed on the phone, where she was texting so fast that her fingers were a blur.

Though the room smelled of pizza, cigarette smoke and weed, Maura herself looked better than JJ had seen her on this trip. She was clean, her hair was styled, her dress was snug and flattering, and her makeup was expertly applied. She wore a pendant with an ornate *E* of glittering diamonds set in brilliant rubies—a hand-me-down from an 1800s-era Evans—a delicate watch, an even more delicate necklace and a stunner of a yellow diamond ring.

After a moment, she set down her phone. "I don't suppose you saw Zander out there. I've been texting him for twenty minutes, and he hasn't answered."

JJ smiled. "He could be busy."

"Or he could be in jail." She huffed, folded an empty pizza carton in half and shoved it into the trash can in a small closet. JJ was impressed. Maura didn't appear to have learned a lot in five years, but she'd figured out garbage didn't get in the can by itself.

"Dating a bad boy—that would have driven your parents crazy, wouldn't it?"

"Oh, they expected—" Maura broke off, her forehead wrinkling before finishing. "They expected me to be a good girl, to marry someone just like Daddy and to grow up to be just like Mom."

"They just wanted you to be happy."

Maura gave her a disdainful look. "If that was true, they would have given my money to me, not Winchester. Do you know what it's like to have to ask for something that belongs to you in the first place? Like a little kid saying, 'Please, can I have a candy bar?'" Then her gaze shifted from JJ's hair, down her clothes to her feet and back up again. "Of course you don't. You don't have any money."

"I'm not exactly poor," JJ said drily, "and what I

have, I spend responsibly. You know, I live within my means. Your means are a whole lot grander than mine, and you still don't manage to do that."

Maura raised one hand as if to comb it through her hair but stopped before mussing it. "I'm not having this discussion." She picked up the cell and fired off another text before laying it on the island and spreading her hands flat on the countertop.

JJ silently acceded by changing the subject. "I remember that ring."

The look Maura gave it was careless, as if she'd forgotten which dazzler she was wearing. "It was my mother's."

"Your grandmother's. On your father's side. His sisters wanted it buried with her, but she went behind their backs and put it in the lawyer's care to be given to you when you turned twenty." JJ tried not to roll her eyes again, this time at herself. Yep, she was a small-town cop. She knew those kinds of stories about half the people in Evanston.

"Whatever."

Whatever, especially in that tone, was JJ's least favorite word in the world. To hide her annoyance, she bent closer to study the ring. The central stone was a large marquise cut, nestled in a mass of smaller round stones. The Evans family had owned bigger diamonds—and emeralds, rubies and sapphires—but this yellow was gorgeous.

And not quite right.

JJ's stomach knotted, and she forced in a breath that smelled of Maura's apple-and-cinnamon vaping liquid. The ring was on the middle finger of her right hand. The perfectly shaped middle finger, long, slender and straight, tipped with a coppery-hued nail. Right next to the perfectly shaped ring finger.

The last time JJ had seen those fingers, they'd crooked to the right at the middle knuckle. Considering that Tako had outweighed ten-year-old Maura by twenty-five pounds or more, the Evanses had decreed that two slightly crooked fingers were an outcome they could live with. Maura had used that splint to twist everyone in the household around her uninjured little finger even more than usual, including JJ, who'd felt so guilty that she'd suffered the fractures in the first place.

The crookedness had still been noticeable at her parents' funeral. Barely so, but for someone who knew it was there, who knew where to look, easily identified.

A motorcycle engine roared outside, causing both of them to jump. Maura was delighted with Zander's return. JJ just felt sick. Before he could interrupt, she quickly asked, "Hey, Maura, the other day you said you spent a whole winter at ice hotels in Switzerland."

The younger woman was too busy anticipating his arrival to care how odd the statement was. "Yeah, what about it?"

"Oh, nothing. I just thought that bit of snow the other day would freeze me solid."

Like the ice hotels Maura had stayed at in *Norway*. JJ had seen multiple references to the winter wonderland vacation in Mr. Winchester's files. She'd even pulled up pictures on the hotel websites to see for herself what lengths people were willing to go for a new experience. The photos of the ice dishes had made her shiver, and the ice-block beds had left her in need of a steaming-hot bath.

She had thought she'd considered every possibility for the changes in Maura's behavior over the last few months, but one had never crossed her mind.

That this woman wasn't Maura.

Oh God.

A crash came from down the hall—presumably Zander's helmet landing wherever he'd thrown it—then faded beneath the clomps of his boots as he strode into the kitchen. He stopped so suddenly that his upper body actually moved forward a few inches while the expensive black imperial-forces-in-outer-space motorcycle boots planted on the stone. His head swiveled from her to Maura, back to her, back to Maura, and a sneer curled his lip. "What the hell is she doing here?"

"I told you we were having lunch."

"And I told you not to go."

He stepped forward and grabbed Maura's—Mel's—arm, but she jerked away. "You're not my boss, Zander. Where have you been? I've been texting you forever. Why didn't you answer?"

"You're not my boss, either. I don't have to tell you—"

JJ drew a calming breath, folded her arms across her middle and felt the satisfying presence of both her Taser and her pistol in their holsters. "Why don't I wait in the living room? Give you some privacy?" Give *her* some privacy so she could text Quint to get the hell down here and bring all the backup he could get.

Zander's gaze jerked back to her. "Why don't you stay right where you are and shut the hell up? Come on, Maura." He grabbed her arm, his grip just short of vicious, and pushed her ahead of him to the nearest

French door. He slammed the door so hard behind him that the glass panes rattled, sending crazy reflections through the air.

JJ's chest was tight, her breathing constricted. She knew deep inside what had Zander so rattled and why: the discovery of the body part. Because he or Mel or the two of them together were responsible for it.

They had killed Maura.

Sorrow rose, swift and powerful. JJ had felt a lot of things for Maura over the years: frustration, affection, amusement, annoyance, irritation, pity, sympathy and, recently, dislike. But no, that dislike was for Mel. Obnoxious, rude, low-class and brainless. The best things anyone had to say about her.

And murderer.

On the patio, Zander and Mel argued, both exuding anger, neither scared by the other. Mel was in his face, poking his chest, and color was rising up his throat into his cheeks. When she finished her rant, she gave him a shove that knocked him back a step and started to walk away, but he caught hold of her again.

Sadly, despite all the emotion, their voices were nothing more than a murmur through the glass. JJ was torn between dashing out the front door to safety and tiptoeing over and easing the door open so she could hear. She settled for turning her back to hide her actions, took out her phone and began texting. At the same time, she casually strolled toward the hallway, focusing on giving the appearance of total nonconcern for the tension, the arguing or anything beyond having a nice lunch with Maura.

She'd made it two feet into the hall when a hand

grabbed her hair and yanked it with enough force to make her stumble back. Frantically she fumbled with the cell, trying to hit the Send key even though her message was only half-written. The pain in her scalp brought tears to her eyes, and a muscle in her back spasmed as a second jerk bent her so far off balance that she fell to the floor.

Damn, she was too old for this physical crap, was her first irrational thought.

Damn, damn, *damn*, she was in trouble, was her second thought as the back of her head hit the stone, sending a shock of pain through her entire body. The hand that clenched her phone involuntarily released, and the cell hit the floor, skidding out of reach. Dear God, she hoped the text to Quint had gone through.

Before her vision cleared, before the desire to retch faded, someone shoved her sweater to each side and removed her weapons. She blinked rapidly, clearing her eyes, expecting to see Zander standing over her, holding her gun, but it was Mel. Obnoxious, rude and evil. So evil.

How had she missed it?

Was it now going to cost her her life?

Chapter 10

Quint wasn't much of a fidgeter, but the longer he waited in the fast-food lot, the harder it got to sit still. It was twenty minutes past twelve, and there'd been no sign of JJ and Maura. She'd said it would probably be closer to one. He got that. Linny's biggest flaw had been her inability to be on time for anything besides work.

It still made him antsy this time. Maybe because Zander had driven past five minutes ago in his usual bat-out-of-hell mode. He'd skidded around the corner at the nearest intersection, then cut across three lanes of traffic to turn onto Willow Street, avoiding three other vehicles with inches to spare, and gunned the bike onto its rear wheel before arrowing toward the Madison house.

Zander always made him antsy.

Realizing he had a tight grip on the steering wheel, Quint eased it and checked the time—12:21. He texted Sam about the leg and got back a terse reply: Definitely human. Dog digs along Cedar Creek. Starting to search north.

Mr. Latham's house was about a mile south, though it was nearly twice that far navigating the streets that meandered with the creek. It crossed this street a half mile east, then angled to the northwest to form the property line for the Madison place.

Zander had been coming from the south.

No big deal. There were businesses, stores and restaurants down that way. Plenty of houses. Zander had a couple of buddies who lived near Two-Mile Park, where they used to hang out at night and drink—

Near Two-Mile Park. And Mr. Latham's house.

Quint's fingers nervously tapped the steering wheel. JJ was a cop. Maura wasn't a threat to her. Zander might not like her, but he wasn't stupid enough to hurt her. There was no reason for Quint to change the plan.

But he started the engine anyway. Backed out of the space. Turned onto Willow and drove the short distance to the house. The Challenger was parked in the driveway. Zander had left the motorcycle at the foot of the steps. When Quint climbed the steps, he saw that the door was open a few inches. Zander had been in too big a hurry to close it.

Every nerve inside Quint urged him to rush in, gun drawn, and get JJ safely out of there. But he didn't know she wasn't safe. She wouldn't appreciate being rescued if she didn't need it, and he couldn't go in aggressively when all he had was a faint niggling in his gut.

Standing to the side, he pushed the door open. The entry, the hallway and the small portion he could see of the kitchen were empty. "Hello? Zander, Maura, it's Quint Foster. I have a message for JJ."

Stillness dropped over the house, broken soon by rustling in the back. A moment later, Maura walked into view, stopping at the island, her right arm resting on it, her fingers toying with the leather bag that sat there. She smiled seductively and poured on the Southern charm. "Hello, Officer Foster. Why is it I always get weak in the knees when I see you?"

I don't think you'd like to hear my guesses. "Where is JJ?"

"She's over there on the couch. Come and say hello, JJ."

Quint had closed about half the distance to the kitchen when JJ stopped near Maura. She was smiling, too, but it looked… Wrong. Her expression was bland, her posture relaxed, her long sweater pushed back and her hands shoved into the pockets of her gray trousers. She looked fine but not fine. A shade too serious. A fraction too brittle.

"Hey, Quint." Her tone was bland, too. "Who's the message from?"

He'd stopped walking, he realized, when he saw her. Now he moved to take another step, but the tiniest shake of her head stopped him. "Chief Chadwick." He worked hard at making his voice sound normal. "He's been calling Sam, complaining that he can't get in touch with you."

She carefully turned her gaze to Maura, and a muscle twitched in her jaw, as if the action hurt. He searched but found no signs of injury. Her hair was mussed a little, but it was always a windy day in Cedar Creek. Her posture was good, though was her breathing a little shallow? And the hands in the pockets…he'd never seen her do that, but—

He stilled, did a double take. Aw, jeez, the holsters for both her Taser and her Glock were empty. Damn it to hell, how badly had they misjudged these people?

"You remember Chief Chadwick, don't you, Maura?"

Bored, Maura shrugged. "Yeah. He was a friend of my parents."

JJ smiled then, one brow lifted. Quint racked his brain, scanning through everything he knew about Bryan Chadwick. He was a dipstick. Had lived in North Carolina. Liked women in their place. Good ol' boy. Bad-mouthed his own officers.

And he'd come to Evanston four years after the murders of Maura's parents. He hadn't been their friend, and she couldn't have remembered him. So Maura was…a liar? Had indulged in too much booze and too many drugs to remember her past? Damn it, JJ was trying to show Quint something, but he couldn't see it.

She offered another clue. "Speaking of memories, Maura, do you remember Tako?"

Tako's not a respectable name for a sheepdog, he'd told her last night. But it was a memorable one. Especially when the dog had broken two of Maura's fingers.

"Taco?" Maura put a world of annoyance into that one word. "What are you babbling about tacos?"

Cold spread through Quint. Hell and damnation. Maura wasn't a liar. She hadn't fried too many brain cells with her substance abuse. She just couldn't remember the past JJ was bringing up. It made horrible sense: Maura cutting off contact with her friends at home. Her new hostility toward her godfather. Forgetting the an-

niversary of her parents' deaths. Breaking off her ten-
tative friendship with Miss Georgie. Not recognizing
her childhood babysitter. Expecting to get her entire
inheritance on her twenty-fifth birthday.

Maura hadn't been herself the past three months because she *wasn't* herself. This was Mel, Maura 2.0,
pretending to be Maura, and the real Maura...

He thought bitterly, sorrowfully, of the body part the
dog Angel had found.

The real Maura was dead.

And JJ was in the room with the woman who had
killed her. Who'd stolen her life. Who'd stolen JJ's weapons. Who had no intention of paying for her crimes.

He'd begun to feel sorry for Mel. Poor, needy Mel.
Never had the opportunities Maura had been given.
Picked up off the streets and shown a lifestyle she
couldn't even have dreamed about. Given everything
her heart desired as long as she let herself be remade
into Maura's image.

Let herself? He and JJ had assumed the whole makeover had been Maura's idea, but they'd been wrong.
Mel had taken advantage of their mutual resemblance,
had seen an opportunity too good to pass up. She'd
persuaded Maura, probably with flattery, to model her
into another version of herself.

Too bad Mel's heart had desired literally everything:
Maura's looks, her name, her status, her jewels, her money.

Her life.

He looked to JJ for confirmation and found it. She
gave him a long, steady look, accompanied with a tiny
smile and said, "Tell Sam I'll call Chadwick later. You'd
better get back out on patrol."

Leave? Walk away? Without her? She must be crazy. Not when he'd just found her. Not ever. So Maur—Mel had her gun. Probably in or under that bag on the island that her fingers kept touching. He was a damn good shot. This was what he'd trained twenty years for: a fast draw and a double tap to center mass. Mel would be dead before her own weapon cleared the purse.

"Yeah," he said at last. "I'll tell Sam." Let Mel think he was leaving, that he didn't have a clue what was going on. In the seconds it took him to get to the bottom of the stairs, she would have shifted her attention back to JJ, and he would have the advantage of surprise.

But the surprise was his when he finally spun around to walk away: Zander, standing a few feet behind him, the baseball bat he held already on a path to collide with Quint's head. The bone-jarring blow spun him back around, and agony dropped him to his knees, everything around him going fuzzy and distant except one thing.

JJ. Not whimpering, not screaming, but roaring like an enraged animal. JJ, in full-on protective mode.

That's my girl.

For an instant, everything froze. JJ stared, her lungs tight as if starved of air even though her breaths came so quickly and deeply that they made her entire body tremble. Quint, dear God, sprawled on the floor, his head turned to one side, blood puddling on the tile. Zander, standing a few feet behind him, trembling even more than JJ, his face gone white, his eyes popped open wide with horror.

And Mel, smiling like the crazy psychotic bitch she

was. Approval for his assault radiated from her. "Zander, sweetie, I didn't know you had it in you."

Zander's boneless hands dropped the bat, the clattering echoing off the high ceiling, and he staggered past Quint and into the kitchen. "Oh God," he muttered. "Oh God, oh God, I can't believe—I didn't—"

He turned his distraught gaze on JJ. "I was aiming for his arm. I didn't expect him to move. I didn't mean—"

He stumbled around the island, jerked open the utility closet door and emptied his stomach in the trash can there. With a put-upon sigh and a roll of her eyes, Mel reached for the gun. "An accident. Of course he doesn't have it in him."

Her gaze still locked on Quint, half-coherent prayers churning in her mind, JJ reacted instinctively. She grabbed Mel's hair in both hands and slammed her face onto the island, then, ignoring her scream, she brought her knee up into the other's woman's midsection before shoving her to the floor.

Mel hit the stone hard enough to slide a few feet, blood streaming from her nose. She touched her hand to it, turned pale at the sight of her own blood and shrieked, "Zander, get the damn gun!"

She tried to scramble to her feet, but before she made it halfway, JJ punched her, square on her already-injured nose, and was rewarded with Mel falling back and the bellow of an enraged animal in pain. JJ's hand hurt like hell, and she suspected her own blood was mingling with Mel's, but damn, it was a good hurt.

"Call nine-one-one, Zander," she commanded. His retching had stopped, but hers felt as if it was about to start. For a few minutes, adrenaline had made her forget that she'd taken a knock to the head, too, but pain flooded back, intensified. Her skull throbbed, her vision went blurry again, her stomach was heaving and that damn muscle in her back was twinging hard.

Her family joked about how hardheaded she was, but right now she felt shaky and weak. She wanted nothing more than to curl up in Quint's arms and let him make everything all right.

She needed nothing more than to hold him in her arms and make his everything all right, too.

Holding on to the island with her scraped hand, she took a careful step toward the hallway. In her peripheral vision, she could see Mel, in the fetal position, wailing and swearing. On the opposite side, Zander was still hunched over the trash can. "Zander!" she snapped. "Nine-one-one now, or Zoey's gonna kick your ass." And when his sister was done with him, JJ would put on her pointiest-toed boots and do it again.

He straightened, focused vaguely on her, then Quint. "My dad's gonna kill me," he muttered. "My *mom's* gonna kill me. Oh God—"

Abruptly he shot off. JJ hadn't spent enough time in the house to have noticed the louvered door between cabinets in the corner that connected to the dining room. Zander's boots thudded through the rooms, then he came into sight again in the foyer. Instead of leaving, though, he ran upstairs first. He returned in seconds with two backpacks, fully stuffed, grabbed his helmet and ran out the front door.

Glad to be rid of him, JJ pushed Mel's purse aside to find her gun, but it wasn't underneath. She dumped the oversize bag and found a lot of stuff, but no gun, no cell phone. When Mel had yelled at Zander to get the gun, he must have taken it. Thank God, he hadn't been enough under her sway to use it. JJ didn't have it to use, but neither did Mel.

JJ inched along the counter, moving cautiously to keep the spasming back muscle as still as she could, to keep as still as possible her brain that was punishing her with every pain receptor in her body. When she reached the island's end, she took one step and swayed to one side, took another and tilted to the other side.

Making it to Quint was an exercise in pure stubbornness. He needed her, and she would slide on her belly if that was necessary. She tried to kneel beside him, but her balance deserted her, and she sank to the floor instead, gathering her clumsy limbs to reach the pocket where he kept his cell. Focusing on the numbers and guiding her useless fingers to the proper numbers took an eternity, and the Send button wavered, watery, when she reached for it.

Thank God, a familiar voice came on the line. "Nine-one-one. Do you need police, fire—"

"Morwenna, it's JJ. Quint's hurt...ambulance... Madison house." She drew a breath, and it turned into a sob. "Please hurry."

"Oh my God. Hold on, sweetie."

JJ sagged against the wall, head back, eyes closed. She couldn't rest, not yet, not with Mel still conscious and ranting in the other room. She needed to get back on her feet, to take Quint's weapon and—

"You ruined everything, you bitch." Mel stood in the doorway, her pricey dress stained with blood, her nose swollen to twice its size. She had one hand on the door frame, and her other hand was empty. No sign of JJ's gun or her Taser. But a weapon lay nearby, within inches of her expensively shod feet. Before JJ could do more than register its presence, Mel swooped down, grabbed the baseball bat and ran her hand lovingly over the wood.

As the phone slid from JJ's hand, she heard Morwenna's voice, distant and worried. "JJ? Help's on the way. JJ? Can you hear me?"

"This is my lucky bat. It's what I used on Maura. Stupid woman. One thing. That's all I asked her to do. Get more money from the old man. She wouldn't even try. Idiot."

"You would have killed her anyway. No matter how much she gave you, it never would have been enough."

"That's probably true. But I would have let her live longer." Mel shifted her gaze to JJ's face, her expression dreamy and ghastly and chilling. "If you had left me alone, I would have let you live."

"I'm not dead yet, bitch," JJ muttered. It wasn't the right answer.

Mel swung the bat with surprising force, not at JJ, but at Quint. At the last instant, she drew it aside, letting it crash into the floor a few inches away. Vibration traveled through the wood and into her arms and must have hurt like hell, but JJ suspected she wasn't feeling anything beyond rage that her plan had gone so wrong and pleasure that she got to punish the people responsible.

"You will be." Her smile was so perfect, so practiced, and made her look so much like Maura that JJ shuddered. "You're going to die, pretty Officer Foster's going to die, and then I'm disappearing. I'm very good at disappearing. I'll change my name, my hair, my voice, everything. I did it before, when all I had to work with was my brains. Now I have a lovely pile of money and a million dollars' worth of jewels. It'll be so easy."

She moved a few steps closer, bat raised over her head, and JJ launched herself at her. Mel crashed to the floor with a grunt, trying to kick free, but JJ held on tightly, an armlock around her knees. She loosed one hand to jerk a thousand-dollar shoe off Mel's foot, then jabbed the narrow heel over and over into the hand that still clenched the bat. After too many times to count, Mel let go of the bat and wrapped her fingers tightly around JJ's hair again.

Damn, this was why she hated girl fights.

Eyes watering, strength flagging, JJ dug her nails into Mel's wrist, then forcefully pulled the psycho's fingers from her hair. Two of them made loud popping noises, and JJ viciously hoped they'd broken. She wanted Mel to live a long time with a constant reminder that she'd been beaten by a woman half again her age.

Not true.

She wanted Mel to die.

As soon as she peeled away the last finger, she drew back her fist and was ready to try her best at seriously hurting the bitch when a quiet, intense voice came behind her.

"JJ, it's okay." It was Sam, his face grim, his gun drawn.

She focused on him, shaking her head to clear her confused brain. She hadn't heard sirens, cars, voices, footsteps—nothing at all to indicate that backup had arrived. When she looked back at Mel, Ben Little Bear and Daniel Harper flanked her from behind, their guns also drawn. Had they gone around her, passed within inches of her, without her noticing? She preferred to think they'd known about the dining room door Zander had used, and not that her entire being had blindly concentrated on hurting—killing—Mel.

Sighing heavily—sure, it was a sigh and not a groan—she sank back, then crawled over to Quint again. This time when she touched him, he wasn't motionless and lifeless. He opened one eye, squinted, then pulled her closer.

Everything else became background. She let herself slide to the floor, then laid her head on his shoulder. He wrapped his arms so tightly around her that she could take only shallow breaths, but that was all right. Sometimes, like when she hurt like the devil, being lightheaded wasn't a bad thing.

"You're okay," she whispered, patting his chest.

"So are you." He laughed, then winced at the action. "Chaos on two feet."

She lifted her brows in question, but he just smiled faintly and brushed a kiss to her forehead. "It's a long story."

"I've got a long time to hear it."

"Here with me. Or there with you."

She assumed he was referring to their homes a thousand miles apart, but it didn't matter. The only thing that mattered was that they were alive, and together. "I'm not picky."

With that, and the sounds of sirens outside that promised imminent medical attention, JJ closed her eyes, pressed her cheek to his chest and peacefully smiled.

* * *

It would take a two-by-four to knock some sense into his kids, Quint's father had once declared. He idly wondered if a baseball bat counted, because even though everything else had gone wonky for a while after Zander's home run hit, one thing had become heart-achingly clear.

He wanted JJ in his life. Now. Forever.

Even though he hadn't known her long.

Even though she lived half a country away.

Even though he'd thought he would spend the rest of his life grieving for Linny. And his family didn't know JJ. And the doctors had urged him to not make any significant decisions until his brain had had time to heal.

He wanted her. She was beautiful and sweet. She made him smile. Hell, she'd made him laugh while lying in a puddle of his own blood. She might talk tough, but she had a soft spot for the vulnerable, the needy, the hungry, the sad. She stayed to fight when no one would have blamed her for leaving him behind. She'd saved his life.

She hadn't given up on him.

She wouldn't ever give up on him.

Time is fleeting. Life is short. Such clichés. But true. He'd thought he had forever with Linny, but it had lasted only twelve years. He could wait with JJ. He could let her go home without saying anything. They could spend the next six or twelve or twenty-four months traveling back and forth between Oklahoma and South Carolina.

And the next time she needed backup on a call, it might not arrive in time. She could be killed in an ambush. She could get shot making an arrest. She could die in a car chase, or fall down the stairs, or get struck by lightning, have a heart attack, slip in the bathtub or drown.

She could die any day by a million means, natural, accidental or homicidal.

And so could he.

He wanted to spend whatever days they had together.

At his feet, Chica, who'd stopped patiently when he did, had had enough. She began walking, tugging lightly on the leash to get him moving again, then suddenly lunging ahead. It pulled him off balance, rattled his head a little, but he followed. "Okay, Chica, I'm coming."

It was Saturday evening. The sun was low on the horizon, a blazing crimson ball just above the tree line, and the colors edging out from it included every shade of the rainbow. The air was warm and still and smelled sweetly of mown grass. Who'd known all it would take was a concussion to get his dad and brother to mow his yard?

It had been a busy couple days. Quint and JJ had been confined in the hospital Thursday night while Sam oversaw the crime scene. He wondered how long it had taken the nursing staff to discover that JJ had escaped her room and crawled into his bed. The most memorable hospital stay he'd ever had.

Mel had been hospitalized, too, under constant guard. Her nose was spectacularly broken, the doctor had said, making JJ preen, as were three fingers on her right hand. All of them had concussions, Mel had a broken tooth caused by the application of fist to face, and JJ had bruised and tender knuckles caused by that same application.

Now Mel was in jail. Sam and the department were still looking for Zander. Turned out those backpacks he'd taken with him had contained only the essentials: a few changes of clothes, toiletries and as much cash as he could stuff in there. Hank and Marisa had come to the house last night, and Hank had apologized a dozen times. Marisa had hung her head, a lost, bewildered look in her eyes, and said nothing.

Chica found an interesting clump of something. Maybe weeds missed by the mower, but more likely the daffodils, limp now that their blooms had faded. She sniffed, circled and sniffed more before raising her leg. Finished, she turned, directing her steady stare behind Quint for a long moment, then lifted her chin and walked away.

"If she thinks she's going to be the alpha bitch in this house, she's sadly mistaken," JJ said.

Quint watched her carefully cross the grass. Her color was better, and she lacked that head-about-to-explode fragility that had plagued them both most of yesterday. Muscle relaxers and a session with a physical therapist wielding acupuncture needles had given her enormous relief on the muscle strain, and her hand was sore but manageable. That left her only one injury to complain about.

"My scalp hurts," she said as she reached his side. She'd said it too many times to count.

"I know." He'd been sympathetic too many times to count.

"My grandmother Raynelle used to threaten to snatch us bald if we were really bad. I always thought it was such an odd threat, but now I know. Are you sure all my hair is still there?"

He pretended to look. "More or less."

"What?" She raised both hands to the top of her head, then winced.

Quint pulled her hands down, slid his free arm around her and kissed her forehead. "It's all there." Minus the eight strands they found clenched in Mel's hand at the ER.

JJ's scowl was fierce. "I hate girl fights."

"Next time I'll take the girl, okay?"

Just like that, the scowl turned into a sweet smile. She didn't say anything. She didn't need to. There *would* be next times for them, for anything and everything.

Well, maybe not facing another murdering psychotic bitch, but then again, who knew?

Chica reached the length of her leash, but instead of returning to them, she dug in her paws and forged ahead. JJ slipped away from his hug and claimed his hand in hers so they could follow the princess. "You know, if Mel had done only two things differently, she would have gotten away with this," she said ruefully. "If she'd controlled her greed, remembered she was playing the long game and been satisfied with the hundred grand a month… It was more money than she'd seen in a lifetime, and she should have been happy with that until the fraud eventually paid off."

But greed had been her driving force. It had been beyond her control.

"And if she'd treated Mr. Winchester like a person, like the godfather Maura had loved, instead of a servant beneath her notice," he finished for her. Then Winchester wouldn't have gotten worried, he wouldn't have asked for help from the police and JJ wouldn't have been sent to check up on Maura.

Quint's world would have been so much bleaker than it was now.

JJ's fingers tightened around his. "He'll be all right. Him and his wife."

"Eventually."

Sam had visited them at the hospital Thursday evening and told them he would break the news to the lawyer. The tension in her had visibly eased. *I never do death notifications*, she'd said, because they freaked her out. She must have been truly dreading telling Mr. Winchester, whom she respected, that his goddaughter had been beaten to death with a baseball bat and buried on the creek bank like so much nothing.

Poor Maura. All she'd wanted was a friend, but instead she'd invited her killer right into her home.

Quint lifted his gaze to the western sky. A few swaths of color remained, but mostly it was a soft, dark blue. The first time he'd looked at this property, he'd stood right here, watched the sun go down and absorbed the peace and stillness around him. Sometimes he thought he'd bought it more for that than the house or its location. While he liked the house, it was just a place. This spot right here, it was a feeling.

JJ gazed up, too. "I got a text from Chadwick after you two came out here. He wants me back at work on Tuesday."

He studied her, keeping his own expression bland, and waited.

"I told him I wasn't coming back. At least, not to

work." Insecurity flickered across her face. "I told him to consider the text my notice. I quit."

Tension Quint hadn't known he had disappeared, making a big imaginary *whoosh* as it left his body. He felt ten pounds lighter and twenty years younger. Relieved, easy, hopeful. "Even though quitting means he wins?"

She shook her head, grimacing at the movement. "I don't know how I ever convinced myself that letting him abuse and misuse me for however many years until he dies or retires means winning. He gets to be a prick, and I get to tolerate it. I'm a good cop, and I deserve better than that."

He couldn't help it. She was so serious, so sincere, that he laughed. Before she could voice her insult, he laid his hand to her cheek. "I've known you deserved better from the moment I heard about Chadwick. I'm glad you see it now, too."

She pressed into his hand, just slightly. "The problem is, I'm currently unemployed. Chica and I might end up living in my car—"

"Or your parents' garage," he added helpfully.

"And there's really no vehicle or garage big enough for us to cohabit in harmony."

He slid his arm around her waist and snugged her closer, careful of her back. "You cohabit quite well in a house with a big yard."

"With a stabilizing influence to keep her under control."

He glanced at the dog, alert and watching them, gaze shifting from one to the other as they spoke, as if she was actually following the conversation. "Or to keep you under control," he amended, then shrugged when

JJ frowned at him. "I'm just saying it depends on perspective."

For a long moment, he stared down into JJ's face. A week ago, he hadn't known her. Now, he wanted her in his life every day.

He stroked her cheek so lightly that her eyes fluttered shut for a moment. When he spoke, his voice was gruff and hoarse, but this time it wasn't from months of near silence. "It just so happens I have a house with a yard. And I'm also a stabilizing influence."

"Who told you that?" she teased.

"Chica. She bares her teeth at you. She snuggles with me."

JJ lightly punched his chest, then winced, settling her tender hand on his shoulder instead. "I knew you'd seen her do it. I bet you reward her with a *good girl* when I'm not looking."

"You're both good girls. My girls." He buried his face in her hair, breathing deeply of the scents that were her. "Stay with me, JJ. Chica's happy here. You're happy here. Sam's not hiring right now, but the county might be, and Tulsa PD always is. Stay. Please."

She went still for a long time, and for the first time, fear began a little tap dance in his brain. Did she think he was crazy, asking her to give up everything for him? Was a calendar tap-dancing in her brain, the pitifully few days they'd known each other flashing in neon? Was she thinking about her family, her home, her entire life that didn't include him?

After an eternity, she cupped his face in her hands, stared up into his gaze and smiled. "Okay."

The fear vanished, relief and pure gratitude taking its

place. He wasn't at all surprised that she'd answered his heartfelt plea so simply. It was good. It fit. Like a kiss, like her many smiles, it said a whole lot with very little.

"I love your house and yard. I love Cedar Creek. I like your friends and family, and I love you." Her features softened in the dim light. "Besides, I need a stabilizing influence in my life."

"Like I need chaos in mine."

"You still haven't told me that story."

Instead, he kissed her, holding her body close to his, focusing his entire being on the feel and the smell and the shape and the taste of her. How she fit so perfectly against him. How heat radiated from her body into his, growing, spreading. How soft and malleable and needy and demanding she became.

How she'd changed his life and lightened his soul and given him hope again.

How hard and hungry and greedy she made him with just one kiss.

She shifted her hips against his erection, made him groan and pulled away with a wicked grin. "Later," she said breathlessly, grabbing his hand and starting toward the house. "You can tell me later."

And, damn, how she'd taught him to appreciate *later*.

* * * * *

*Don't miss out on any other suspenseful stories
from Marilyn Pappano:*

Killer Smile
Killer Secrets
Detective Defender
Nights With a Thief
Bayou Hero

*Available now from
Harlequin Romantic Suspense!*

WE HOPE YOU ENJOYED THIS BOOK!

HARLEQUIN®

ROMANTIC suspense

Experience the rush of thrilling adventure, captivating mystery and unexpected romance.

Discover four new books every month, available wherever books are sold!

Harlequin.com

The memories flooded back so fast and hard, slamming into him like a physical blow, that he stumbled behind Anna, and had to catch himself with a hand against the wall.

How could he have forgotten all of that stuff?

Anna stopped abruptly in what looked like a dining room and turned to face him, tipping up her face expectantly to the light. The curve of her cheek was worthy of a Rembrandt painting, plump like a child's and angular like a woman's. How was that possible?

"Well?" she demanded.

"Uh, well what?" he mumbled.

"Are my pupils all right?"

He frowned and looked into her eyes. They were cinnamon-hued, the color of a chestnut horse in sunshine, with streaks of gold running through them. Her lashes were dark and long, fanning across her cheeks as lightly as strands of silk.

Pupils. Compare diameters. Even or uneven. Cripes. His entire brain had just melted and drained out his ear. One look into her big innocent eyes, and he was toast. Belatedly, he held up a hand in front of her face, blocking the direct light.

She froze at the abrupt movement of his hand, and he did the same. Where was the threat? When one of his teammates went completely still like that, it meant a dire threat was far too close to all of them. Without moving his head, he let his gaze range around the room. Everything was still, and only the sounds of a vintage disco dance tune broke the silence.

He looked back at her questioningly. What had her so on edge? Only peripherally did he register that, on cue, the black disks of her pupils had grown to encompass the lighter brown of her irises. He took his hand away, and her pupils contracted quickly.

"Um, yeah. Your eyes look okay," he murmured. "Do you have a headache?"

"Yes, but it's from all the sanding I have to do and not from my tumble off your porch."

Don't miss
Navy SEAL's Deadly Secret *by Cindy Dees,*
available January 2020 wherever
Harlequin® Romantic Suspense
books and ebooks are sold.

Harlequin.com